TO STEAL A MARQUESS

The Sisterhood of Independent Ladies
Book Two

by Maeve Greyson

ARE YOU SIGNED UP FOR DRAGONBLADE'S BLOG?

You'll get the latest news and information on exclusive giveaways, exclusive excerpts, coming releases, sales, free books, cover reveals and more.

Check out our complete list of authors, too!

No spam, no junk. That's a promise!

Sign Up Here

www.dragonbladepublishing.com

Dearest Reader;

Thank you for your support of a small press. At Dragonblade Publishing, we strive to bring you the highest quality Historical Romance from some of the best authors in the business. Without your support, there is no 'us', so we sincerely hope you adore these stories and find some new favorite authors along the way.

Happy Reading!

CEO, Dragonblade Publishing

Additional Dragonblade books by Author Maeve Greyson

The Sisterhood of Independent Ladies Series
To Steal a Duke (Book 1)
To Steal a Marquess (Book 2)

Once Upon a Scot Series
A Scot of Her Own (Book 1)
A Scot to Have and to Hold (Book 2)
A Scot To Love and Protect (Book 3)

Time to Love a Highlander Series
Loving Her Highland Thief (Book 1)
Taming Her Highland Legend (Book 2)
Winning Her Highland Warrior (Book 3)
Capturing Her Highland Keeper (Book 4)
Saving Her Highland Traitor (Book 5)
Loving Her Lonely Highlander (Book 6)
Delighting Her Highland Devil (Book 7)
When the Midnight Bell Tolls (Novella)

Highland Heroes Series
The Guardian (Book 1)
The Warrior (Book 2)
The Judge (Book 3)
The Dreamer (Book 4)
The Bard (Book 5)
The Ghost (Book 6)
A Yuletide Yearning (Novella)
Love's Charity (Novella)

Also from Maeve Greyson
Guardian of Midnight Manor (Novella)

CHAPTER ONE

En route to Lionwraith Estate
The northernmost border of the Lake District, England
June 1816 (The year without a summer)

"**A**RE YOU QUITE certain about this, my lady? Would it not be better for your husband to address it?" Mr. Parkerton, the Ardsmere family solicitor from London who somehow managed to sit upright even though he obviously possessed no spine, peered at her from the other side of the coach like a cornered mouse about to be hit with a fire iron.

Lady Francis Croyden, Marchioness of Ardsmere, informally known as Frannie, waved away the small-minded man's worries. "Firstly, Mr. Parkerton, my husband has been ill for quite some time now. According to his physician, there appears to be no good estimate of when the marquess may resume travel and once again take an active role in overseeing our ventures. And secondly…" She leveled a flinty glare on the man that he would do well to heed. "How many times have I handled business affairs with not only my husband's blessing but also that of his esteemed mother?"

"Yes, my lady." Parkerton tipped her a nervous nod, then stared down at his white-knuckled fists in his lap.

A hard gust of wind buffeted the coach, making it shudder and sway as if adding furor to her scolding. Rain and sleet pelted the rig, making further conversation too difficult to attempt.

Frannie gathered her fur-trimmed cloak closer around her. Thank goodness she and Mother Ardsmere had possessed the foresight to bring their warmest clothes for this unseasonably cold visit to England. Belgium was just as damp and dreary. It made one wonder if the entire world had displeased the Almighty. It certainly felt like a frigid punishment during what would normally be a most pleasant time of the year.

"You mustn't take a chill, my lady." Daisy, Frannie's lady's maid, confidante, and dependable rock who never failed her, spread a sumptuous wool blanket across her lap. "You would think it's the dead of winter rather than the start of summer."

"Thank you, Daisy." Frannie bumped Mr. Parkerton with the toe of her boot and raised her voice. "Blanket?" Between the storm and the vehicle battling the muddy roadway, it was next to impossible to be heard.

The man squinted at her through his smudged spectacles and leaned forward. "Beg pardon, my lady?"

Frannie shook her head and leaned toward Daisy, who sat beside her. "A blanket for Mr. Parkerton, please."

Daisy pulled another folded blanket from the stack beside her. She offered it with a tight smile that revealed her low opinion of the solicitor who had done nothing but whinge and moan since they had left London.

Without even so much as a thankful look or nod, Mr. Parkerton snatched the blanket out of her hands and covered himself from his jawline to his boot tops. "Dreadful weather," he shouted. "Thank heavens we reach our destination today."

"Indeed." Frannie refused to allow herself to roll her eyes again. Mr. Parkerton had triggered that response in her so many times, it was a wonder she hadn't become permanently stuck with her eyes pointed at the back of her head.

She settled deeper into her comfortable cloak. Thank heavens Mother Ardsmere had remained in London with Celia, the Duchess of Hasterton, and her husband, Lord Elias Raines. Mother's rheumatism had been more severe of late, and this wretched weather would have made her temperament even more unbearable than usual. Frannie smiled at the thought of Celia and Elias's precious new baby, little Oliver. Mother would be much better served remaining in London and enjoying that sweet little cherub in the warmth of friends who were more like family.

Her mind turned to poor Mr. Judson and Mr. Marcus, the more-than-reliable Bow Street Runners that her dear friend, Lady Sophie, had insisted come along in case the Duke of Lionwraith lived up to his dark reputation. The men had refused to ride inside the coach or even on top beside the driver. Instead, they rode their own mounts, insisting a little rain wouldn't trouble them or their horses.

Frannie huffed a silent laugh. A little rain, indeed. She hoped neither of them would fall to illness brought on by this dreadful weather. If they did, the dratted duke would be to blame. After all, this entire trip was that infernal man's fault. How dare he target her imports? His unreasonable declaration of some sort of commerce war would be bad enough during prosperous times, but the losses he had recently incurred would be difficult to recoup with the growing season crippled by the weather. Every supplier she traded with offered nothing but dire projections if Mother Nature didn't settle her moodiness and return to a warm, sunshiny countenance.

"My l-lady," Mr. Parkerton said in a hesitant stammer she barely heard. "Do you truly think it wise to show up in force without an invitation?"

"On the contrary," she answered loud enough to be heard over the din. "The Duke of Lionwraith issued several *invitations*." Although the duke's odd missives had sounded more like summonses than invites. "I am sure His Grace will be delighted to see us." Frannie smiled, knowing her sarcasm would not be wasted on the solicitor.

Mr. Parkerton didn't respond. He merely sat there, looking somewhat ill.

The coach lurched to a rather sliding stop, making Frannie tingle with the anticipation she always enjoyed when meeting an adversary head-on. She adored the element of surprise. They always expected the Marquess of Ardsmere, not realizing that her illustrious husband of several years now did not exist.

Frank Croyden, second Marquess of Ardsmere, was an elaborate farce that was born on the same day as Frannie. Months after the first Marquess of Ardsmere was killed in a shipyard accident, her mother gave birth to her, praying Frannie would be a male. But it was not to be. Frances Isabella Marie, the only child of the late marquess, was a girl.

To keep the Ardsmere wealth, entitled lands, and privileges of the title away from a heartlessly cruel cousin, Frannie was proclaimed a ward of the family rather than the daughter who could inherit nothing. In due time, she *married* the fake Ardsmere son that her mother and the townsfolk of sleepy little Chanticlare, Belgium, not only created but kept *alive*—and to such a successful degree that the imaginary man was quite the legend in exports and imports. Because of Frannie and her mother's astounding talent for business, the Ardsmere empire provided the most sought-after wines and rarest goods to the wealthiest families in the realm—up to and including the prince regent.

The coach door flew open and a blast of cold, wet air blew inside as Mr. Judson stuck in his head. "We are here, my lady." The stout man blinked the rain out of his eyes. "I feel Tom and I should accompany you and Mr. Parkerton inside." He set his grizzled chin to a leery angle. "I assume you are aware of the duke's temper?"

Frannie pondered the suggestion, finding some merit in it. Not only had the Bow Street Runners provided a report about the duke's disposition, but Celia had also filled her in about His Grace's surly mother and the rumors circulating about why the man rarely emerged from his country estate, which stretched from the northernmost portion of the Lake District up into Scotland. Alec Douglas, the Duke of Lionwraith, was rich as

Croesus, relentless to the point of cruelty, and trusted no one.

"Yes. I do believe you and Mr. Marcus should accompany Mr. Parkerton and me inside." She set aside the blankets and noticed the cowardly solicitor wilting in relief. "Mr. Parkerton," she said, not bothering to curb her snappish tone. "You may remain in the coach if you wish."

The man's eyes rounded in surprise and his bulbous nose and pockmarked cheeks flared to a deeper red, presumably from the embarrassment at being called out as a coward.

"I shall go inside with you too, my lady," Daisy said as she deftly refolded all the blankets and tucked them into a neat pile.

"Of course I shall go in, my lady," Parkerton said, his tone defensive in a whiny sort of way. He bumbled his way out of the coach, then turned and offered to hand Frannie down. "Whatever this dreadful business turns out to be, I am certain legal advice will be required."

Accepting the man's help to alight, and watching to ensure he also helped Daisy down, Frannie came to the irritating conclusion that she should have left the annoying solicitor back in London. She would definitely replace him at her first opportunity.

"Mr. Parkerton, you will allow me to do the talking. Understood?" She locked eyes with him, determined to impress upon the bottle-headed fool that she meant that as an order, not a suggestion.

"Whatever you wish, my lady." He offered his arm. "Mind the cobblestones. They seem quite slick."

She accepted his offer while ducking deeper into her fur-lined hood to avoid the frigid sleet. It was June, for heaven's sake. Was the world coming to an end? They carefully picked their way up the broad stone steps of the main entrance, leaving the coachman to continue along the circular drive to an impressive shelter, which rivaled any covered colonnade or portico in Roman architecture, and get his team into the dry.

With any luck, once she firmly put the duke in his place, she could convince the man that it would be common courtesy to put them up for the night on account of the weather. After all, from the sheer massiveness of the elaborate manor, any number of people could inhabit the place and never cross paths. However, if his reputation held true, and he refused, they would simply return to Caldbeck and stay at the inn.

She pounded the door knocker on its large metal plate three times. The heavy bronze paw of a lion with its claws unsheathed made quite the clacking bang that could be heard echoing into what was probably a high-ceilinged entry hall. Frannie braced herself for what she would face within Lionwraith's lair.

The door swung open, revealing a tall, older man scowling down at her through bushy white eyebrows so wild and full it was a wonder he could see.

"Yes?" he drawled.

"Marchioness of Ardsmere here to see the Duke of Lionwraith." Frannie took a step forward to enter, but the infernal servant remained rooted to the spot, blocking her passage. She pushed back her hood and glared at him. "Is your master aware that you keep his guests standing outside in unholy weather while you decide whether or not to let them in?"

"His Grace is not expecting any guests and is quite adamant about his privacy. Good evening." The man stepped back to shut the door.

"Oh no you don't." Frannie charged ahead and hit the door with her shoulder, knocking it open wider as she pushed inside. Daisy scuttled in after her, followed by Mr. Judson and Mr. Marcus. Mr. Parkerton hesitated outside, obviously unable to decide whether to join the fray or tuck his tail and run.

"Stay out there and drown for all I care," Frannie called back to the solicitor as she sidestepped Mr. Wild Eyebrows when he tried to take hold of her arm. "And you will not lay hands upon me, sir!" She fixed her sternest scowl on the servant, then took in the magnificent marble interior of the atrium that resembled a tomb more than a residence. Her wet boots would be treacherous on this floor. She needed to take care of her foothold or end up on her behind.

"Lionwraith!" she bellowed at the top of her lungs as she widened her stance. "Lionwraith! Come out this instant and face me!" Her roar echoed through the cavernous structure better than she had expected. It filled her with a pleasingly warm sense of certain victory.

Mr. Wild Eyebrows quick-stepped over to a black and gold velvet bellpull hanging beside the door and furiously yanked on it, no doubt summoning reinforcements to oust them.

Frannie held out her hand to Mr. Judson. "Give me your pistols. I shall fire them into the air until the blackguard deigns to acknowledge me."

"That will not be necessary," a deep voice rumbled from the landing above. A gray and white striated marble staircase gracefully curved upward to the next floor, flanked by matching columns that probably came from the same quarry. "You are?" the mighty voice intoned with such ringing authority that Frannie felt as though she stood before the Almighty Himself.

She moved closer, trying to see the speaker possessing the rich, throaty baritone, but the man remained hidden in the shadows. Probably afraid she would shoot him. "I am the Marchioness of Ardsmere, responding to your invitation—or should I say *summons*? That is—if you are the Duke of Lionwraith."

"I am, and I neither invited nor summoned you." He remained out of sight, irritating her even more.

She pulled three tightly folded letters from her reticule and held them up for him to see. "I have them right here. You and I have much to discuss."

"Are you illiterate?" The notorious Lionwraith stepped into the light.

The sheer grandeur of the man looming above her made Frannie stumble back a step and momentarily forget his rudeness. He was fiercely exquisite, breathtaking with a regal aloofness that suited him well. No wonder his home appeared to be sculpted entirely from expensive stone and adorned with precious metals. Even the rarest wood wouldn't suit his lair. His pristine white shirt of what looked to be the finest lawn was open at his throat. The material strained across the impressive width of his muscular chest. Buff-colored pantaloons tucked in polished Hessians showcased his long, powerful legs. His thick, unruly black hair somehow seemed out of place to Frannie. For some reason, she had expected the duke to be crowned with a tawny mane. Due to the *Lionwraith* title, she supposed.

She blinked, fighting the urge to turn tail and run. She would not. Too much was at stake. Once she gathered her wits enough to notice his heavy-lidded smirk, his insult roared through her veins.

"I assure you I am quite literate," she said, doing her best to sound composed and forceful. "Are you always this rude?" She stormed closer, reclaiming the ground she had lost when retreating from his entrance. "You demanded a meeting." She shook the notes at him. "Three times, in fact, over the past four months. Well, I am here to meet with you."

"So I see." He slowly descended the stairs with the graceful indifference of a royal deigning to join his court. "And yes, I am this rude when the invitations I extend are weeded away from their intended recipients." As he reached the base of the stairs, he offered her a deprecating nod. "Not one of those missives was addressed to the *Lady* Ardsmere." After a slow, dark look around the chamber, his chiseled jaw flexed as though he clenched his teeth. "MacGinnis," he said to Mr. Wild Eyebrows. "Stand down and send the lads back to their duties."

"Yes, Your Grace." The butler spared a glance at the six footmen who had shown up in force to his harried ringing of the alarm. Even though each of them nodded and then left the same way they had entered, MacGinnis remained in place, obviously hoping for further orders on how to torment the unwanted visitors.

The duke shot another insolent glance at Frannie, although it seemed somewhat milder. "You and I have no business to discuss, Lady Ardsmere. It is your husband I seek."

"Since my husband has been ill for several years now, and unable to leave our home in Belgium, I have handled the Ardsmere accounts in his stead. Handled them quite well, I might add." She took another step toward him. "I have evidence that shows you as the culprit for the false accusations of smallpox that resulted in the burning of two of my ships and one of my warehouses. You and I have a great deal of business to discuss, Your Grace." She removed her cloak, shook the water off it, then held it out for MacGinnis to take. "Shall we continue this conversation in the entry hall? After sitting for such a long carriage ride, I have no problem with standing while we speak."

Something about Lionwraith's demeanor changed. The strong, lean lines of his face hardened even more, as if he braced himself for a shift in the battle. "That is not possible."

"I assure you, sir, it is quite possible that I am tired of sitting."

He shook his head and growled, "Not that. The fact that your husband has been too ill to leave your home in Belgium for the past few years."

"First you call me illiterate, and now you call me a liar." Frannie stormed to MacGinnis and shoved her cloak into the startled man's arms. "Take it. I am staying until your master learns some manners!" After a nod at Daisy, Mr. Parkerton, and the Bow Street Runners, she turned back to Lionwraith. "Well? What say you? Stand here and speak, or retire to a room where everything we say does not echo so loudly that it resounds in your staff's ears?"

"To my library. Now." Once more he cast a furious scowl at everyone present, then pointed at her. "You. With me. Alone."

Mr. Judson stepped up beside her. "I do not think that wise, my lady."

Her own reservations had Frannie quivering inside, but she couldn't very well back down now. Not after forcing her way into the man's home and demanding he speak with her. She offered the Bow Street Runner an appreciative nod. "I am sure it will be quite all right, Mr. Judson." She sidled a taunting look the duke's way. "I believe our host is only rude. Not dangerous." That was a lie, but she wasn't about to wilt beneath Lionwraith's gaze.

"I have yet to harm any woman, no matter how irritating they are," Lionwraith said with an unreadable glint in his haunting eyes. He shot a curt nod at MacGinnis. "Show the rest of Lady Ardsmere's company to the blue parlor."

"Yes, Your Grace." The butler included Daisy, Mr. Parkerton, and the two Bow Street Runners in a displeased, squinty-eyed look as he pointed at an archway to the right. "This way."

Frannie allowed herself a hard swallow as she watched her allies file out of the entry hall through a doorway decorated with a lifelike sculpture of a lion's head, its teeth bared in an angry roar.

"Follow me," Lionwraith said, then turned and strode down a wide hallway off the cavernous atrium without a glance back to see if she would obey.

Frannie hurried to catch up while trying not to look like some silly goose girl chasing after her flock. Never in all her days had she met a man as bad-mannered and exasperating as the Duke of Lionwraith. She wasn't a fool. She knew he was trying to rattle her because she had him dead to rights on the accusation of sabotaging her warehouse and ships, and would take him to the courts for restitution if he forced her hand. It was her hope, however, that they could settle this privately. After all, going to court was dangerous, since producing an actual Marquess of Ardsmere—or even a convincing facsimile—would be expensive and carry risks of its own.

By the time she reached the door the duke had disappeared through, she was nearly out of breath. She skidded to a stop in front of it, her wet boots slipping on the highly polished marble. She grabbed on to the door trim to prevent herself from landing in an unladylike heap on her backside.

"You are the most infuriating, ill-mannered man I have ever

had the misfortune to meet," she said. She composed herself, then strode into the room. It looked more like a disorderly cave crammed full of books than the sort of opulent library she expected in such a grand manor.

"Thank you," Lionwraith said without glancing her way. He removed stacks of tomes from a pair of burgundy leather wingback chairs angled in front of an enormous hearth that took up that side of the room. "Might I remind you it was your choice to invade my home?"

"*Invade* is a strong word."

He spared her a narrow-eyed glare. "What would you call it, then?"

She refused to rise to his bait. Instead, she squared her shoulders and wound her way through the seemingly endless columns of books. The disorderly stacks cluttered the floor, reaching impressive heights, as if striving to touch the ceiling. "A larger room might serve you better as a library."

"I like this room." He pointed at the chairs in front of the hearth. "Sit and explain what you said in the atrium."

The warmth of the crackling fire was inviting after the bone-chilling ride. Frannie chose the chair on the right, pleased to discover the fine leather of its ample cushion warmed quickly beneath her bottom. "I have evidence that you instigated the destruction of not only my London warehouse but my ship at that same port and another of my ships at Liverpool. Why are you attacking my assets?"

"Why are you lying about your husband?" He circled the other chair like a restless predator, then grudgingly lowered himself into it.

What did the man suspect? Frannie drew on her years of subterfuge and deception to maintain her composure. "Why are you attacking my assets?" she repeated, choosing to behave as if he had not thrown down his own gauntlet.

He studied her for a long moment, making it very difficult for her not to squirm beneath his gaze. The firelight flickered in his hazel eyes, turning them as haunting and dark as a rich jade.

"Revenge," he finally answered in a low, throaty growl.

Frannie could almost see the angry wraith of a man-eating lion in the way the duke held his masterful body. Even though she forced herself to breathe evenly and appear calm, her heart pounded into her throat. "Revenge? What has the Ardsmere line done to you?"

"For four months, I have been unable to locate your husband. You expect me to believe he has been at your Belgium estate all along? For the past several years, even? Unable to travel because of illness?" He slid forward in his chair as though ready to spring. "According to my men, the marquess has not been there since I began looking for him." His eyes narrowed. "As a matter of fact, your husband has not been *anywhere*."

"The townsfolk of Chanticlare are very protective of us," Frannie said, easily reciting the lie she had used many times before. "We care for them, and they take care of us." Not a lie, as such, depending on one's perspective. "They know my husband needs quiet and solitude as he struggles to regain his health. Your men discovered nothing because those at Chanticlare ensured they discovered nothing. The devoted people of our quaint little village are quite loyal."

Lionwraith did not appear convinced. He pushed up from his chair, made his way to the edge of the mantelpiece, and yanked down on a heavy gold cord that she hadn't noticed until now. The library door opened before the duke had time to return to his seat.

"Yes, Your Grace?" MacGinnis asked from the doorway.

"Bring her here," Lionwraith ordered the butler through clenched teeth.

Without a word, MacGinnis bowed and disappeared.

"Bring who here?" Frannie couldn't resist asking.

The duke behaved as though she had not spoken. Instead, he moved to stand in front of the fire and stared down into it, giving her his broad, muscular back.

She clasped her hands in her lap, trying to remember every detail of the Bow Street report she had read several times. Nothing about the man stood out as unusual for a duke of the realm. Most of the information was about his heroism during the war, his vast holdings, and his political affiliations. Celia and her mother's information had been slightly more helpful. If their gleaned gossip held a kernel of truth, it somewhat explained Lionwraith's penchant for privacy and his almost hermitlike existence since returning from the Continent. His wife had died in childbirth while he was at the front battling Napoleon. The babe had not survived either. Such a heartbreaking loss, along with the horrors of war, would undoubtedly alter a man—or so Frannie supposed, since business was her area of expertise, not men.

"You wished to see me, brother?" a soft, almost ethereal voice asked from the doorway.

Frannie shifted to see the person calling the duke *brother*. None of her contacts had mentioned any of his relations other than his dragon-lady mother.

The candlelit sconce beside the entrance illuminated a delicate girl who was probably the same age as Frannie's four and twenty years, or maybe even a little younger. Fine-boned and tiny, the young woman was the polar opposite of the duke. Their only resemblance was their hair. Her ebony curls, caught up in the latest style, reflected the light like the richest black silk.

Lionwraith turned and actually assumed a kind and caring air for the first time since Frannie's arrival. With a sad, yet tender, smile, he motioned for his sister to join them. "Lady Ardsmere, allow me to present my dearest sister, Lady Violet."

Frannie rose to return a polite greeting, but before she could utter a word, the duke's demeanor hardened with such ferocity that it rendered her speechless.

As the duke's sister moved closer to him, he caught hold of her gown and stretched the material tighter across her middle, revealing the barely visible swell that the lines of the dress had concealed. "And allow me to introduce you to your husband's unborn child."

CHAPTER TWO

A LEC KEPT HIS arm around his beloved sister, holding her close and praying she understood his motives. He would smooth it over with her later. This had to be done. Her child deserved to be acknowledged, and Vivvy deserved vengeance, even though she was too meek to seek it for herself. As her brother, the duty fell to him, and he would see it done.

He eyed the stunned Lady Ardsmere. It appeared he had finally discovered a way to silence the lovely yet belligerent woman. Her furious blush matched the deep red rose of her lips that currently formed an astonished *O*. The brilliance of her sapphire eyes had darkened to the intensity of a building storm. *Good.* Just as he had intended.

"Lady Ardsmere?" he prodded. "Did you hear me?"

The marchioness blinked, batting her lashes as if dust motes had flown into her eyes. Her dazed look kept sliding from him to Vivvy, and then to Vivvy's middle.

"Lady Ardsmere?"

She jerked as though startled and cleared her throat. "Yes, Your Grace," she uttered softly. "I heard you quite clearly." An unexpected expression that strangely resembled concern furrowed her delicate brow. She moved forward and extended her hand. "It is an honor to meet you, Lady Violet. Pray, do not feel ill at ease. I would never cause you or your precious child any harm. I swear it."

"Your husband already took care of that," Alec growled, unable to resist the accusation.

"Brother." Vivvy gave him a gentle glower of reproach. She managed a tremulous smile and took Lady Ardsmere's hand. "I am so sorry, my lady. The marquess promised me he was not attached."

"I understand." The marchioness patted her hand. "And do call me Frannie—if you would feel comfortable doing so."

Vivvy bowed her head and clasped her hands to her heart as though ready to drop to her knees in prayer. "You are most kind," she whispered. She turned to Alec and looked up at him with an expression of such pain that his heart, or where he had once had a heart, ached like an open wound. "Excuse me while I go find MacGinnis and order tea for our guest."

He wished he could shield his sister from this ugly business, but it had to be done. She was as fragile and delicate as the flowers for which she was named. "I can ring for it, Vivvy. There is no need for you to fetch him."

"I insist." She cast a quick glance at the marchioness, tried to smile again, and failed. She squeezed his hand and tearfully whispered, "Please."

"Very well." He didn't have it in him to force her to stay and forge the particulars that would make her life easier—or, at the very least, more tolerable.

She skittered out the door, faster than a shadow retreating from the sun.

He turned back to Lady Ardsmere. "Now, do you understand?"

The lady released a heavy sigh and bowed her head. "I do indeed." She returned to her chair, eased herself down into it, and stared at the fire. Her pensive expression shifted to one of frustrated bleakness. She caught her bottom lip between her teeth and barely shook her head before returning her fathomless blue-eyed gaze to him. "I was not lying when I told you my husband has not traveled from Chanticlare in several years. I can't remember the last time he ventured from home—or to put a finer point on it, even emerged from his private chambers."

She tossed a troubled glance over at the door. "Did Lady Violet say where she met the man who called himself the Marquess of Ardsmere?"

"You cannot expect me to believe someone posed as your husband in order to debauch my sister?" The subtle rustling of the marchioness's skirts distracted him. She was trembling. A sure sign she was lying. "Are you cold, Lady Ardsmere? Shall I add wood to the fire, or do you merely quake when you lie?"

"For your information, I sometimes jiggle my feet when I think terribly hard. It helps." She lightly stomped her way to stillness, then scowled at him. Her infuriating yet glorious fight had returned, straightening her spine and fueling her indignant yet beautiful glower. "Do you have it within you to carry on a civil conversation and work constructively to solve this dilemma? Behaving like a pigheaded bully does your sister no good whatsoever."

"My sister is ruined." He forced himself to speak calmly even though he raged inside at the injustice of it all. "Lady Violet's tender heart has been ripped out and crushed into a pulp beneath the heel of your cruel husband."

With an incredibly unladylike snort, Lady Ardsmere yanked open her reticule and rummaged through it as though the thing was bottomless. She withdrew a small oval object trimmed in gold and shoved it under his nose. "This is a miniature of my husband. As you will see by the date inscribed in the ivory on the back, the portrait was done this past Christmas. A gift to me, and I must say the artist captured an accurate likeness of Frank. Does this image match Lady Violet's description of the brute who so callously misused her?"

He took it from her. Before examining the picture, he flipped it over and noted that it was indeed inscribed: *To my darling Frannie, Merry Christmas 1815, All my love, Frank.* He stole a glance at her as he turned it back over, not missing the vainglorious tilt of her head. Stubborn woman. She was determined to clear her husband's name—from love, loyalty, or to keep from suffering any additional business losses. He wondered which of the three truly ruled her actions. He tore his scrutiny from her and fixed it on the miniature in his hand.

The man's eyes were as black as his wavy hair. The set of his strong jaw and the smirk on his lips portrayed an air of amusement that bordered on the devilishly wicked demeanor of a schoolboy about to get into mischief. This man looked entirely capable of seducing an innocent woman and leading her to ruin.

Even though his blazing temper begged him to crush Lady Ardsmere's precious memento beneath his heel, he carefully placed it on the arm of the chair with the image facedown. He couldn't bear the gleam in the portrait's eyes for another second. "When Lady Violet returns—if she finds the strength to return—I will ask her if this is the hellhound who debauched her."

The marchioness stared at him as if he hadn't spoken. Within seconds, her infernal skirts started twitching again.

"Are you unable to sit still, Lady Ardsmere?"

She flattened her hands on her knees and dipped an apologetic nod. "Sorry. As I alluded to earlier, it's an uncontrollable habit I have had since I was a child. I have always done it when faced with a problem begging to be solved." She pulled in a deep breath and slowly released it, still eyeing him as though wondering what size casket he would take.

"What?" he bit out, not liking how this woman had the uncanny ability to unnerve him so easily.

She caught her bottom lip between her teeth again—apparently another of her habits. "You don't intend to send your sister away or force her to do anything she doesn't wish to do, do you?"

The question caught him off guard. Why would this woman care about what happened to one of her husband's conquests? "Lady Ardsmere—"

"Frannie," she corrected him with a flip of her hand. "You

might as well call me Frannie. I believe this terrible situation warrants it." Then she smiled—a real smile filled with compassion. It lit up her eyes and complemented the sleek sculpting of her high cheekbones. At his stunned expression, she continued, "Even though I know my husband is not the rogue you seek, I would like to help your sister. She seems so…" Another belabored sigh left her. "She needs everyone's help at this time."

"What do you want?" No one helped anyone without profiting from it. He would not have Vivvy abused and shattered further.

She gave a bewildered quirk of her head, reminding him of his hound pups when they didn't understand the command. "Whatever do you mean?" she asked.

"It has been my experience that when so-called *help* is offered, there are always strings attached. In fact, the cost can be quite dear."

Her bewilderment shifted to an injured pout. He almost laughed out loud. Did she actually expect him to believe he had hurt her feelings? "Well?" he said. "What do you want?"

"To help your sister." She resettled herself in the chair and frowned at the fire flickering in the hearth. "It strikes me that Lady Violet is a gentle soul. Meek and kind." As her gaze slid back to him, her eyes narrowed. "My instincts are never wrong about people. The dowager marchioness tells me it is a rare gift that serves me well in the Ardsmere ventures. As soon as I meet someone, my intuition tells me who they *really* are—not who they are trying to be."

"Does it now?" He leaned back in his chair, wishing Vivvy or MacGinnis would hurry and return to put an end to this frustrating interruption that had made this dark and dreary night even less bearable. "Pray tell, Lady Ardsmere, what does your intuition say about me?"

"That you are an insufferable arse who hates the world and most of the people in it because of the way life has treated you." One of her expressive brows shot higher, and challenge flashed in her eyes. "What say you to that?"

A snort of laughter escaped him before he could stop it. He raked a hand through his hair and found himself smiling. "I would say that pretty much sums me up, Lady—"

"Frannie," she said. "I understand why you attacked my business, and will not be pursuing reparation. If anyone I cared about had such a thing happen to them, I would gleefully destroy the culprit responsible for such cruel mistreatment. It must not go unpunished." She tossed her head, sending her mass of honey-colored curls that were fashionably arranged at the back of her head into a nervous twitch as fast as her skirts. She must have noticed his glare at her jiggling, because she clapped both hands on her knees and stilled herself again. "Sorry."

Instinct warned him to be wary of *Frannie*. It was not normal for those of so-called *Polite* Society to treat a woman in Vivvy's situation with care, compassion, and consideration. Quite the opposite, in fact. The *ton*, once they got wind of his sister's ruin, would cut all ties with her and make her the helpless victim of every ball or gathering. She would become the pariah of the Season.

"We shall see what Lady Violet says of the miniature and then go from there," he said.

"I understand." Frannie rose and moved closer to the fire, extending her gloved hands to warm them.

The silence between them grew, becoming a suffocating fog of unease that filled the room. The only sounds were the pop and hiss of the damp wood on the fire and the clock ticking on the mantel.

"What was your husband's reaction when you informed him you were coming to confront me?" Alec watched her stance, the set of her shoulders, the tilt of her head. He took note of the slightest changes. The way a person held their body always betrayed a lie—unless that liar possessed no conscience whatso-ever. He also picked up on the faintest scent of lilacs laced with the mouth-watering hint of vanilla that disturbed him no small amount. Apparently, as the lady warmed, her delectable scent activated to foul his senses and outmaneuver him.

He snorted to clear his head. Neither her beauty nor her fragrance would be allowed to veer him from his course.

She faced him and backed toward the fire, holding the material of her blue wool traveling dress tighter across her shapely behind, apparently to better heat her curves—or distract him. She twitched a shrug and scooted even closer to the flames. "I didn't tell my husband. His physician recommended complete calm, with nothing more exciting than the sun breaking through the clouds."

Before he could comment, the library door opened and MacGinnis announced, "The tea, Your Grace, and Lady Violet insisted that the visitors in the blue parlor be served as well."

Alec watched the empty doorway. "And will Lady Violet be joining us?" He already knew the answer. Poor Vivvy had retreated to the sanctuary of her rooms.

MacGinnis set the tray on the table in front of the wingback chairs, then straightened and leveled a sour look on the marchioness. "Lady Violet offers her apologies. She finds herself suddenly quite unwell and has chosen to retire early."

Just as Alec had known she would. He pulled in a deep breath and let it slowly ease out. "Once Lady Violet is settled, please ask Jennet to come down."

"Yes, Your Grace." MacGinnis disappeared back out the door.

"Shall I pour while you explain who Jennet is and how she might help us?" Frannie asked. Before he could respond, she poured their tea and paused above his cup with a small pitcher. "Milk or lemon? Sugar or no?"

"Nothing." He took his drink from the tray before she could hand it to him and settled back in his chair. "And Jennet is Lady Violet's maid. With your consent, I intend to send the miniature up to my sister, and have Jennet report not only what she says but also her reaction."

"I have no issue with that plan at all, as long as you are certain it won't upset Lady Violet further." Frannie offered him the small plate of biscuits.

"No, thank you, and why would it upset her any more than she already is?"

Frannie eyed him as though she thought him a cod's head.

"What is it now?" he growled after burning his tongue on his tea. How could this infernal woman poke him in the eye with just a look?

"When she sees my husband is not the man responsible for her condition, do you not think she will become even more overset?" She returned to basking her attractive backside in front of the fire while sipping her tea. The wood crackled and popped, but she stood her ground. Apparently, her trip had quite chilled her.

The acrid scent of burning wool reached him, and a hint of smoke rose in a delicate tendril behind her. Alec set his tea aside, dragged her forward, and slapped at several smoldering spots on her skirt.

Her outraged shriek reminded him that she already thought him an ill-mannered arse. "Forgive me, my lady," he said with forced sweetness. "But you were on fire."

"Oh, no. Not again." She twisted around, trying to see the dress's damage, and slopped a trail of tea down the front of her fine woolen gown.

He clenched his teeth to keep from laughing out loud as he took the cup from her. "Pouring it down the *back* of the dress would be much more effective at putting out any remaining embers that might have reached your petticoats."

"Heaven help me," she groaned. "I swear to you, I am not always this *graceful*. I just get distracted and don't pay attention sometimes." She propped herself against the arm of the chair and yanked the material around to better inspect it, revealing a delightful peek at the slender curve of her calves. "Daisy will be overwrought trying to mend this. It is surely ruined."

Alec didn't dare speak. To do so would be his undoing and

unleash a torrent of mirth that would be extremely ill-bred of him, even though he still wasn't sure he trusted her. "It could happen to anyone," he finally managed to say with a modicum of politeness.

Her worried frown at her skirts turned into a narrow-eyed glare at him. "You are too kind," she said, delighting him with her acerbic tone.

Perhaps Frannie interrupting his evening wasn't as odious as he had first thought. Before he could taunt her further, Jennet entered after lightly tapping on the door.

"Ye wished to see me, Your Grace?"

He couldn't resist a smile as the marchioness hurried to throw herself back down into her chair to hide the damage to her dress. He waved Jennet closer. "How is she?"

With a worried wrinkling of her freckled nose, the maid sadly shook her head. "Heartbroken, Your Grace, and prepared to wear sackcloth and ashes for bringing such shame upon the family."

"If Mother comes at her again, I am to be summoned immediately." The situation was bad enough without the dowager duchess unleashing another torrent of cruel bitterness toward Vivvy. If Mother tried it again, he would banish her to their small manor house near Castle Douglas. Solitude in Scotland might teach the old demoness some manners.

He held out the miniature to Jennet. "Do you think Lady Violet would be well enough to look at this and confirm whether or not it is the father of her child?"

Jennet took it from him and studied it. The longer she eyed the small portrait, the more her head tilted to one side. She kept stealing glances at him, then looking back down at the painting. "If ye dinna mind my saying so, Your Grace, this looks like yourself."

Frannie burst into a coughing fit, hurried to set her tea aside, and pressed a napkin to her mouth.

"Are you quite all right?" he asked. This lady appeared to be a mishap waiting to happen.

"Fine," she said, waving the cloth like a white flag while trying to recover from choking.

He turned his attention back to Jennet. "Personally, I do not see the resemblance. However, do you consider my sister calm enough to look at it and confirm or deny if this is the blackguard in question?"

"I dinna ken, Your Grace." Jennet nervously fidgeted, appearing unsure whether to speak her mind or not.

"Speak freely, Jennet. I would know your thoughts." He braced himself, knowing the maid probably knew his sister better than anyone.

"She might feel even more the fool when she sees this." Jennet wrinkled her nose again.

"Tell her we want to help her make this predicament as bearable as we can," Frannie said. "She and her child deserve every chance at happiness. We are not trying to overset her even more, but we need as much information as she is able to provide."

Jennet bowed her head and blew out a heavy sigh. "Then I see no need to fash her about it with this wee thing. The man in this painting is not Lady Violet's lover."

Alec smelled an accomplice he had previously been unaware of. He clenched his gut as though about to be punched. "And why would you say that?"

After a cringing shrug, the maid gently placed the miniature on the tea tray while keeping her head bowed. "I went with Lady Violet whenever she went to see him." She stole a glance up at Alec before continuing. "To seem all proper and such with a chaperone, mind ye. I would wait in the carriage while she…" Her voice trailed off, and she swallowed hard. "I saw him once when he handed her up into the carriage during a storm. Forgive me, Your Grace."

"Describe him." Alec fisted his hands so tightly his knuckles popped.

"A fair-haired man," she said. "So fair that the fringe of his curls popping out from under his hat was almost white as wool."

She shuffled in place and lightly coughed. "Pale blue eyes. Not nearly so tall as yerself, but tall enough for Lady Violet to have to tiptoe when she whispered in his ear." Jennet rolled her narrow shoulders as though in pain. "Not a Corinthian, but dapper enough, I reckon." She eased back a step. "May I go now, Your Grace? I should be getting back to Lady Violet in case she should need anything."

"Go." He waved the girl away, then sagged forward and dropped his face into his hands. Hell and damnation, what a bloody mess. He dragged his head up out of his hands and locked eyes with Frannie. "It appears I owe you and your husband an apology, Lady Ards—Frannie." He angled his chin higher. The lady should strike him for his behavior. "As well as a great deal of money."

He pushed up from the chair, made his way to his cluttered desk, and lit the stub of the candle in the glass lamp. "I assume you brought a full list of the damages. If you would kindly provide it, I shall see you repaid in full plus interest."

"I told you I would not seek reparation," she said quietly. "Were I in your position, I would have done the same, and I cannot imagine how difficult it would be to find a man going by the name of another—especially when you had no description. Only a name." She rose from her chair and sauntered closer. "I still mean to help you and Lady Violet."

He raked both hands back through his hair, unable to fathom this woman's motives. "And why would you do that?"

"Because whoever the culprit is cost me a great deal too. Not only in expensive goods but also reputation." Frannie moved closer still. "I mean to see him pay and see Lady Violet vindicated. How dare he traipse off unscathed while she bears the consequences?" Her eyes flashed with righteous fire. "Impersonating a peer for the sole purpose of tossing a lady into ruin? Disgraceful!"

A bitter laugh escaped him. "Your offer is admirable, my lady. But I fail to see how you can help."

"I cannot form a successful plan until I know every detail of the crime." She unleashed that beguiling smile of hers again. "I assure you, Your Grace, I have access to untold resources when it comes to ferreting out secrets."

"Alec."

She blinked and angled a bit closer. "Beg pardon, Your Grace?"

"If I am to call you Frannie, as well as partner with you on championing my sister's cause, then you might as well call me *Alec*." He cast a glance around the room. "At least when we find ourselves in a relaxed and private atmosphere such as this."

"I do not know that I would call the current atmosphere relaxed," Frannie said with a self-deprecating laugh. "I set my dress on fire, and you just discovered that you are back to the beginning in bringing a slippery devil to justice."

"Indeed." He exhaled a disgusted huff. "Might I interest you in something stronger than tea?" He needed a drink. Badly.

"Very much so. This unbelievable weather has me chilled to the bone." She patted her behind. "So numb, in fact, I couldn't even tell when my skirts caught fire."

"I shall make you a deal, Frannie. You swear to tell no one about my favorite smuggled brandy *or* my sister's dilemma, and I give you my word that no one shall ever hear about the unfortunate landing spot of a few stray sparks. Agreed?"

Her soft, joyous laugh filled the shadowy room with a refreshing lightness he hadn't felt in years. She slipped off her glove and stuck out her hand. "Agreed. I shall even shake on it."

He shook her hand, then, on an unexplainable impulse, kissed it. "Thank you, Frannie. You are the first hint of pure brightness I have seen in a very long while."

Surprising him with a flush of rosiness across her cheeks, she ducked her head and squeezed his fingers. "You are too kind." And this time, her words didn't drip with biting sarcasm.

A disturbing warmth, one he barely remembered because he hadn't experienced it in so long, stirred in his chest. He cleared his throat to dislodge the inexplicable feeling and awkwardly released her hand. "And now for our drinks. I know it is not a lady's usual choice, but I pray you enjoy a good brandy?"

A delightfully amused wickedness flashed in her eyes. "As long as it was provided by West Belgium International."

"But of course." He made his way over to the only piece of furniture in the room not buried in books and papers: the liquor cabinet. He selected the decanter of rich, dark brandy and poured a generous amount into two glasses. "Blackcurrant brandy. One of my favorites, but strong. I hope you find it suitable."

He watched as she tried a sip, noting with no small amount of disquiet that as she licked her luscious lips after that first taste, the disturbing warmth in his chest surged into an even more alarming sensation below his waist. *Absolutely not.* Not only was she married, but he fulfilled those needs with mistresses who clearly understood his terms. No messy entanglements. No professions of love.

But he couldn't help but wonder about the situation with her ailing husband. How long had it been since they had shared a marriage bed? *Not my bloody business.* He forced the thought from his mind and concentrated on the problem at hand. "Since it is quite apparent that any information I gathered is useless, you realize catching the true scapegallows could take some time?"

"I do not care how long it takes." Frannie enjoyed another sip, then held up the glass and swirled it in the candlelight. "Exquisite. Just as promised. I must thank Monsieur Grandon yet again when next I see him." She meandered back in front of the hearth but halted a safe distance from the fire. "You will find I am quite relentless. Not only when it comes to my business assets but also in defending those I care about. I know I just met Lady Violet. But turning my back on her would be like abandoning a starving kitten. I have as much time as it takes to bring this heartless blackguard to his knees, and look forward to the opportunity to do so."

Surprisingly, the tension in Alec's shoulders eased for the first time since his sister came to him pleading for help. Must be the brandy. "In that case, you and your traveling companions are welcome to stay here, if that would be to your liking."

"That would be very much to my liking, and most convenient as you and I work together to solve this mystery." Frannie held up her glass. "To a joining of forces."

He touched his drink to hers while trying to ignore a growing attraction to this unusual woman. "To the raging lion and the cunning fox as they save the helpless lamb."

Her smiling eyes made his swallow of brandy burn even hotter all the way down.

CHAPTER THREE

"HERE IT IS June, and we've yet to have a day warm enough for you to wear one of your nice muslin gowns." Daisy hissed like a disgruntled teakettle as she deftly fastened the small buttons of Frannie's lightweight wool dress in a shade of cornflower blue.

Frannie glanced at the nearest window and smiled. "At least the sun is out. I take that as an omen that today's endeavors will be prosperous." She smoothed her hands across the coolness of the white marble top of the dressing table. The impressive piece of furniture was littered with tiny, ornate metal boxes and crystal vials of perfumes that looked to be quite dear. "Have you ever seen such lavishness?"

"No, indeed, my lady."

While Frannie's homes would never be found wanting, none of them were decorated so luxuriously. Opulence dripped from every surface at Lionwraith Estate, from the exquisite crystal chandeliers to the plush carpets and everything in between.

Last night, she had found herself nearly lost in the uncommonly large canopied bed with its velvet curtains. Its sumptuous counterpane and throw pillows of the deepest rose had provided a most comfortable nest. The bed was a masterpiece in and of itself, lending a feminine awe to the room. Curtains in the same shade of rose adorned the tall, narrow windows that framed the bed. Ivory wallpaper decorated with nosegays of pale pink miniature roses shone with a satiny sheen.

"But Belgium Hall is quite fine," Daisy hurried to add, sounding as if she feared she might insult her mistress.

Frannie laughed, then winced as the maid tugged harder on a snarl in her hair. "I am quite thankful and proud of all the Ardsmere prosperities. Make no mistake."

"If you don't mind my asking, are you really going to tell Mr. Parkerton to take his leave and hire the first available carriage back to London?"

Frannie didn't miss the anticipation in Daisy's voice. The maid despised the solicitor, and Frannie didn't fault her for it. Not after witnessing Mr. Parkerton's rudeness to those he considered *lesser*. "Rest assured, I intend to dismiss him as soon as I see him this morning. I have no further need of the sniveling little man and cannot imagine what Mother Ardsmere ever saw in him."

"Lady Emmeline won't be angry with you for dismissing him, will she? It hurts my soul the way she treats you sometimes." Daisy hit a particularly tangled lock and yanked harder.

"Daisy!" Frannie grabbed her hair before the maid pulled it again. "If tangled that badly, then cut it free rather than rip it out. Please?"

"Your curls always tangle so," the maid complained. "Wavy and thick as can be, but finer than strands of silk and twice as easy to snarl. Take heart, my lady. I am nearly done."

Frannie squared her shoulders and braced herself for the hairbrush's final onslaught. In the girl's defense, her hair always did become a frightful mess quite easily.

"While I appreciate your concern," she said, "no, I do not think Mother Ardsmere will be upset at the loss of Mr. Parkerton. After all, Celia's husband insists on keeping his position as a solicitor even though Celia is *officially* a duchess now. Lord Raines will be an exemplary replacement for Mr. Parkerton." She relaxed as Daisy set the brush on the dressing table. *Thank heavens.* The attack was over. "And Lord Raines fully understands the needs of the Sisterhood."

The Sisterhood of Independent Ladies. A remarkable endeavor that enabled three families to foil unfair patriarchal laws and traditions. The founding ladies of the secret society—Thea Tuttcliffe, the Dowager Duchess of Hasterton; Nia Redwell, the Dowager Countess of Rydleshire; and Frannie's mother, Emmeline Croyden, the Dowager Marchioness of Ardsmere—shared three things. They all debuted in the same London Season, all made prosperous matches, and all became widowed before the birth of their first child. The three also shared a furious determination to ensure their daughters suffered no losses just because they were born female.

Each mother had created an inventive ruse to keep possession of the title. They also instilled a driving desire within their daughters to excel in what most considered a man's world. Lord Elias Raines had discovered the truth of the Sisterhood when he had fallen madly in love with his precious Celia, the Dowager Duchess of Hasterton's daughter and one of Frannie's sisters by choice.

"In hindsight," Frannie said, "I should have retained Elias as soon as he and Celia married." She rose from the cushioned dressing table stool and headed for the door. It was time to descend for breakfast. She paused with her hand on the latch and turned back to Daisy. "You are quite certain the Lionwraith servants are being kind to you?"

The maid's contented look reassured her. "Oh, yes. Quite kind, my lady. As soon as they heard of your intentions to help Lady Violet, they no longer saw us as enemies storming the manor."

"I am glad to hear it." Frannie opened the door a crack and peered out into the hall before turning back to Daisy. "Note all that you hear. We know little of the duke, and it never hurts to be informed."

"You have my word on it, my lady." The maid's cheerful demeanor shifted to one of almost pleading. "And please mind the fires in the hearth. I am not sure I can mend yesterday's dress.

We may have to save it for the modiste, and that leaves you with naught but the one traveling gown that's fit to wear."

"You have *my* word on that." Frannie exited before the tea stains or the missing buttons on the sleeves of yesterday's outfit also came up. She really needed to make a more concentrated effort to be mindful of her things. Good heavens, sometimes she was as clumsy as a newborn foal. Her heart had nearly stopped when the duke leapt from his chair and started swatting her backside to put out the fire. What must he think of her?

A smile tickled her lips as she descended the stairs. She knew what she thought of him. Handsome. Dashing. Protective of his loved ones to a fault. A bit foolhardy—rushing to act before fully knowing the situation. "Wounded," she said quietly, as she remembered the torment in his mesmerizing eyes. And he trusted no one. She wondered if that was because of the war or if something else had made him so leery. Most veterans she knew wrestled with demons begat from their experiences on the battlefield. It was sometimes guilt over their survival when many of their comrades died. Perhaps that was what troubled him.

And wasn't it odd how the miniature she had painted to prove her imaginary husband's existence resembled the duke? What an eerie revelation that had been. A shiver flitted across her at the memory of it.

Frannie released the musings with a sigh as she reached the bottom of the stairs and realized she had no clue where the dining room was or where breakfast might be served. She supposed she could attempt to follow her nose, but in the vastness of the high-ceilinged place, sniffing out a delectable cup of chocolate might prove difficult. Apparently, there was nothing to do but wander about until she found what she felt would be a lovely breakfast buffet. She chose the hall to the left and started down it. Soon after, the sound of hurried steps clicking behind her made her stop and turn.

"Lady Ardsmere!" A short, plump woman in a dark dress and pristine white apron huffed and puffed, approaching as fast as her legs could churn. The matron soon reached her, gasping for air as she dipped a curtsy and pointed a pudgy finger in the other direction. "I am Mrs. MacGinnis, my lady. Housekeeper here at Lionwraith. Do forgive me for not making it to your rooms in time to bring ye down to breakfast."

"There is nothing at all to forgive," Frannie said to the harried woman, doing her best to put her at ease. "With a manor as boundless as Lionwraith, I am sure your duties are endless. Besides, I would have found the dining room eventually. A cup of chocolate cannot hide from me for very long."

Mrs. MacGinnis bowed her head. "Ye are too kind, my lady." With a sweep of her hand, she directed Frannie the other way. "Come with me, and ye shall have that wee cup of chocolate in no time."

"Thank you so much, Mrs. MacGinnis. Do you know if Mr. Parkerton has come down yet?"

The housekeeper's cheeriness immediately soured. "Indeed, he has, my lady. Ye will find him waiting for ye." The silvery-haired woman gave a disgruntled hiss, and it had nothing to do with being out of breath. She angled a sympathetic look in Frannie's direction. "Ye traveled all the way from London with that man?"

"Yes, and didn't kick him out of the coach a single time. Are you not impressed?" Frannie wanted Mrs. MacGinnis to know she could speak her mind without fearing rebuke.

The housekeeper quietly chuckled as they strolled down the endless hallway. "Immensely impressed, my lady."

Just as Frannie decided they would never reach the dining room, Mrs. MacGinnis stopped beside a set of open double doors and bobbed a happy nod. "The dining room, my lady." She rolled her eyes and added, "And Mr. Parkerton there at the table waiting for ye."

"Thank you, Mrs. MacGinnis."

As Frannie entered, Mr. Parkerton rose from his chair, and a pair of footmen stepped forward with expectant looks. "Chocolate and perhaps one of those lovely pastries, please," she told the footmen before turning her attention to the solicitor, who appeared to have gotten a sampling of every item from the vast breakfast buffet that ran across the entire end of the dining room. The small plates littering the man's place at the table held enough food to feed several people.

"Are you quite famished, Mr. Parkerton?" Frannie asked as she seated herself across from him.

The pinch-faced gentleman shook his head. "I simply have found nothing to my liking. The quail's eggs don't suit, the honey cake is far too rich, and the kedgeree is too…" His picky voice trailed off, and he scowled upward, appearing to have exhausted his vocabulary of disparagement.

She could not abide a complainer. Nor could she tolerate such wastefulness. Especially when a guest behaved like a spoiled child, taking a nibble of all the treats and spoiling them for anyone else. "Perhaps you should make haste in arranging for a carriage back to London, since the food there better suits you."

The solicitor hovered his hand over each of the three cups in front of him as though trying to decide which to drink from. One contained coffee. One appeared to hold a milky tea, and the other chocolate. He selected the chocolate and lifted it in a toast. "I shall see to it immediately, my lady." Then he faltered and appeared confused. "But we already have your coach. Did it somehow become impaired during the last leg of the trip last night?" He gave her a knowing nod. "I noticed the ride became quite uncomfortable just before we arrived."

"To the best of my knowledge, my coach is quite fit." Frannie slowed the pace of her dismissal of the man by taking another sip of the most delicious hot chocolate she had ever tasted. She made a mental note to discover Lionwraith's supplier. "The carriage is for you, Mr. Parkerton."

"For me?" The man's Adam's apple zipped up and down his long, narrow throat in a hard swallow. "Alone?"

"Yes." She nibbled at the flaky butteriness of her pastry. The warm, sugary treat melted in her mouth. "You are to return to London and relinquish all Ardsmere files to Lord Raines. Moving forward, he shall represent the family."

Mr. Parkerton slowly returned his cup to the table and stared at her as if she had just sprouted horns. "You no longer require my services?"

"I do not." She realized he might not appreciate her bluntness. But in business matters, straight and to the point was always best. "Lord Raines will expect the transfer. I sent off a letter this very morning. It should reach him before you reach London." She locked eyes with the man to ensure he clearly understood. "I expect your departure today."

"There is no way I can sway your decision?" He swallowed hard again, now looking somewhat pale.

"You cannot." She wished he would excuse himself so she could enjoy her chocolate.

"Very well, then." He scooted back his chair, slowly stood, then offered a formal bow. "It has been my honor and pleasure to serve the Ardsmere family. Good day, my lady."

"Good day." Frannie kept her gaze fixed on him, willing the man to leave the room in a dignified manner. She didn't wish him ill. She merely wished him gone.

As if reading her mind, Mr. Parkerton gave a curt nod and hurried out.

It didn't escape her notice that both footmen were now smiling. She made eye contact with the closest one. "Have Mr. Judson and Mr. Marcus been down yet? The other two men who arrived with me last night?"

"I believe they are with Mr. Kirby, Lionwraith's stable master, my lady. Mrs. Kirby always makes a fine breakfast for all the hands who work in the stable. Your coachman, Mr. Hardie, is probably there too, since the place has quite nice quarters of its own for the visiting servants who tend to their master's animals."

"Thank you." She understood completely. The Bow Street Runners would be more at ease in the company of Mr. Hardie and Mr. Kirby's family rather than joining her at the duke's table.

"Your solicitor just ran past me. I believe the man was crying," Alec said as he entered the dining room and swept the area with a guarded scowl.

Now it was her turn to swallow hard. The apprehensive duke had tamed his unruly jet mane and dressed quite handsomely in a golden brocade waistcoat, tan pantaloons, and tall black boots that gleamed with a fresh polishing. The whiteness of his cravat complemented the aristocratic lines of his sculpted jaw, and the cut of his black, single-breasted jacket made his broad chest look even wider. This morning's vision of the man was more delectable than her hot chocolate.

"Lady Ardsmere?" He angled a quizzical look her way as he went to the buffet and prepared his own plate rather than allow the servants to see to the task.

"Yes, Your Grace?" She had already forgotten what he had said. She really needed to focus.

"Your solicitor in tears?" he prompted.

"Ah. Yes." She sipped her chocolate while silently scolding herself for behaving like a complete ninny. "I severed our association and suggested he hire a coach and return to London. Today."

"I see." Alec seated himself at the head of the table to her right, then appeared to allow himself a rueful smile. "That is a relief to hear. I feared further tragedy had found its way to us."

She glanced at the doorway, then at the footmen before leaning toward him and asking in a lowered voice, "Will Lady Violet be joining us this morning?"

He paused with his fork in midair. "That is my hope," he said quietly, then gave her a meaningful arch of a sleek, dark brow. "But I ask that any discussions that should remain private be held in the proper place."

"I would never do otherwise," she assured him. As she finished her chocolate and toyed with the thought of treating herself to the rare indulgence of a second cup, the duke's sister entered.

The poor lady looked wan and bleary-eyed. Frannie's heart went out to her. "Good morning, Lady Violet."

"Good morning, Lady Ardsmere." Lady Violet curtsied before seating herself on the other side of the table to the duke's right.

Alec set down his fork and took his sister's hand. "Good morning, Vivvy. I pray you rested well?"

His sister gave him a tense smile and shifted with a deep, shuddering breath. "The sun is shining today. Did you notice?"

"I did indeed." The duke rested his hands on either side of his plate as though he couldn't decide whether or not he was finished. "Perhaps after we are done with breakfast, we might enjoy a stroll through the gardens."

As Lady Violet accepted a cup of tea and a small plate of toasted bread from one of the footmen, she barely shook her head. "It will still be far too wet in the gardens, brother." She cast a hesitant smile at Frannie. "I believe the conservatory would be a much better choice. We wouldn't wish to ruin our slippers. Would we, Lady Ardsmere?"

Frannie sensed the two were trying to find a place other than the library where they might speak without being overheard. Still feeling the need to win Lady Violet's trust, she leaned across the table as if about to share a secret. "Indeed, we would not. If I ruin any more of my things," she said in a loud whisper, "my poor maid will scold me to no end." She tipped her head the duke's way. "Last night, while warming myself in front of the hearth, sparks popped onto the back of my dress, and I was totally unaware of them. Thankfully, your brother acted quickly and put them out." She gave a little laugh. "I fear my poor traveling gown is ruined. My dear maid is beside herself."

Lady Violet's dark eyes danced with mirth, and the taut set of her slender shoulders relaxed the slightest bit. "Thank goodness my brother was in a chivalrous mood. He is not usually so quick to help those he has just met."

"I could not very well allow the lady to burst into flames in my library," the duke said.

"You were simply worried I might set your books on fire." Frannie had to tease him. His broody spirit so needed uplifting.

"The thought did cross my mind." Amusement finally gleamed in his hazel eyes.

She released a dramatic sigh and pressed the back of her hand to her forehead as though about to faint. "I knew it. Chivalry is dead."

"Oh no, my lady," he said with a devilish grin. "If chivalry were dead, I would have simply tossed you out the window."

Frannie laughed. "How fortunate for me, then!"

"I believe I am quite finished with my breakfast," Lady Violet said, quietly ending their banter. "If the two of you are ready, might we go to the conservatory now? I would prefer to—" She interrupted herself with a hitching intake of air and bowed her head. "Get this behind me," she finished so softly that Frannie barely made out the words.

Alec turned to Frannie. The turmoil in his eyes had returned, and her heart hurt for him. "Would you like to see our conservatory, Lady Ardsmere?"

"I would indeed."

With a grim air, he rose to help her from her chair and then attended to his sister. "The portico that crosses the garden should be dry enough to avoid ruining your slippers. Shall we give it a go?"

Frannie waited for Lady Violet to decide, but when the troubled young woman remained silent, she forged ahead. "I would love to." She slid her hand through Alec's arm, even though he had failed to offer it.

As if spurred on by her action, he patted her hand, then offered his other arm to his sister.

Looking as though she was about to be led to the gallows, Lady Violet took his arm and turned toward the wall of double doors that opened out into the gardens. A lovely design indeed, if only the rains and chilly days would grant them a reprieve.

Without the necessity of being told, the nearest footman hurried to open the doors and stand aside.

"I believe it is more like early spring rather than mid-June," Frannie remarked as they stepped outside. Thank goodness Daisy had selected a woolen dress for her for the day. While in the shade of the covered cobblestone walkway, the air was quite cool.

"Are the two of you warm enough?" Alec halted as if reading her mind, and eyed them both with concern. "Do we need to turn back and fetch your shawls?"

"I am quite fine," Lady Violet said while frowning at something off in the distance. "Thank you."

Frannie wasn't about to relent and turn back. If Alec's sister could bear it, then she would too. "Let us carry on. I am sure the conservatory will be much warmer."

"To the conservatory, then," Alec said.

A light breeze brought the clean, fresh smell of damp earth to Frannie. She inhaled deeper, relishing air unspoiled by London's smoke and the stench of too many people living in one spot. It made her miss Belgium's countryside and the sweetness it held. While well-populated areas supported her import business admirably, she despised the noise, the filth, and the dangers that came with them.

"It is quite lovely here," she said while lifting her nose and pulling in another deep breath. A thrill washed across her. "You have lilacs!"

"They are Alec's favorite," Lady Violet said with an affectionate smile up at her brother.

"Mine too." Frannie closed her eyes and took in another sampling of the sweet scent, her spirits buoyed by the fragrance. It had to be a good omen. They would find the rogue who ruined Lady Violet and bring him to justice.

"I feared they wouldn't bloom and maybe not even survive because of the lateness and severity of the frost." Alec opened the door to the conservatory and ushered them in with a smile. "But I have more in here. Rare lilacs I think you will enjoy."

"I shall wait in the sitting area while you show her, brother." Lady Violet slipped away before either of them could protest, disappearing through a verdant, leafy screen.

It suddenly hit Frannie that it might not be in Lady Violet's best interest to find the father of her child. Could the lady bear to see him again and confront him about what he had done? "Have you asked your sister what she wishes for us to do to help her?"

"Asked her?"

"Yes. Asked her if she wants to face the man who has caused her so much pain?"

"He should pay." He bared his teeth as if about to gnash them.

She touched his arm in a silly attempt at calming him. "I quite agree. But what if Lady Violet simply needs to move on? Have her baby and find a way to make the best of it." She lowered her voice and prayed he would take her advice with the sympathy and caring she intended. "Maybe she only wishes for her family to accept her and help raise the child."

"Are you insinuating I have not given my sister all the acceptance and support possible?"

She decided it was better to change course. "Absolutely not. It is quite clear you have offered her nothing but love and as much comfort as possible. I merely wish to do what your sister truly wants and needs. I can always pursue the blackguard to recover the losses caused by his using my husband's name, but if Lady Violet wishes, we can keep her out of it. We should ask her what she wants." Amazing even herself, she squeezed his arm as though they were on familiar terms. "I do not wish us to hurt your sister any more than she has already been hurt."

"You are a strange woman, Lady Ardsmere."

"Frannie in settings like this. Remember?"

He snorted like a bull. "Frannie—you are a strange woman."

"You are not the first to accuse me of such, and I am sure you will not be the last. Now, shall we join your sister? You may share the lilacs with me later, and I shall hold you to doing so." She tried the same stern look that Mother Ardsmere always used on her, but realized it failed miserably when the duke rolled his eyes. "Rolling your eyes is very rude, Your Grace."

"I am a very rude man, or have you not noticed?"

"It has not escaped me."

He huffed a mirthless laugh and held out his hand. "This way to my sister."

She took his hand without hesitation and followed him through the screen of greenery, catching her breath at the cozy seating area beneath a glass vaulted ceiling that was as grand as any ballroom. "Oh my."

"I take it that means you like it?" He tugged her toward the table covered in a fine linen cloth where his sister waited.

"Is the prince regent not jealous of you?" She craned her neck to take in the glass ceiling, still fogged and covered in rain droplets but revealing as much of the azure sky as possible.

"Prinny owes me many favors," he said, looking as though the admission pained him.

She decided not to pursue that line of conversation, for all their sakes. Instead, she hurried to seat herself at the table with Lady Violet. "We decided to chat before I enjoyed the lilacs. You are more important than any flower."

After a weepy-eyed attempt at a smile, Lady Violet bowed her head. "I am a fallen woman. Deserving of no one's kindness."

"Stop repeating Mother's rubbish," Alec gently scolded. "The woman thinks of no one but herself." He seated himself beside his sister and covered her clasped hands with his. "It is you and me against her, Vivvy. As it always has been. We shall best her now as we did when we were children."

Frannie was thankful Lady Violet had her brother to depend upon. If not, who knew what would have happened to the poor girl and her child? "What do you require of us to make your life easier?" she asked her. "Do you want us to find the father of your baby so you might confront him with his responsibilities?"

The lady's deep brown eyes glimmered with so much emotion and pain that Frannie's heart lurched. "He loves me, Lady Ardsmere. I will never believe otherwise."

"Does he know you carry his child?" Before the girl said a word, Frannie knew the answer. "You didn't tell him."

"How could I?" The overset lady sagged forward and buried her face in her arms.

"You didn't even give him the opportunity to do the right thing?" Alec's tone concerned Frannie. The man's frustration had reached a dangerous level.

"I could not," Lady Violet said, her voice muffled because she didn't raise her head. "I just couldn't. Not with all his responsibilities and worries."

He reared back and opened his mouth as if about to roar, but Frannie held him off with a pointing finger and a look she hoped would silence him—at least temporarily. "What responsibilities does your false marquess have, my lady?" she asked his sister.

Lady Violet sat up and gave a woeful shake of her head. "He brings goods in and sells them. Like your family does, my lady. Sometimes it is very complicated and always done at night because it is so dangerous."

"My goods travel through highly finessed channels," Frannie said. "Neither my husband nor I are smugglers."

"Apparently, he is," Alec growled. He pushed away from the table and shot to his feet, obviously unable to sit any longer. "A smuggler, Vivvy." He shook his head. "Where, in heaven's name, did you meet this devil?"

"Here," she whispered. "At Mother's Twelfth Night masked ball that infuriated you so."

"A masked ball," Frannie repeated. "How appropriate."

"And how convenient," Alec said.

CHAPTER FOUR

ALEC PACED IN a tight circle in front of the table. He noticed the folds of its cloth quivering the slightest bit. Apparently, as Frannie sat frowning at something off in the distance, her annoying habit of jiggling had returned. The woman said she always did that whenever deep in thought about a problem. If her incessant twitching could solve this dilemma, then so be it. He would kiss her full on the mouth for it.

The suddenness of that improper thought slowed his pacing. She was married. Even though he didn't know the man, he would not dishonor her husband in such a manner. Never would he do to another what his late wife had done to him. But in defense of his immoral, wandering mind, Frannie distracted him. More so than any woman had in a very long while. She was so…so damned odd, for lack of a better word. He had never met another woman like her. She intrigued him like a rare, newly acquired book waiting to be opened and enjoyed.

"Does your fidgeting have any insights to offer?" he asked, trying to focus on more appropriate thoughts. The tablecloth immediately stilled, and he struggled not to smile at her narrow-eyed glower.

"As a matter of fact, it does." She cast him a disparaging glance before turning to his sister. "Try as I might, I cannot recall receiving an invitation to your mother's Twelfth Night masquerade, and if she sent one to the Ardsmere townhouse in London, I would have been informed. How did the false Lord Ardsmere gain entry?"

Vivvy nodded at Alec. "Lord Ardsmere said you invited him when the two of you met at White's. Mother took him at his word."

"After Mother's behavior at the last ball she hosted, she knew very well I would never sanction another. Why would she believe I had invited a guest, especially a new acquaintance, to one of her arrogant *haut ton* affairs?"

"Are they ever anything but arrogant?" Frannie blew out a very unladylike snort. "The *haut ton* puts the *haut* in haughty." Her lovely blue eyes flared wider, as though she immediately regretted speaking her mind.

"And yet you, my lady, are an esteemed member of that dubiously Polite Society. Are you not?" He couldn't resist goading her. She always came out with something unexpected and, more often than not, quite amusing. And, at present, he needed as much amusement as he could get.

She fidgeted in place as if her backside was once again smoking with red-hot embers. "I am not so sure about *esteemed*." She rolled her eyes, entertaining him immensely. "But I have endured my share of balls and parties in Belgium, and an evening at Almack's with the dowager countess once or twice."

"I shall never be allowed entry to Almack's ever again," Vivvy said. With a heart-wrenching wail, she hid her face in the shelter of her folded arms once again.

"Oh dear." Frannie leaned over and patted his sister's shoulder while casting a panicked look his way. "I should not have said that. Please forgive me, Lady Violet."

Vivvy sobbed harder, howling like one of Alec's best hounds when it caught the scent of the hunt.

He scrubbed his hand across his mouth to keep from ordering her to find her backbone and fight for herself. His dear sister had always been the weepy sort, and since getting with child, that trait had only worsened. "Vivvy," he said as calmly as he could manage. After several minutes of being ignored while she hiccupped and wept, he tried again. *"Violet."*

Frannie rose from her chair and gently took hold of his sister's trembling shoulders. "Lady Violet. Please pull yourself together, dear lady. You are going to make yourself quite ill. Think of your child."

"What do you know of my troubles?" The lady erupted with a feral growl and jerked away from Frannie. "You are a married woman and not burdened with a bastard." Vivvy shot to her feet and ran away without looking back.

In wide-eyed amazement, Frannie stared after her. "My goodness."

Alec sank into his chair and unleashed a heavy sigh. "Please accept my apologies on my sister's behalf. Under normal circumstances, she would never speak to you in such a vulgar manner."

"Do not give it a second thought. The poor thing withstood all she could bear." Frannie slowly returned to her seat, still staring after Violet. After a slow shake of her head, she turned to him. "It will be up to us to find this man. I do not believe she is capable of taking an active part in trapping the rakehell. Nor did she seem inclined to tell him he would soon be a father. I am sorry, but I found her excuse about his smuggling operation questionable."

Her suspicious tone filled Alec with misgiving.

"I would never accuse your sister of lying," she said, "but I believe in her heart, she knew her lover was not the Marquess of Ardsmere. Do we have any way of knowing if that was the name the rogue actually gave her or if she came up with it on her own? After all, she compared his business activities with that of West Belgium International's imports. Few in London think of the Ardsmere family when dealing with West Belgium International. It's almost as if my company is a peer in and of itself."

"I cannot imagine her lying." But as much as he hated to admit it, Frannie's questions were valid. "Why would she lie?

Especially to me? All I have ever done is help her."

"I am not saying she did." Frannie twitched her nose as if smelling something foul. "Well, perhaps I am saying that, but please understand, I do not mean it maliciously." She nervously patted the table. "Surely you have heard of ladies falling in love with men their families would never approve of."

"And they sometimes do it deliberately to defy their families." He scrubbed his face with both hands this time. Had meek little Vivvy chosen this as a way to strike back at their cruel mother? Gads, that meant he would have to confront the old demoness herself to discover if what Vivvy had said about the Twelfth Night masquerade was true. Discussions with Mother never went well. Neither of them attempted to control their contempt for the other.

"And perhaps none of what I suggested might be true," Frannie said. "I am simply saying we must consider all options as we attempt to unravel this mess."

"A mess indeed." A suffocating need to grant his mind a small reprieve in order to think more clearly churned within him. He rose from his chair and offered his arm. "I need to walk, and I promised to show you some of my favorite lilacs."

Much to his relief, she appeared to welcome the change of subject and took his arm. As they followed the winding path toward the fragrant bushes, she beamed like a child headed for a table of treats. "Do you cultivate your lilacs, or do you have a gardener who cares for them? They are so lush and beautiful."

"I know enough about plants to get them safely here to Lionwraith. After that, my gardener, Sir Henry, tends and nurtures them as if they are his children."

"Your gardener is a knight?" She paused and buried her nose in a cluster of star-shaped purple flowers.

Alec realized with something of a start that this moment in time felt as natural as could be. He couldn't shake the eerie feeling that he and Frannie were old friends. Or had known each other for quite some time, even though they had never met before last night.

"Alec?" She turned back to him and patted his arm. "Have I lost you to your worries?"

"Forgive me." What the devil was wrong with him? He resettled her hand more comfortably in the crook of his elbow. "Sir Henry was part of my regiment. He suffered an injury that left him slightly rattled and thinking that he had received a knighthood for an act of valor in saving the queen. Which, in a roundabout way, he did. But just not as he now remembers it." Alec reached up and plucked a cluster of small white flowers tinged in purple. "I didn't have the heart to tell him that his knighthood was only imagined. So, I brought him here. To live out the rest of his days. Tending my gardens." He held out the mass of blooms to her. "*Syringa pubescens.* I obtained this variety from China. Its scent differs from most lilacs in that it not only smells sweet but also somewhat spicy."

"Its fragrance is so much stronger too." Frannie cradled the cluster of blossoms in her hands. "Its sweetness isn't delicate like my usual favorites."

"It is like you," he said before he could stop himself.

"Like me?"

"Sweet, yet strong, and impossible to be ignored or overlooked." While he couldn't attest to the spiciness of the lady in question, he wouldn't mind discovering it. But that would not be right. *True. But it would be safe,* his conscience argued. With her a married woman, there would be no danger of entanglements or messy declarations of love. What was it about Frannie that made him so ready to toss his morals and convictions aside?

He needed to convince her that his ill-spoken observation was a jest—even though it wasn't. "You did burst into my home uninvited and threaten to use pistols to get my attention. Did you not?"

She rewarded him with a laugh that lightened his battered heart. "I did at that. But rest assured, I would not have shot you. Your churlish butler was being obstinate, and I had to make him realize I was quite serious about seeing you."

"Yes, I fear you wounded MacGinnis's pride immeasurably." He directed her to the next fragrant island of woody plants thriving in large tubs. "This species of lilac tends to be more blue than purple—symbolizing happiness and tranquility."

"We could all use more happiness and tranquility right now." She buried her nose in the delicate bundle of petals and smiled. "Ahh…now this one is closer to the scent I have always loved."

He didn't understand why, but he couldn't resist an unreasonable need to know about her relationship with the marquess. The longer he was around her, the more it nettled him. Like an itch he couldn't reach. "Do you and your husband share a love of flowers?"

She turned and stared at him with a jerk, as though he had startled her, but then she quickly recovered her composure. "We used to," she said, then turned back to the path and strolled deeper into the conservatory. "This direction seems warmer. Oh my goodness. Lemon trees too? This place is absolute heaven."

"Yes, lemon trees too. And oranges, limes, and pineapples. Sir Henry keeps the braziers going to ensure the temperature suits what the plants and trees need to thrive." He barely stopped himself from holding out his hand for her to take. What the deuce was wrong with him? He had no right to such familiarity. Offering his arm was one thing. Attempting to take her hand and hold it as they walked was quite another. "On the far side of the building are the hibiscus, oleanders, camellias, and vegetables and herbs for Cook to use year-round."

As the path opened into a wider area, Frannie stretched out her arms and slowly turned in a circle. Her happy smile lifted skyward. "So beautiful. I could stay in here forever."

If only she could. Alec shook away the not only unsettling but also ridiculous idea. "I come here often. To think."

She let her arms fall to her sides and gave him a sympathetic nod. "And you have had much too much to think about of late."

"Indeed." A heavy sigh escaped him. "And after this latest

conversation with my sister…" It was better he not voice the rest. Although he treasured sweet Vivvy, he was not at all pleased with her. "I fully intend to speak with my mother and have my men renew their search for the father of her child."

Frannie pursed her lips in a thoughtful look that gave him pause. "I too planned to send my Bow Street Runners in search of the man, but now I am not so sure that is the first action we should take."

"Meaning?"

"Firstly, we need to ensure that the scoundrel was the one who assumed my husband's name and title and that it wasn't merely a subterfuge devised by Lady Violet." She paced back and forth between the orange and lemon trees with her arms folded across her front, lightly tapping her chin as she spoke. "And secondly, the invitation to the ball must be confirmed or denied by the dowager duchess."

"I intend to address that with my mother, but how do you propose we discover if the devil told Vivvy he was Lord Ardsmere, or if she made it up to throw us off his trail?" He fell in step beside Frannie, joining her pacing.

She abruptly halted, and her eyes narrowed. "Jennet has seen the man, and if she and Lady Violet are as close as I am with my maid, Jennet would know the name the man truly used—but will she tell us?"

"She will if she values her position here at Lionwraith."

Frannie rolled her eyes. "That is not the tactic you should use to get her to talk."

"You told me rolling one's eyes was very rude, and yet you keep doing it." He glared at her, needing her to be on his side.

"It is not rude when I do it because I am trying to emphasize my point." She cleared her throat and fixed him with a reproachful frown. "May I continue now?"

With a mirthless huff, he bowed. "By all means, my lady."

"We need to convince Jennet we need as much information as possible in order to help her mistress."

"And then what?" He mimicked her stance by folding his arms across his chest.

"If the man posed as Lord Ardsmere merely to seduce unsuspecting innocents, then we set a suitable trap using the soirees of the London Season. But if his fraudulence was merely a means of gleaning more contacts to further his smuggling operation, our snare would be better served wherever smugglers exchange their goods. Once we surmise which is the more accurate, then we use my investigators and your men to gather the information needed to make our ambush a success."

Alec stared at her. It was a shame the woman hadn't been born a man. Her ability to strategize would have been a boon to the war effort—probably ending it much sooner. "And what if Jennet is unable to tell us any more than she already has?"

"I cannot believe she does not know more." Frannie winced and ceased chewing on the corner of her lip. She touched her mouth, then frowned at her fingertips as though checking for blood. "She simply has to. Jennet said she accompanied Lady Violet every time she met with *her* Lord Ardsmere. We will simply speak with her and write everything down so we do not miss a single clue." Her focus shifted from her fingers back to him, and the look in her eyes set him on edge.

"What now?"

"You do realize that no matter which scheme we decide would render us the best results, you are going to have to remain calm and control your temper?" She arched a brow, intensifying her critical scrutiny of him. "Your reputation as a raging lion is still quite alive and well in London." She studied him, barely tilting her head as she did so. "I wonder if it would be in the best interest of your sister for you to remain here at Lionwraith and behave as though nothing has gone awry. I can handle things and keep you informed."

"You underestimate me, my lady. Not only am I an adept hunter, but I am also quite good at, shall we say, *reading* people?" He moved closer, so close that she unconsciously took a step back to keep an appropriate amount of space between them. Her reaction made him smile. "You see? I knew you would move back when I pressed the boundaries of your propriety."

She wet her lips, making him wonder what they would taste like in a stolen kiss. "Point taken," she said, then cleared her throat and opened her mouth to say something further, but was interrupted by a very loud and demanding *meow*.

"Wellington, it is bad form to interrupt a lady." Alec reached down and held out his hand. "Come out, old man. Show yourself and apologize to Frannie."

The enormous, long-haired ginger cat with only one ear and three legs emerged from the depths of the garden platform without rustling so much as a single leaf. He assumed a regal pose, proudly seating himself on the wide beam of the raised plant bed before casting a discerning look at Frannie. He licked his nose, flicked his ear, then yawned.

"May I pet you, Wellington?" She allowed him to sniff her hand, then risked scratching him under his chin.

The feline angled his head so she might reach the perfect spot and rewarded her with a loud, rumbling purr.

"What a handsome gentleman." She continued scratching him as she glanced up at Alec. "You named your cat Wellington?"

"*Wellington* named Wellington." He lowered himself to the wide beam and sat beside the cat. "This valiant beast staggered into our camp one evening. A half-starved kitten covered in blood and dragging what was left of his leg behind him. One man started to shoot him to end his suffering, but neither Wellington nor I would stand for it. The surgeon took care of the leg, and we nursed him back to health. He traveled with us on several campaigns and cheered us on at Waterloo."

"You are a surprising man, Your Grace," Frannie said with her adoring look fixed on the cat.

"Alec."

"Alec," she repeated softly. Shifting her attention to him, she seated herself on the other side of the purring feline. "And how is it that Wellington came to live with you rather than with his namesake?"

"The duke's wife was not of a mind to open any of her homes to a…'crippled battle cat,' I believe is how she put it."

"Well, how rude was that? Was it not, Wellington?" she stroked the proud beast and scratched him behind his lone ear.

The cat looked up at her, twitching his whiskers as he slowly flipped the white tip of his fluffy tail.

"You are quite the handsome gentleman, and your service to the regiment is much appreciated," she added, then leaned down and kissed the top of his head.

For the first time in his life, Alec found himself jealous of the cat. A snort escaped him at such silliness. "Wellington now assists Sir Henry in protecting the conservatory against attack. One must never let down one's guard."

"Indeed." Something about Frannie shifted and her expression became unreadable. She suddenly seemed almost wary. Then she took in a hurried, deep breath and returned to her self-assured demeanor. "Shall I accompany you to see Her Grace?"

"That depends."

"On what?"

"Do you enjoy battles?"

Her smile turned mischievously wicked and lit up her eyes. "Only the ones I win."

Her attitude inspired him. Alec rose, offered her his arm, and gave Wellington a nod. "Wish us luck, old man."

Wellington blessed their endeavor with a slow, lazy blink of his amber eyes and another enormous yawn.

"Let us make him proud." Frannie took his arm and fell in step beside him. "I am prepared, you know. While readying for our confrontation, information about your mother's *personality* became available as well."

"I doubt it took much effort for your contacts to discover that Mother is known for her delight in throwing off and rumping those who dare displease her. And she always ensures her cuts and insults are performed in the presence of the largest and most powerful audiences possible."

"The reports hinted at such."

"You are being polite," he accused.

She cleared her throat and tried not to smile but failed. "I am trying."

As they followed the portico back to the main house, he noticed dark clouds gathering once more. Apparently, even the sun refused to show its face when his mother was discussed. He didn't blame it one damn bit. Once they had exited the dining room, he veered to the left. "The demoness's lair is this way, and I hope you enjoy walking. For the sake of all concerned, it was best for her apartments to be located as far from mine as possible."

"I am surprised she is not in London. After all, it is the Season." Frannie tugged on his arm. "I would appreciate a slower pace, Your Grace. Your stride is much longer than mine."

"Forgive my thoughtlessness, my lady." And he meant it. While she was tall for a woman, she was still a full head shorter than his six-foot-three frame. "I tend to charge into battle with little thought to anything else."

"Nothing to forgive. I understand completely, but I do wonder why your mother is not in London rather than here?"

"This year was to be my sister's debut, and Mother will not risk word getting out about Vivvy's difficulties." He snorted a bitter laugh. "Mother is a coward. She hides here, feigning illness and also using that as an excuse for Vivvy to wait until next year to dominate every event of the Season. After all, as a diamond of the first water, *Lady Violet* could not possibly negotiate Society without her esteemed mother guiding her."

"Wisely played." Frannie lightly trailed her hand along the banister as they climbed the stairs to his mother's floor.

"If the demoness is anything, she is a cunning schemer." He nodded at the footman standing outside the set of double doors of the dowager duchess's suite. "Has she emerged from her lair yet?"

The footman didn't react other than to bow his head. "Her Grace breakfasted in her dressing room, but I am told to inform you she is quite well, Your Grace." He opened the doors and kept his head bowed as they passed through.

"That is code for 'she is aware we have guests,'" Alec said in a lowered voice to Frannie. "Consider yourself warned, my lady."

"I wonder if she knows who I am," she whispered back.

"I am sure she does." He pulled in a deep intake of air and slowly released it through tightly clenched teeth to control the age-old rage his mother always stirred. "I have yet to discover her informant, but she misses nothing that goes on in this household." Upon entering the private parlor, he yanked on the bellpull beside the door. "And so it begins."

The ivory door decorated with gilded roses on the other side of the room creaked open. It took forever for Mother to choose to step forward and enter the room. The woman always had a penchant for the dramatic.

"Alec." She spat out his name as though she hated saying it. And he knew very well that she did. Her icy gaze settled for a fleeting moment on Frannie, then slid back to him.

"Your Grace," he said in a disgusted tone intended to infuriate her. "Allow me to present the Marchioness of Ardsmere." He stepped forward, keeping Frannie on his arm. "Lady Ardsmere— the Dowager Duchess of Lionwraith, my mother."

Frannie stepped away from him and curtsied. "Your Grace. It is a pleasure to meet you."

"I doubt this meeting will be a pleasure for either of us." His waspish mother angled her sharp chin to a haughtier angle. "I take it your husband sent you?"

"He did not." Frannie's smug expression revealed she had purposely not used the customary *Your Grace* this time. "I came here of my own accord to discover why Lionwraith had declared a commerce war upon West Belgium International."

"And did you?" The dowager resettled her bony hands atop a replica of the gleaming black cane she had often used to crack across her children's backs until the day Alec had snatched it away, broken it in half, and threatened to use what was left of it on her. "Did you see the mess that man left for us to clean up?"

Completely unflustered, Frannie shook her head. "I found no mess of my husband's doing. However, I did meet the lovely Lady Violet and intend to help her in any way I can."

"The Ardsmere line has done quite enough for that little hedge whore." The surly matron shifted her dark gaze back to Alec, as if dismissing Frannie from her presence. "How dare you interrupt a most pleasant morning by throwing this family's failure in my face yet again?"

He instinctively placed himself between his mother and Frannie. "Were you aware that Vivvy first met Lord Ardsmere at your Twelfth Night masquerade ball I refused to sanction? I would say that makes you a part of that failure, Mother."

"Her name is Violet, not *Vivvy*!" The dowager sneered at him, baring her yellowed teeth like a cornered rat. "And you are the one who invited the man! Not I."

"Why would I invite a man to a ball I refused to attend?"

"To irritate me," she growled through clenched teeth. Her gray curls trembled, revealing the depths of her anger. Her ebony eyes glittered even darker, matching the soullessness of her austere black gown. She pointed her cane at the door. "Get out." She narrowed her eyes at Frannie. "And take that with you."

A satisfied coldness settled over Alec, and a smile came easy to him. "Thank you, Mother."

"For what?"

"Martha!" he bellowed, knowing his mother's maid stood on the other side of the door, waiting for her mistress's summons. As expected, the door flew open, and the elderly maid scurried to stand in front of him with her head bowed.

"Yes, Your Grace?"

"Pack Her Grace's things and have her ready to leave for the manor house at Castle Douglas by this afternoon. From this day forward, that will be her permanent residence." He savored the fear registering in his mother's beady eyes.

"You cannot mean to—" the dowager whispered.

"It is done, and your allowance will be lowered accordingly to prevent you from wandering too far from home." He turned and offered his arm to Frannie. "We found out what we came here for. Did we not, Lady Ardsmere?"

"Yes, Your Grace." She took his arm and didn't spare a look back as they left the room.

Once they stepped out into the hallway just outside the double doors, Alec paused and bowed his head, listening.

"Alec?" Frannie whispered.

Bloodcurdling shrieks and the sound of breaking glass came from his mother's rooms.

He lifted his head and smiled. "Do you find champagne agreeable, Frannie?"

"Of course. But why?"

"Because it is definitely in order."

CHAPTER FIVE

FRANNIE PULLED HER notes from her reticule and slowly thumbed through them yet again. She reread everything that Lady Violet's maid, Jennet, had not only told her about the infamous Lord Ardsmere but also shared with Daisy. She glanced up at her maid where she sat across from her in the carriage. "Thank you for convincing Jennet that we really are trying to help her mistress."

"Even if you find the devil and confront him," Daisy said, "do you think he will do right by her?"

"I cannot say." Frannie wouldn't even begin to speculate about that. The man might not even have the opportunity to do the right thing if Alec flew into a rage and did away with him. "And I am not sure that is what Lady Violet wants him to do, either."

Daisy leaned forward, as if fearing the walls of the coach might overhear. "Maybe the Sisterhood could help her."

"That would be a risky and complicated endeavor because of her brother, the duke." Frannie leveled a meaningful look on the well-intentioned maid. "Lionwraith must never learn of the Sisterhood. Not ever."

"Understood, my lady." Daisy lifted the flap covering the window and wrinkled her freckled nose. "Still raining. The trunks will be good and soaked when the lads bring them inside."

"Well, we are nearly to Mayfair, so I suppose we might as

well resign ourselves to the weather being as dreary here as on the road. Lady Sophie sent word to her staff to get the house ready, since she has yet to arrive from France. So, our settling in shouldn't be too difficult." Frannie shoved her notes back inside her reticule and peered out the window for herself. Such a dismal day. The chilly grayness threatened to sap the joy out of everything.

"And why did you say we are staying with Lady Sophie rather than opening Ardsmere House?"

"We can't very well entertain at Ardsmere House and expect the false Lord Ardsmere to show up there. Surely the man would not be so bold as to do that—or so foolish. Lady Sophie's home, or rather, the home of her brother, the Earl of Rydleshire, will suit much better than our home or Lionwraith's home here in London." Frannie found herself hoping she hadn't forgotten anything as she reviewed every detail of what she and Alec had discussed and planned. "And Celia said we may also use Hasterton House should the need arise—although I would rather not. After all, little Oliver is merely a few weeks old, and Celia is still in her confinement."

Daisy made a disgruntled clucking noise. "The Duchess of Hasterton's maid was fair beside herself, what with trying to keep Her Grace from doing too much. Why, the duchess hasn't even been churched yet, nor the babe christened, and she's already talking of giving parties? That is asking for bad fortune, I say."

Frannie smiled at the maid's superstitions. "Celia does not suffer boredom well, and she is quite the determined lady. But she won't endanger herself or the little one." She peeked beyond the window flap again, noting the change of the buildings through the somber curtain of rain. "At least Rydleshire is across the way from Hasterton House. Perhaps we can help keep Celia entertained for the remainder of her lying in."

"Jennet said His Grace's home is near there too." Daisy squinted as though trying to see her memories. "In fact, if I remember correctly, I believe she said Lionwraith Place is next to

Lady Sophie's home. Seems like they share a mews."

"That would be fortunate." Frannie fought to tamp down the excited fluttering that troubled her of late whenever the Duke of Lionwraith was near or even mentioned. "After all, His Grace wishes to be an active accomplice in our hunt."

"If I may be so bold," Daisy said with a sly smile, "His Grace has a certain way about him whenever you are around." She cleared her throat with a dramatic *ahem*. "And you with him, I might add."

"As far as His Grace is concerned, I am a kindhearted, yet *very married*, woman who is trying to help him and his sister." And that was all she could ever be, she realized with a sudden heaviness that made it hard to breathe. Even though she was always surrounded by people, she was so unbearably alone. Rank and privilege were cold and heartless companions, and she was weary of them.

But her attraction to the handsome duke would never be anything more than an unattainable wish. The supposedly fearsome man whom she had discovered to be a soft-hearted protector of wounded veterans, stray cats, and his hapless sister abhorred liars and deceivers. Of which she was both—and had been all her life. For the safety of all concerned, as well as her blossoming friendship with the dashing Duke of Lionwraith, Alec must never learn the truth. The truth would destroy everything.

The coach halted, saving her from further reflection on what could never be.

"Finally," she said a little too sharply. "Let us get dry and settled in with a nice cup of tea. Strangely enough, the trip back to London wearied me infinitely more than the trip north to Lionwraith Estate."

The carriage door opened and a young man who Frannie supposed was one of Sophie's footmen placed the steps for her to descend upon while holding an umbrella overhead to keep her dry. Another man, one who appeared to be a great deal older than the first, waited with an umbrella much larger than the footman's.

"Welcome to Rydleshire House, my lady," he said with a prim nod, while ensuring she remained untouched by the rain as they ascended the front steps. "I am Thornton, the butler here at Rydleshire."

"Thank you, Thornton." Frannie cast a glance back and was pleased to discover that another footman held an umbrella over Daisy as she supervised more servants unloading the trunks. Apparently, Sophie had spared nothing for her home in London, even though she and her mother spent most of their time at their villa in France.

As they pushed through the grand doors of the townhouse, Frannie was met by the servants lined up in the entry hall to greet her. She clenched her teeth against unleashing a weary sigh. All she presently wanted was a warm seat by a crackling fire and a cup of tea. But she didn't have the heart to disappoint them and dash their expectant looks. They were all trying so very hard to make the perfect first impression.

She paused in front of the gray-haired matron at the head of the line who kept shooting stern glances at the young men and women standing at attention beside her. Frannie offered the lady a kind nod. "You must be the housekeeper. Thank you so much for seeing that the house is ready in such a short amount of time. All this damp weather, and yet not a hint of mustiness in the air. Everything looks shining and perfect."

The older woman's rosy cheeks plumped with an appreciative smile that crinkled the corners of her eyes. After a perfect curtsy, she bowed her head. "Mrs. Thornton here. I am the housekeeper. Just as you said, Lady Ardsmere. Thank you for your kind words. Anything you need shall be seen to immediately. Lady Sophie said to make it so, and we shall." She waved a hand at the line of servants. "All of us have served Lady Sophie for years, and are proud to serve you as well."

Frannie took that to mean they could be trusted, but she still felt the need to be careful—at least until she spoke with Sophie.

She removed her cloak and handed it to the butler. "I know I am in the best of hands, Mrs. Thornton. Would you be good enough to show me to my rooms so I might freshen up and enjoy a relaxing cup of tea by the fire?"

"Of course, my lady." Mrs. Thornton arched a stern brow at the servants, and, without her saying a word, they scattered like birds flushed from the trees. She turned back to Frannie, politely nodded, then headed for the staircase to the left of the wide entry hall. "This way, my lady. The lads should already have your trunks delivered, and I told them to show your maid the way to your suite."

The rich, reddish tones of the staircase's mahogany handrail warmly coaxed Frannie to slide her fingers along its smooth finish. The steps were adorned with gleaming brass stair rods that perfectly set off the burgundy, gold, and royal blue of the plush carpeting that cushioned each footfall.

Even as weary as she was, Frannie recognized Sophie's touch everywhere. Paintings with golden frames decorated walls covered in satiny wallpaper. Delicate porcelain figurines and vases adorned the shelves and tables. Sophie and her mother had created their own little piece of France in the midst of London.

"Your suite, my lady." Mrs. Thornton opened a set of double doors on the first landing and stepped back with an expectant smile.

"Lady Sophie does love purple," Frannie said as she entered a sitting room as delightful and welcoming as a field of lavender.

"And her ladyship wrote that your favorite flowers are the lilacs." Mrs. Thornton pointed out several vases overflowing with the fragrant purple blooms.

A door on the other side of the room opened, and Daisy joined them. "Come, my lady. Let's get you out of those traveling clothes, so you'll be more refreshed."

"Your tea will be up shortly, my lady," Mrs. Thornton said as she headed for the door. She tapped a dark purple bellpull hanging beside it. "If you should need anything at all, do ring.

Each room has a pull."

"Thank you, Mrs. Thornton."

The housekeeper gave her a kindly nod, then left and quietly closed the door behind her.

"I have a fresh chemise and stockings warming by the fire." Daisy herded Frannie toward the bedchamber. "I am sure you're damp from head to toe."

"It is good to be in the dry after so many days on that wet road." Frannie peeled off her gloves and added them to the drying rack.

"The hearth had a kettle of water already warming. I've added some to the bowl so you can enjoy a nice wash." Daisy unbuttoned the wool traveling dress that had seen entirely too many days of wear since Frannie had ruined her other one. Soon, Daisy had her out of the stale clothes and washed and dressed in fresh attire. A knock on the sitting room door announced that tea had arrived.

Daisy went to let them in but stepped back and frowned. "Uhm...Lady Ardsmere."

The maid's strained tone made Frannie turn from breathing in the sweet scent of a vase overflowing with lilacs. "What is it?"

Thornton stood in the hall, his broad forehead creased with worry. "Forgive me, your ladyship, I understand this cannot possibly be the best time for visitors, but the Duke of Lionwraith insisted upon seeing you. His Grace is in the drawing room."

"Do you wish to change, my lady?" Daisy asked while turning toward the bedroom door.

Frannie glanced down at her simplest morning dress, then touched the bandeau confining her unruly hair. She despaired how it curled with even wilder abandon whenever it rained. "No. I shall see His Grace as I am. After all, the man has seen me with my skirt tails on fire."

Thornton's shaggy brows shot higher, but he didn't comment. With a tight-lipped expression, he gave a curt nod and asked, "Do you require refreshments in the drawing room, my lady?"

"Most definitely, Thornton. A proper tea, if you would." Frannie clasped her hands tightly against her middle and followed him. "But first, show me the way to the drawing room, please."

"Of course, my lady." The butler squared his shoulders and marched forward as if walking at the head of a parade.

Frannie followed, thankful the townhouse wasn't so large as to make it difficult to commit to memory which room was which. Later, after she'd had the opportunity to settle in properly, she would tour the place so she didn't have to be led around like a child.

At the bottom of the stairs, Thornton led her to the first set of double doors on the other side of the entry hall. "I shall see to the refreshments personally, my lady," he said before excusing himself with a polite tip of his head.

Frannie pulled in a deep breath, blew it out, and armed herself with what she hoped was an air of serenity and calm. "Your Grace," she said as she swept into the room. "I didn't expect to see you again so soon."

Alec turned from the window overlooking the street. His smile made the treacherous fluttering in her middle beat its wings even faster.

"I know it pompous and rude to visit when you have only just arrived, but that should not surprise you," he said.

She couldn't help but laugh and shake her head. "It does not. Although, I must say, you've sent poor Thornton into a terrible spin when he is doing his level best to make an impeccable first impression." She directed the duke to a sitting area of couches and chairs closest to the ornate hearth decorated in white and gold scrollwork. "Come and sit. A proper tea will be here soon, and you can tell me what could not possibly wait."

His smile disappeared and his strong jaw flexed as though he gritted his teeth. Once she seated herself, he strode over to the couch opposite her and uncomfortably sat on the front edge of its cushions, as though ready to leap to his feet at a moment's notice.

She glanced at the doors, then leaned forward and whispered, "What has you so unsettled, Alec? Has something happened I should know about?"

He barely shook his head while scowling at her as though ready to fly into a rage. "I simply needed to see you. That is all."

A light knock on the doors, then Thornton's entry, thankfully prevented Frannie from saying something foolish. At least for now.

"Shall I serve, my lady?" the butler asked as he set the tray on the oval marble table centered between the sofas.

Even without looking, Frannie sensed Alec's wish that they be unencumbered by overly helpful servants. "No thank you, Thornton. I always enjoy pouring for my guests. That will be all for now."

The man bowed and quietly left the room. The firm click of the double doors as they closed somehow assured her they would not be disturbed again unless they requested it.

"No milk. No sugar. Only tea," she said as she filled Alec's cup and handed it to him. "Or would you prefer I ring for some brandy?"

"Tea is fine, thank you." But rather than drink, he set it on the table, then clasped his hands together and stared down at them. "Forgive me, Frannie. I should not have come."

"Of course you should be here. We are partners in this valiant scheme, remember?" Knowing it was a risk but not caring, she stepped around the table and sat beside him rather than return to her more appropriate seat across from him. "Tell me what is troubling you. Are you worried about Lady Violet staying behind by herself?"

"Actually, I think Vivvy was relieved to be left in peace." He raked his hands through his dark hair, tousling it to the same spiky, unkempt mane he had possessed the first time they met. Somehow, it made him even more handsome. A dark, dangerous man with a lion's heart—a heart that cared deeply and raged to protect those who could not protect themselves.

"You weren't this uneasy when we stopped at any of the inns on the way here. Was your house not in order when you arrived?" She needed to find a reason for his unsettledness, a reason other than he *simply needed to see her*. Remembering the way he had said those words thrilled her more than it should have.

"My house has not been in order for years now," he said with a bitter laugh, then sat straighter and squared his shoulders. He fixed her with such a pained expression that she ached to pull him into her arms and comfort him. But she dared not go down that path of folly.

"I am so sorry, Alec," she said gently, apologizing for more than he would ever know.

"I needed to see you because when I walked into that cold, soulless townhouse next door, I realized I wouldn't be able to laugh with you and scold you about your infernal jiggling every day, as I have since you barged into my home almost a fortnight ago and demanded I speak with you." The rich baritone of his voice rasped softer and became heartbreakingly hopeful. "You brought light to me where there was only darkness and despair. Now, I am loath to be without it for even a day."

Frannie found herself trapped in his stare and not caring if she ever escaped. She swallowed hard, her loneliness fighting to overpower her ability to reason, her need to keep a sadly safe distance between them. "I shall always cherish our friendship," she forced herself to say. She hated minimizing what she knew they could share if only circumstances were different.

He tore his gaze away from her and stared downward for a long, uncomfortable moment. "Friendship," he repeated softly, then lifted his head and gave her a smile that wasn't mirrored in his eyes. "I consider our friendship a priceless treasure as well."

With a thankful nod she didn't feel, she rose and prepared her own cup of tea, then returned to her seat on the other side of the table. She prayed the safe distance would keep her from making a dangerous mistake. "Lady Sophie should be here as early as tomorrow or the next day, and then we can start planning our first snare. You intend to survey White's for any sign of our man, yes?"

"Yes. I shall make some discreet inquiries." He picked up his tea, then appeared to change his mind and returned it to the table. "To protect Vivvy, I intended to say that Lord Ardsmere had yet to pay his vowels and requested I meet him at White's so he might properly settle up." He shrugged. "Innocent enough way to spare reputations. Gentlemen taking care of their gambling debts."

"A good ploy that protects everyone involved." She hated the beastly unease that squatted between them like an ugly toad. Her heart wished they were back in the conservatory at Lionwraith, strolling through the lilacs with one-eared Wellington leading the way. "And if your venture at White's is unsuccessful, I shall try Almack's—even though I despise the place."

"I could escort you there when you choose to go." The intensity of his stare made it feel as if he were waiting to see if she was brave enough to accept his dare. "Since you would be there in search of your husband, who presumably arrived earlier, no one would think anything of our arriving together."

"Lady Sophie could come with us, making us a party of three and quite respectable."

"Nothing about me has ever been deemed as *quite respectable*." Something about the set of his mouth and the look in his eyes assured her he meant that in the most sinfully delicious way possible.

"Indeed." She inwardly cringed at the nervous squeak in her voice, then turned aside and coughed to cover it. "My goodness. It must be the weather troubling my throat."

He rose and made use of the bellpull hanging beside the hearth.

Thornton appeared at the doors faster than immediately. He threw out his chest when he noticed the duke standing closest to the narrow strip of embroidered tapestry that served as the pull for the summoning bell. "Yes, Your Grace?"

"Your mistress and I require brandy—warmed with a stick of cinnamon and a slice of orange to stave off the chill of our trip." Alec cast an unreadable look Frannie's way, then returned his attention to the butler. "I fear the weather is attempting to make our lady ill."

Thornton bowed. "Right away, Your Grace." He disappeared before Frannie could protest.

"Usurping my servants?" she gently teased.

"Nothing of the sort." He calmly strolled back to the pair of sofas but sat beside her rather than returning to his seat on the other side of the short, bandy-legged table. "I am merely behaving as the concerned *friend*, since you admitted to being unwell." He leaned back and draped one of his muscular arms across the back of the sofa behind her and the other atop the pillows to his left. After a slow, critical look around the drawing room, he frowned. "You need a cat."

She stoked her courage, determined not to let either her racing heart or the sly duke trick her into tipping her hand. But this was no simple game of whist. It was her loneliness begging to be put out of its misery. "This is not my home. Remember?"

He relinquished the point with a nod. "Fine. Then Lady Sophie needs a cat." He angled closer, as though completely entranced with the silliness of the subject at hand. "Do you have cats at your home in Belgium?"

"Uhm…no." She lifted her teacup from the saucer to stop the infernal thing from rattling and giving away that she trembled. "Mother Ardsmere is allergic to animals. Even a brief ride on her favorite mare sends her into a frenzy of coughing and wheezing."

"Pity." He twitched a shrug and edged closer still. "I assumed by the way you warmed to Wellington that you had a fondness for cats."

"I love all animals," she admitted. "I love their ability to love unconditionally." The aching loneliness in her tone made her immediately regret saying the words. "A long ride through the

Belgium countryside is the best tonic I have ever found."

"And does your husband share your love of riding?" Alec spoke with a quietness as gentle and coaxing as a lover's caress. "He is a damned fool if he doesn't."

"His—his health." Why was it that the standard lie she had used for the past several years became so difficult to repeat to Alec? "Frank is quite bedridden, I am afraid. Poor dear doesn't have the strength to leave his rooms." Frannie twisted to glance at the doors and used the opportunity to put more space between them.

"How long has your husband suffered with his malady?" Alec stretched to collect his teacup, then settled back down beside her. The hard, muscular length of his leg brushed against hers. The feigned innocence of his expression didn't fool her one bit. "If memory serves, you earlier mentioned several years," he said. "So, I take that to be more than three. Did it strike him suddenly or come on gradually?"

"It had been coming on for a while." Then, for good or for ill, she abandoned all subtlety. "What are you trying to accomplish here, Alec?"

"An arrangement that will soothe both our lonely souls," he said with dangerously enticing gentleness.

Before she realized what was happening, he slipped his warm, calloused fingers up the back of her neck and into her hair. He tipped her head back and covered her mouth with his while gently shifting her deeper into his embrace. The heat of him not only wrapped around her but ignited a fire of her own. And then the taste of him… The hard, insistent urgency of his lips. His tongue. She slid her hands up his chest and into his hair, hanging on to keep from spiraling out of control. Dear heaven above, his kiss sent her reeling. She should push him away. Stop this madness. But—as his arms tightened around her—she couldn't. Or perhaps *wouldn't* was the more appropriate wording.

He lifted his head and gazed down at her. The golden-green depths of his eyes pulled her in and refused to release her. "I will not say I am sorry to have done this," he rasped, then kissed her again to keep her from forming a sane, logical thought.

She had never been kissed before. And even if she had, she doubted very much it could ever compare with the powerful yet aching tenderness of this claiming. Heaven help her. He had rendered her as powerless as a newborn kitten. The stubble of his cheek grazed her palm, exciting her immeasurably. His familiar scent of sandalwood, citrus, and a hint of clean male musk made her yearn to breathe him in and possess his soul as he was trying to possess hers.

"I will never apologize for this," he whispered as he lifted his head again. "Never."

"We cannot do this," she managed to utter. Or, at least, she *thought* she said it out loud. From the look in his eyes, perhaps she only said it to herself. "Alec—this must not—"

"I do not believe in *must not* any more than I subscribe to *if only.*"

She touched the warm softness of his parted lips, and he kissed her fingers with such a ravenous look that she caught her breath. Drawing upon every ounce of self-control she had ever possessed, she halfheartedly attempted to push him away. "I…am…married to another." The lie sounded weak even to her. There was no intention behind it, and she hadn't the will nor the wish to fabricate any. "This is folly," she whispered. That, at least, was the truth.

"We could have all this and so much more," he said quietly. With a gentleness that almost made her sob, he brushed her fallen curls back from her face and offered her a tender smile. "I know I am a rude man who has little use for Polite Society, but I give you my word, I am the epitome of discretion. No one would ever know but us."

"Your sister should be our focus. Not…this." She swallowed hard and breathed him in again, inwardly crying out to toss all caution to the winds and just *feel*. After a gentle pat on his chest, she pushed at him again. "Please, Alec," she said softly.

"You want this as much as I do. I see it in your eyes."

"We cannot always have what we want." With more regret than she had ever felt before, she softly touched his cheek. "And this is one of those times."

"You will find I do not give up easily, Frannie." He shifted, putting more space between them, as if sensing he had almost pushed her too far. "In fact, I never give up. Ever."

"In this case, you must." She rose and went to the window, not trusting herself to remain on the sofa beside him. A harsh gust of wind sent sheets of rain slashing across the glass. Her ragged emotions rivaled the pace of the storm, and her spirits sank like the water rippling down the panes. "You should go, I think. We are both weary from long days of travel and at risk of doing something we might regret."

"I would not regret it, and I do not believe you would either."

"Eventually," she whispered, "we would both regret it. Trust me on this. I know."

CHAPTER SIX

"I WAS QUITE shocked when I received your note, Lion. What the deuce convinced ye to leave your lair and come to London?"

"Business that could not be ignored nor handled from Lionwraith Estate." Alec looked up from his desk at one of the few people he had ever trusted or called a friend. His favorite Scotsman, Robert Galloway, Viscount of Dunkeld. He pushed up from his chair, stepped around the desk, and grabbed the viscount's forearm in a warrior's brotherly handshake. "I needed someone I could trust at my side, and you came to mind. Up for the task, Dun?"

"Always." Dunkeld eyed him as though bracing himself for bad news. "What *business* couldna be handled by either your solicitors or your private men who put even the infamous Bow Street Runners to shame?"

Alec unleashed a heavy sigh, hating that it was necessary to reveal Vivvy's plight to yet another individual. The more who knew, the greater the danger of the gossips getting hold of the blasted debacle and tearing poor Vivvy to shreds.

"Gads, man. Is it that dire?"

"In several ways." Alec poured them both a drink. A grimness settled over him as he handed Dun a glass of the man's favorite whisky. "Here. From your very own distillery."

Dunkeld didn't smile. Instead, concern filled his pale blue

eyes. "Thank ye, old friend. Now what are these *several ways* that are so dire?"

Alec propped back against his desk and crossed his legs at the ankles. "What do you know of the Marquess of Ardsmere?"

"Nothing other than his wife is as shrewd at handling the family business as she is beautiful to look upon." Dun sipped his drink, then held the glass up to the light and swirled the honey-colored liquid, appreciating it with a satisfied smile. "It was she who finalized my distillery's latest contract with West Belgium International, and I must say, she did a damn sight better by us than the East India Trading Company." A snort of amusement escaped him. "Of course, the crafty lady insisted the lucrative contract be for seven years rather than the two I was prepared to close on."

Alec didn't doubt that for a minute. Frannie might be a bit accident prone and rather unusual, but she was fearless and possessed the wit and cunning of the slyest fox. "She is an intelligent beauty at that." The desolate sense of being denied something he yearned to possess made him grind his teeth until his jaws ached. Then another question came to him. "When did she complete that contract?"

Frowning, Dun idly tapped the rim of his glass as he slowly circled the room. "A year or two ago. I would have to check the documents to be certain. Why?"

"And why was it she who finalized it rather than her husband or West Belgium International's solicitors?"

"The solicitor was there with her," Dun said, "as was the dowager marchioness." He paused for another sip of the whisky, then shifted with a vague shrug. "Seems like the marquess had taken ill or something and couldna make the trip from Belgium to Scotland."

"And I am sure your habit of never closing a deal without looking a man in the face rather than dealing solely with his solicitor caused them some issue?"

Dun shook his head. "No issue at all. Lady Ardsmere seemed

quite at ease with taking care of things in her husband's stead. What is this about?"

"Vivvy has named Lord Ardsmere as the father of her unborn child."

Dunkeld flinched as though Alec had punched him in the midsection. "Gads, man. I am sorry. Has the man agreed to at least provide for the bairn?" He rolled his shoulders as though uncomfortable in his own skin. "Not that ye need the black-guard's coin, of course, but he should be made to pay, or at least help ye find somewhere to place the wee one so your sister might overcome the scandal."

Alec set his untouched drink on the desk. "My men discovered Ardsmere's name as the one who ruined Vivvy. When the man ignored my requests for a meeting, I *arranged* for two of his ships and one of his warehouses to be destroyed. Spread the rumor they harbored smallpox. Then, over a fortnight ago, Lady Ardsmere showed up at my lair demanding to know why I had declared war on West Belgium International."

The viscount's eyebrows ratcheted higher, rising almost to his sandy hairline. "She did, did she?" He snorted a humorless laugh. "I thought she might be a fiery lass. Ye can tell by the way she comes straight to the point rather than dancing around with words. What did ye tell her?"

"The truth." Alec folded his arms across his chest. "Or, at least, what I believed to be the truth."

"And what the devil does that mean?"

"The miniature self-portrait that Lord Ardsmere gave to his wife this past Christmas looks nothing like the man who debauched Vivvy. My sister's maid attested to that." He slowly shook his head. "And as you yourself stated, Lady Ardsmere said her husband had been too ill to leave his bedchamber in Belgium for several years."

"So, ye think someone lied to Lady Violet? Gave her a false name?" Dun's face darkened. "Have ye found the bastard yet, so we might take care of him?"

"Not yet. That is the primary reason for my being in London."

"And the secondary reason?" Dun thumped his glass down on the liquor cabinet and shook his head when Alec glanced at the decanter to offer him more.

"Lady Ardsmere." Alec pulled in a deep breath and whistled it out through clenched teeth. "Frannie," he repeated softly.

"*Frannie?*" Dunkeld perked with interest. "Did ye cuckold the man before ye knew he was innocent of ruining your sister?"

"No." Alec pushed off the desk and paced back and forth across the library that was entirely too neat and organized for his liking. "Not that I didn't wish to."

"The lady is quite lovely." Dun fell in step beside him. "Ye might as well tell me the rest. I can see there is more."

"Lady Ardsmere accepted my apology for wrongly attacking her business. But she refused to accept remittance for the destruction of two fully loaded ships and a warehouse full of goods due to ship out the following week. She is determined to help me find the devil responsible for Vivvy's downfall and make him pay for not only what he cost West Belgium International—but also Vivvy."

Dunkeld halted and puckered a dubious scowl like a headmaster interrogating an errant pupil. "Why do I sense that is not the entirety of your dilemma with the lovely Lady Ardsmere?"

Alec glared at his trusted friend, debating whether to tell the man and risk being damned by him. Dun had always possessed a strong sense of morality and justice. "I want her, Dun. More than I have ever—" He cut himself off and turned away.

"More than Charlotte, even?"

Alec thought about the wife he had once loved. Until she had died giving birth to another man's child. A child she had conceived while he was away at war. "I said I wanted Frannie. Not that I loved her."

"Not only are ye being an arse about this, ye are splitting hairs. Ye ken that, aye?"

"And your Scots speak becomes more pronounced when your high and mighty morals kick in."

"Were ye not the one who told me ye would never do to another man what had been done to ye?" Dunkeld angled an infuriatingly judgmental glare Alec's way.

"A genuine friend would not throw a man's own words in his face at a time like this."

"If memory serves, the assignations ye have enjoyed since your wife's death have all been with attractive widows who fully intend to remain as such. Is that not true?" Dunkeld's attitude grated on Alec's nerves. "Well, man? True or not?"

"Meaning?" Alec glowered at him, knowing full well what the smug devil was about to say.

"Meaning, ye have taken great pains to avoid anything other than physical pleasure, but ye seem different with this one. Why would ye be willing to risk an affair with a married woman? Ye have always kept to your word. Even when ye made foolish vows that were better off broken. Your sheer stubbornness alone kept ye in line with whatever ye had sworn. Why is this one different?"

"*She* is different." There was no lying to Dunkeld. Alec picked up his untouched drink and downed it in a single gulp, trying to burn the foul taste of the admission off his tongue.

"Ye love her." Dun sadly shook his head. "'Tis a fool's errand, man. As near as I can remember from what her solicitors said, her husband is a young man. Probably close in age to her. He could recover from whatever malady he has and return to his husbandly duties. Where would that leave ye?"

"In as much misery as I am in now."

"More so," Dun corrected him. "If ye let this go any further than it already has, ye would suffer even more with the loss of her. At least now, ye dinna ken what ye've never had." He clapped a hand on Alec's shoulder and shook him. "Move on. Find a new widow to bed or take up with one of your old ones again, but move on."

"That's just it, Dun. I do not want to move on."

Dunkeld sank into a nearby chair and kicked back, propping a foot on the overstuffed hassock in front of it. "We do not always get what we want, Lion."

"That is exactly what Frannie said after I kissed her."

With a shake of his head, Dunkeld threw up his hands. "Ye've already kissed her. When did ye become a fool so lovesick that ye have lost all ability to reason?"

"You've met her."

"Aye, but I kept my wits about me." Dun jabbed his thumb at the liquor cabinet. "Pour me another and tell me what ye need of me, other than to help ye find the scapegrace who broke Lady Violet's heart. I think ye are an addlepated fool about that other matter, but I'll not abandon ye in your time of need."

"Back me up at White's when I go there looking for the man to collect what he owes me. I want no one to discover Vivvy's dilemma. As you can imagine, the predicament horrified Mother and kept both her and Vivvy from coming to London for the Season. Society believes Mother to be suffering from ill health, and that loyal and trustworthy Vivvy refused to debut without Mother at her side." Alec poured himself another after he refilled Dun's glass.

"Ye had that old she-devil there with ye at Lionwraith?" Dunkeld shuddered as he accepted the whisky.

Alec allowed himself a gloating smile. "For a while. The old demoness's permanent residence is now back at the manor house just south of Castle Douglas."

"Finally banished her to the wilds of Scotland instead of waiting for old age to take her?" A laughing snort exploded free of Dun. "I told ye the woman would live forever. Evil like that doesna die."

"Yes," Alec said. "I finally came to my senses when she kept antagonizing Vivvy."

"Good on ye, man." Dun held up his glass in a toast, downed it, and then pushed up from the chair. "I'll help ye find the scoundrel." He gave a curt nod and fixed Alec with a hard glare.

"And I'll also try my best to keep ye from doing anything foolish as far as Lady Ardsmere is concerned." He shook his head. "I dinna wish to see ye hurt. Ye are the brother I never had."

"I also need you to help me find out what mysterious ailment troubles Lord Ardsmere. My men failed me there. It appears the good people of Chanticlare, Belgium are quite adept at hiding the man and any information about him."

"It doesna matter what ails him," the viscount replied. "He is still married to Lady Ardsmere, and it is bad form indeed, and probably ill luck as well, to wish a man dead so ye can have his wife."

Alec ignored that. He wasn't superstitious like the blustering Scot. "I am having dinner with Lady Sophie and Lady Ardsmere this evening. Lady Ardsmere recruited Lady Sophie as a fellow conspirator in our grand scheme. Come with me. I want you to meet them."

"I shall go," Dun said with an irritated look. "But only to keep ye from doing anything more foolish than ye have already done."

"Good. And you agree to help me find out more about the real Lord Ardsmere?" Alec knew if he gnawed at Dun long enough, he would wear the man down.

The viscount stared upward as if praying for divine guidance. "I will do what I can. I canna do more than that."

Alec clapped Dun on the back as he walked him to the door. "That is all I ask. I shall see you later. Promptly at seven. Luckily enough, Lady Sophie's home—or, more accurately, the home of her brother the earl—is right next door."

"I look forward to it," Dun said without sounding convinced. "Until dinner, old friend."

"DID YOU EVER stop to think that it might be high time you killed him off? Surely you have made all the arrangements required to become a widow of substantial means? Of course, there is that dreadful cousin to consider. I am not sure what might be done about Lord Vulture." Celia, Duchess of Hasterton—and another of Frannie's sisters by choice, thanks to the tight-knit kinship of the Sisterhood of Independent Ladies—wrinkled her nose and shuddered. "I abhor that despicable little man. Lord Vulture is a blight upon humanity."

"Lord *Vander*," Frannie corrected her. She lovingly gazed down at baby Oliver's sweet little face as he peacefully slept in her arms. "And Celia—really? Killing my imaginary husband off? Must you word it so?"

Celia laughed. "Says the lady whose unabashed bluntness reduced her poor solicitor to tears merely days ago."

Frannie resettled the precious babe more comfortably in the crook of her arm. She enjoyed his cuddly warmth and wished she might someday experience this joy with a baby of her own.

"Who told you that?" she asked without looking up from the adorable angel in her arms.

"The foolish little man not only confessed it but renewed his tearful whinging to Elias while handing over the Ardsmere files." Celia rose and gently eased her baby away from Frannie. When Frannie groaned in protest, Celia cut her off. "It is Sophie's turn for a cuddle. My goodness, this child will never learn to sleep in his cradle with everyone constantly holding him."

"Yes…come see Auntie Sophie," Sophie crooned as she took little Oliver into her arms. "When you are big enough, I shall teach you archery, horsemanship, and espionage. There will not be a sweet treat anywhere in the realm safe from you."

"Now," Celia said, turning back to Frannie. "Back to the delightful matter of the mighty lion roaring to take you."

"He is not roaring to take me," Frannie said, even though that aptly described yesterday's meeting with Alec in the drawing room. "I merely said he kissed me and suggested we could enjoy much more before I insisted that we certainly could not, and that he should leave."

"You did not *merely* say anything." Sophie huffed a wayward curl out of her face, then tucked it behind her ear. "You should see your cheeks. It's as though you used a pot of rouge for each of them."

"She is right, you know." Celia patted the bright bandeau that fashionably held her ebony hair in place. "Our fair skin gives us away every time, dear." She leaned forward and gave a wicked wink. "The duke has kindled a fire in you that's making you glow like stoked embers." Her brow lightly puckered as she frowned. "Did you ever rid yourself of your virginity? That will be a dead giveaway if you and he—"

"Celia!" Frannie resettled herself on the settee upholstered in delicate mauve florals. She tucked a matching pillow under her arm, fiddled with its ruffled edges, then tossed it aside. Unable to sit any longer, she rose and wandered aimlessly around the room while pressing her handkerchief to her throat. "It is very warm in here. Might we open a window?" Perhaps some illness from the dreadful weather had given her a fever. She hadn't slept well at all last night, either—tossed and turned and kicked off her covers, all because of an aching heat at her core that wouldn't leave her be. "I think I am coming down with something."

Sophie erupted with a very unladylike snort that startled the baby and made him cry. "Oh dear. I am sorry, Oliver. Auntie Sophie didn't mean to scare you."

"Here, let me have him." Celia cuddled her fussing son close and made the circuit of the parlor in a slow, bouncing walk that calmed him. She shot an amused glance at Frannie. "You are overly warm, dear sister, because of Lionwraith." A mix of mirth and sympathy twinkled in her eyes. "I remember how it was right before Elias and I… Well, before our first time." She reluctantly handed the baby off to the nanny who appeared at the parlor door. Before the nanny took tiny Oliver away, she kissed the baby's forehead. "Mama loves you, dearest."

Once the nanny was well out of earshot, Frannie said, "My relationship with Alec is nothing like your relationship with Lord

Raines. Your Elias didn't insinuate he wanted you as nothing more than his mistress." She returned to the table in the center of their grouping of seats, picked up her tea, and sipped it. For the first time in her life, she was thankful it had gone cold. "I don't know whether to be flattered or insulted."

"He thinks you are a married woman," Sophie said, while idly winding one of her coppery curls around her finger. "Whatever else could he possibly suggest?"

"That is absolutely right," Celia agreed. "Elias understood I was single and of an age to marry." She twitched a shrug. "Well…that and Mama's urgings for him to marry me."

"Mother Ardsmere has yet to meet Alec," Frannie said with a despondent sigh. "And I am not sure how she would weather the demise of her fictitious son so that I might pursue an attachment with him. You know how she can be."

"You don't have to address her as *Mother Ardsmere* in front of us, dear sister." Sophie leaned forward, her face filled with concern. "Are you that overset about the duke?"

Frannie shook her head. "I have called her *Mother Ardsmere* for so very long. That is how I think of her rather than simply *Mother*. After all, she's never really behaved like a loving mother, now has she?" She twisted her handkerchief, wringing the poor thing so tightly it would never return to its original shape. "Alec and I can never be." Another hopeless sigh escaped her. "He abhors lying and deception, and those happen to be my best traits."

"Lying and deception are all of our best traits," Celia reminded her gently. "We had no choice in the matter. Remember?"

"But he entrusted you with his sister's dilemma." Sophie rose and hugged an arm around Frannie's shoulders. "He even gave you permission to share it with us, so we might help find that scheming rakeshame. That must count for something."

"He trusts me because he does not really know me." Frannie winced as the lacy edging of her handkerchief tore. "And I fear that once he *knows* me, that will be the end of it." She tossed the mangled bit of linen and lace down on the table. "Then I won't even have the pleasure of his friendship." She covered her face with her hands. "I am so tired of being lonely." She turned to Sophie. "Aren't you? Are you not weary of keeping everyone from getting too close?"

"Yes," Sophie admitted with a halfhearted nod. "But what choice do we have?" She hugged Frannie tighter. "At least we have the Sisterhood."

"You must take action, Frannie." Celia took hold of Frannie's hand and led her back to the settee. "Kill off your fictitious husband, and when Lionwraith asks how a woman who was supposedly married for the past six years remained a virgin, tell him your dearly departed husband was not able to perform in the marriage bed—for whatever reason." She tipped her chin to a defiant angle. "He doesn't have to know the truth, nor the history of the Sisterhood of Independent Ladies. Your *situation* is much easier resolved than mine was, or Sophie's has yet to be."

"Continue living a lie," Frannie whispered. That long-ago choice her mother had made had well and surely trapped her.

"Our lies harm no one," Celia said. "In fact, think of all the good we have done by embracing and improving our mothers' hold on our fathers' *titles*. Because of us, all the work we do, many a family has obtained success rather than starvation or a bleak life on the streets. Neither the Crown nor your greedy cousin would have provided them with such opportunities. And my Elias can review the Ardsmere patent and your *husband's* will to ensure that all Lord Vulture is able to get his greedy hands on are the entailed lands and the title once Lord Ardsmere meets his demise."

"I suppose it's true our deceptions haven't really harmed anyone." But Frannie's heart wasn't in the admission. She had always believed if a person was so motivated, they would justify anything in their own mind—whether it be for good or for ill. "I do wish you and Elias could join us at dinner tonight," she told Celia. "Safety in numbers and all that."

Celia sadly shook her head. "I cannot possibly, even though

it's merely across the street." She rolled her eyes. "Heaven forbid if word should get out that I attended a dinner party before Oliver's christening and the official end of my lying in." She patted Frannie's hand. "But the churching and christening are this Sunday. After that, I can become an active participant in this intriguing scheme." She leaned closer and gave Frannie a playful nudge. "And you will invite the Duke of Lionwraith to accompany you to the christening, will you not? After all, you and Sophie are Oliver's godmothers."

"Two godmothers? But Oliver should have two godfathers and only one godmother." Frannie felt it was high time she deflected the conversation away from her dilemma with Alec. Celia had an unnerving habit of worrying a subject to death at times.

"Elias's brother, the Duke of Almsbury, is to be a godfather along with the Marquess of Bournebridge," Celia said.

"Lord Bournebridge?" Frannie couldn't contain her shock. Bournebridge's wife, the condescending dragon lady who ruled the *ton* when it came to gossip, had always been considered a bitter enemy of not only Frannie's mother, but Celia and Sophie's mothers as well.

"Lady Bournebridge turned out to be most helpful when it came to resolving my inheritance *dilemma*," Celia said with a tight-lipped nod. "Favors must always be repaid."

Frannie rose and returned to the window. An uncomfortable, edgy restlessness had plagued her ever since she stormed Lionwraith Estate. "Regarding favors—did your Elias recall anyone fitting the description of the despicable rogue who misused Lady Violet?"

"He said no one came to mind, but dear Frannie, that vague description would fit any number of lordlings in London during the Season." Celia lightly tapped her spoon against her teacup until Frannie turned and faced her. "And what will you and your lion do if the man has assumed yet another name to continue his debauching of debutantes? Has it not occurred to either of you that as soon as he discovers the two of you are in London, he might very well flee?"

"I had wondered about that, but I am not certain Alec thought of it." Frannie bit her lip and turned back to peer out the window, stretching to see Lionwraith's house. "He was planning a trip to White's to try to find the man."

"If he goes to White's, news of his return to London will spread within hours," Sophie warned. "Men gossip as much or more so than women." Wariness tightened her expression. "And he is an eligible duke. The Marriage Mart may have already sniffed him out. Carriages unloading trunks at houses that usually remain empty rarely go unnoticed."

"I should warn him." Frannie chewed on her lip while eyeing the brilliant blue sky of the rare sunny day. "He and I must lurk in the shadows while those we trust set the snares." She turned and took a few steps toward the door before forcing herself to halt. "I cannot believe he and I overlooked such a basic danger."

"I can," Celia said with an arch of her brow. "You two have more—shall we say—heated issues distracting you."

Sophie joined Frannie and tugged on her arm. "Come. We shall pay His Grace a visit and enlighten him on the flaws in his plan."

Frannie hurried to kiss Celia on the cheek, knowing her friend hated to be left behind. "We shall keep you informed, and remember, just a few more days until you are free again."

"My only solace is Oliver," Celia said with a contented smile. "He is worth every minute of my confinement."

"Indeed, he is," Frannie agreed. "Your angel is precious beyond words."

"Keep me informed." Celia walked them to the door. "I shall expect a note from each of you about this meeting. By this afternoon, mind you."

"Promise." Frannie hurried down the steps, then paused, anxiously waiting for Sophie to catch up. "Now, he might seem rude at first, but remember everything I told you from the report."

Sophie snorted as she linked their arms and tugged Frannie forward. "I am certain the man will be on his best behavior. After all"—she gave a suggestive wink—"he is trying to impress his next conquest."

"Sophie." Frannie shot her friend a warning look that she knew would be absolutely useless. "Please behave?"

With a laugh, Sophie banged the bronze door knocker hard upon its plate. "We shall see."

A man who could pass for a younger version of MacGinnis, Lionwraith Manor's butler, opened the door. "May I help you?"

"Lady Sophie, sister to the Earl of Rydleshire, and Lady Ardsmere to see His Grace," Frannie said. She couldn't help but smile, remembering how she had pushed her way into Alec's home at the northern border of the Lake District.

The butler opened the door and granted them entry. As they filed in, he directed them to a doorway on the right of the wide entry hall. "I shall inform His Grace immediately."

"What a lovely shade of blue," Sophie said as they entered a parlor that was much smaller and more intimate than Frannie had expected after all the grandeur she encountered at Lionwraith's country estate.

"This parlor is decidedly masculine. More like an office or a library. Do you not agree?" Frannie couldn't help but laugh as she remembered the chaotic, cavelike state of Alec's other library. "Of course, this room is much too tidy for the duke's liking."

"You know me well," Alec drawled from the doorway.

Frannie's heart leapt, making it difficult to breathe. Now she understood what a thief felt like when they were caught stealing. "Your Grace, this is my friend I told you about. The one I am staying with. Lady Sophie, the Earl of Rydleshire's sister." *What an awkward introduction.* She turned to Sophie. "Lady Sophie, allow me to introduce you to His Grace, the Duke of Lion-wraith."

Sophie curtsied, but the twinkle in her eyes alluded to the

mischief in her mind. Frannie felt like kicking her.

Alec offered a proper nod. "A pleasure to meet you, Lady Sophie, and might I also extend my gratitude for your help in this rather delicate matter."

Sophie gave him a genuine smile, but Frannie still didn't breathe easy. One never knew what her dear sister by choice might say. "I am always happy to help Lady Ardsmere, and when she described the plight that connects the two of you, I could not in good conscience refuse."

Frannie exhaled in relief. "While visiting with the Duchess of Hasterton, we came upon a slight error in our plans."

"I see." Alec's eyes briefly narrowed, and he jutted his chin to a defensive angle. He directed them to a gathering of chairs arranged in front of the sunny window overlooking the street. "Please have a seat while I ring for refreshments."

Frannie and Sophie seated themselves while he returned to the door, yanked on the bellpull beside it, and then spoke quietly to his butler.

Sophie reached over and lightly tapped Frannie's bouncing knee. "Frannie. Please."

Alec's rumbling laugh shattered the uncomfortable air of the rather indelicate visit. "I am glad to see her infernal jiggling irritates someone other than myself."

Sophie blew out a long-suffering breath and shook her head. "She has always done it. Even as a child."

"I am right here," Frannie reminded them both before fixing a stern look on Alec. "You must not go to White's as you had planned. I hope we are not too late in advising you of this."

"What?" He stared at her as though confounded.

"If word spreads that you and I are in London, our target might realize we seek him and choose to either flee or assume yet another identity." She glanced at Sophie for support. "We must stay in the shadows. Be sly and cautious about where we go and where we are seen."

"Not to mention the marriage-minded mothers who would

start circling you as soon they caught the scent of an eligible duke," Sophie added.

"We should have thought of that," Alec said, tightening his mouth into a grim line.

"Yes," Frannie said. "We should have." She would not share the popular opinion as to why they had overlooked such a crucial detail. "You have not gone to the club yet, have you?"

"No." He went quiet as the butler and a footman entered.

After the servants placed their trays on a nearby table, they served the lemonade and offered a selection of biscuits. Mille feuille, sweetmeat, filbert, and some delicate rolled wafers filled the platters.

As soon as they bowed their way out of the room, Alec cleared his throat. "I shall have my friend, Dunkeld, go to the club in my stead." He squinted at Lady Sophie as though trying to read her mind. "And do forgive my impertinence, but I took the liberty of inviting Dun to your dinner party tonight. I hope that is not an inconvenience."

"Of course not." Sophie took a sip of her lemonade, then rose. "And that reminds me, I must get back and finish plans for tonight's repast. Since I only arrived late last night, I fear I failed to give this evening's gathering the attention it deserves."

As Frannie stood to join her, Sophie motioned for her to sit back down. "No, Frannie. You stay. I am sure the duke's company would help distract you from that disturbing letter you received this morning. I know it upset you immeasurably, and I have done all I know to do to comfort you." Sophie turned a beguiling smile on the duke. "Do help lift her spirits, please. I am at a complete loss as to how to console my dear sister."

Already on his feet, he fixed Frannie with a concerned look. "I will do my best, of course. Lady—"

"Good day to you, Your Grace," Sophie interrupted. "I look forward to this evening." Then she swept out of the room before Frannie could foil her devious plan.

CHAPTER SEVEN

"FRANNIE?" ALEC WAITED, as if he knew the resonance of his deep voice softly saying her name would completely unravel her. And it did.

His concern made her clench her teeth even harder. How dare Sophie decide to shove her in this direction and force her hand? Frannie bowed her head, unable to meet his eyes. "A letter from Chanticlare arrived this morning."

"Chanticlare, Belgium?" Rather than return to his chair, he took Sophie's vacated seat next to her. His delectable scent of sandalwood and citrus washed across her, drawing her in as he leaned toward her. "From your husband?"

"Not from him, exactly." She hated lying to him. She longed to have just one thing in her life not tainted by deception. "But from my home," she said, trying to remain as vague as possible and allow his imagination to fill in the gaps.

"Must you leave for Belgium right away?"

The aching disappointment in his voice twisted her heart. He didn't want her to go. Was it because of the need to find his sister's rogue, or did he want her to stay for him?

"There is no need for me to hurry back to Belgium," she said. At least that part was genuine. She kept her gaze locked on her hands clenched in her lap.

"I am so sorry, Frannie." He took her hands and cradled them between his warm, calloused palms.

That was the thing about Alec—he was a man of opposites. Even though he was a duke with servants ready to jump at his every whim, his hands were calloused from years of war and then working alongside Sir Henry in the gardens. He made himself out to be rude, gruff, and uncaring, but she knew better. She had discovered that his tender heart protected those who needed him most.

Except her. He could never protect her.

"What can I do to help you?" he asked quietly.

"Nothing, I fear." She still avoided his gaze. "I tried to prepare myself because I understood this time would come." That was the truth as well. Everything but the entailed properties would belong to her—even West Belgium International would be safely in her name. The indisputable will Lord Raines had helped put in place protected every asset from Lord Vander.

"Forgive me for pressing you on the matter, but are you certain you need not return to Belgium for the—" He cut himself off with a groaning huff and bowed his head. "I am sorry," he muttered. "I should not be so indelicate."

"They buried him immediately," she lied, suffering the untruth like a knife twisting in her heart. "To prevent the spread of the unknown disease, you understand." How shameful that she had researched and read about such things in order to lie convincingly. No amount of prayers or candles would keep her from the hottest levels of hell whenever she died.

She pulled in a deep breath and blew it out. "Of course, now I must go into mourning." She lifted her head and finally risked looking him in the eyes. "But that should not hinder our plans to help your sister. We had already decided it unwise for you and me to attend functions at the risk of that blackguard discovering we were on his trail." She stared down at her hands again, unable to face the caring and compassion in his gaze. "Perhaps it will be easier to keep to the shadows dressed in black and shades of dark lavender. Who knows what I might discover?"

He gently tipped up her face, forcing her to look at him once more. His caring and compassion were still there, but disturbing shadows had joined in, darkening his expression. "Did you love him, Frannie? Your husband?"

In this one thing, she would always speak the truth. She refused to lie about love. "Ours was an arranged marriage. An agreement to benefit all parties concerned." She allowed herself a sad smile and barely shook her head. "There was no love between us. Not ever."

He blew out a deep breath, as though he had held it to prepare for her answer. "But I am sure the loss is still painful. All the changes that must come about now. I am sorry."

"You do not appear sorry." The accusation came out before she could stop it. She bit her lip to keep from saying more.

He drew closer still and brushed the tenderest of kisses to her forehead. "I am sorry you have never known love," he said, "but I will not deny that I am glad you did not discover it with him."

"I am newly widowed and at the start of mourning, and yet you speak of discovering love?" She drew back and fixed him with a chiding scowl. "Have you no shame?"

"None whatsoever, and would never pretend as such. You know me, Frannie. Probably better than most. I am callous to a fault." He gently touched her cheek, staring at her as he grazed his thumb back and forth across her bottom lip. "But I will restrain myself out of respect for you, my lady. For now, at least. Please know I would never do anything to offend you, but I will be waiting for you."

She turned away from his touch and whispered, "You have no idea of what you say."

"Explain it to me, then. Tell me what you need, and I will make it so."

Tears stung her eyes and overflowed, proving her helpless to stop them.

"You weep for him?"

"No," she said with a hitching sniff. "I weep for things you will never understand. Things that can never be changed or remedied."

Without a word, he pulled her into his arms and cradled her to his chest as if she were an overwrought child. He stroked her hair and rained gentle kisses across her brow as she melted into his embrace. "Cry your tears, my precious lady. Let them fall unashamedly. I am here for you—whenever you are ready. The past cannot be changed or remedied, but the future is ours to make into whatever we see fit."

Unable to fight it any longer, she sank against him and turned her face into the warm curve of his throat. A shuddering sigh left her as she closed her eyes. If only this could be her safe haven instead of yet another precarious lie that would require the most careful tending she had ever done in her life.

She went to pull her handkerchief from her sleeve and re-membered she had abandoned the poor, torn thing at Celia's house. Even though it was ridiculous, the act of forgetting such a minor thing triggered another torrent of sobbing that shook her. Forgetting was not acceptable. Forgetting could cost her everything. A pitiful wail escaped her.

"Frannie," he gently crooned. He picked her up and carried her across the room to the sofa in front of the hearth. He settled them on it and rested her atop him with her head on his chest. With a swift tug, he pulled a velvety throw across her, and they lay there partially reclined. After another subtle shift, he pressed a handkerchief into her hands. "Here, sweetling. For your tears."

"This is most inappropriate," she said in a hiccupping whisper into the fine lawn of his shirt. But try as she might, she couldn't bring herself to move. "What if the servants walk in?"

"I shot the last servant who betrayed my trust."

She pushed up and stared at him, still trembling with her storming emotions, and now a sense of shocked dismay shook her even harder. "You didn't!"

His lopsided grin eased her. Somewhat. "No. I did not. But my servants are well aware that if they ever betray me, they will regret it." He gently settled her back down on his chest. "And fear not, sweet Frannie. This is not a ploy to seduce you. This is merely the comfort and care you deserve at a time like this."

She sniffed and wiped her eyes, finding it impossible to refuse him. The hard, muscular expanse of him beneath her, his warmth, the safety of his embrace—all of it felt so indescribably wonderful. But it made the restless aching deep inside her return and burn ever hotter.

Even through their clothing, she became *very* aware of his rigid length nudging against her. Heaven help her. Of course, she had seen statues and paintings depicting a man's *appendage*, but none in the galleries had looked as big as his *felt*.

Once again, she pushed up. But this time, she forced herself to slide off him and sit on the edge of the sofa. With a hurried drying of her eyes, she breathed in deeply and fought to regain at least a tiny bit of composure. After all, what sort of woman tumbled into another man's arms upon the announcement of her husband's death—even if that husband wasn't real?

"I…uhm…should go." Before he could tempt her further and change her mind, she jumped to her feet. "I have yet to tell Mother Ardsmere, and I am most certain she will not take the news well."

"Shall I come with you?" He stood and held an arm around her waist, as if determined to support her. "I can offer condolences to the dowager. Assure her you and she may call upon me for anything you require in the coming days…since there appears to be no direct heir to the title." Something akin to a scowl furrowed his brow. "Unless you have a son you never mentioned?"

She swallowed another sob before it escaped, and forced a sad smile. "No. I have no precious children. The title and entailed lands will go to Lord Vander."

"Vander," Alec repeated, narrowing his eyes as though sighting a pistol. "Never heard of the man, but I will remedy that to ensure that neither you nor the dowager are mistreated."

She couldn't resist reaching out and resting her hand on his broad chest. "You take on too much, my courageous lion. Mother

Ardsmere and I will be fine. You must focus on your sister. There is little time to set things right for her."

"You always think of everyone else."

His pained expression gave her pause. But then he whispered, "Forgive me," and pulled her into his embrace for a kiss that turned her bones to pudding.

She clutched at him to keep from melting into a puddle at his feet. When he finally lifted his head and stared down into her eyes, she struggled to catch her breath.

"What must you think of me?" he rasped, but his smile belayed any sign of genuine remorse. "I could not help myself, my lady."

After a deep inhale that failed to calm her, she stumbled back a step to escape his dangerous spell. "I really must go."

"Frannie… Please…"

She curtsied, then fled to the front door. As she went to open it, a hand on her arm halted her.

"Frannie. Please don't be angry with me." He gently turned her to face him.

She offered him the best consoling smile she could manage. "I am not angry," she whispered as she caught sight of the butler approaching. "I am afraid of all that you make me feel."

Before he responded, she tore out the door, raced down the steps, and hurried up the walkway to Rydleshire House. She didn't breathe until safely inside with her back pressed against the closed door.

"Frannie? Is that you?" her mother called from the drawing room.

Frannie closed her eyes and blew out a heavy breath. Blessed saints, would this day give her no peace whatsoever? Time for the reckoning. Her mother adored the status and benefits the title granted them. This announcement would not go well.

"Frannie?" Mother Ardsmere appeared in the doorway. "What is it? Your appearance is an absolute fright."

Frannie didn't doubt she appeared disheveled. After all, she had just spent entirely too long wallowing in the duke's embrace. She touched her unruly hair and discovered that part of it had become unpinned and was trailing down her shoulder. "I am unharmed, I assure you. Do not worry."

"I was not worried. Merely concerned that someone saw you. You do not wish to be called a hoyden, do you?" Her mother pursed her plump lips and studied her with a more critical eye.

Frannie knew that look. Might as well be done with it and the devil take them both. "We must go into full mourning, Mother Ardsmere. I told the Duke of Lionwraith that Lord Ardsmere has died."

"You did what?" Her mother drifted forward slowly, tilting her head as if to improve her hearing.

"It was time." Frannie glanced up the staircase just in time to catch Sophie darting out of sight. *Well, fine.* Sophie might hide if she wished, but that would not prevent Frannie from including her and Celia in the blame. "Sophie, Celia, and I came to the conclusion that it might be for the best. And you know very well that all we will lose are the entailed properties—and the title, of course."

"Which includes our beloved home in Chanticlare," her mother said with a tight-lipped growl. "Or did you conveniently forget that part? Did it not occur to you for a single moment that you might extend me the common courtesy of discussing it with me first so I might share my opinion with you?"

"I am sorry, Mother. It fell in place before it could be helped—or shared with you."

"And what, pray tell, is that supposed to mean?" Her mother closed her eyes and leaned against the wall as though about to swoon.

Lovely. Time for the theatrics. Her mother's oldest ploy for manipulating everyone and everything to benefit herself. Frannie swept around her, then halted just inside the drawing room and tossed her words back over her shoulder. "If you are quite finished with your parlor games, come and have a seat, so we might discuss this as rationally as possible."

"I did not teach you to speak to your mother with such impertinence." Completely recovered from her presumed fainting spell, Mother Ardsmere marched into the drawing room. She flounced her plumpness into a delicate ivory and gold chair beside a table laid out with an elaborate afternoon tea. "If you wish to join me, I suggest you ring for another cup, since Sophie informed me she did not know when to expect you."

"Perhaps after we have talked." Frannie hoped the tempting array of sandwiches, cakes, and sweetmeats would help the fractious woman digest the conversation more calmly. "First of all, I do apologize for not speaking to you before announcing the demise of your fictitious son. I have always understood your intentions and appreciated them, but the time has come. I need a life other than that of a lonely, virginal wife and a rudder for West Belgium International." She paused to give her mother a chance to comment, but apparently, that was not necessary, since Mother Ardsmere was more interested in a bite of saffron cake. "We discussed this years ago. I am now four and twenty. It is time."

Her mother paused and rested her plump hands on either side of the dainty, golden-edged plate. "I am not an unreasonable woman, Frannie." She dabbed at the corners of her mouth, then returned her napkin to her lap. "It's just the thought of losing Chanticlare." She sniffed and stared down at her plate. "That odious Vander will have it in ruins in no time. The entire village will suffer because of that man's greed and mismanagement."

"It cannot be helped, Mother. It is entailed."

"Why not do what Celia did?" Her mother's petulant frown reminded Frannie of a spoiled child.

"Because you made me a ward of the Ardsmere family when I was born. Not a daughter. Remember? If we were to attempt to untangle that legal snarl, Lord Vander would surely discover the truth and send us both to the gallows." Frannie allowed herself a heavy sigh. Her emotions were raw enough at the moment. She was in no mood to cater to her mother's tantrums. "Everything remains ours except for Chanticlare. You will still be able to enjoy every indulgence, and we can live here in London. Our town-house is not among the entailed properties."

"And what about you?" Her mother leaned back in the chair, cradling her teacup and saucer in her hands. "I assume you chose this timing because your relationship with the infamously rude Duke of Lionwraith holds promise? I also assume, since you intend for us to enter mourning, that His Grace is also oblivious to the truth."

"Our truths must never be revealed to anyone outside the Sisterhood. I have not lost all reason, thank you very much." Frannie bowed her head and discovered she still held tightly to Alec's handkerchief. The sight of it nearly brought her to tears again. "My life has always been a lie. I do not see any way of changing that."

"Your life has not been a lie, Frannie." Mother Ardsmere slowly shook her head. "It has merely been a necessary caution. You were always meant to be who you are today, my brilliant girl. The unfairness of this world forced me to make the choices I made to protect you. To protect us both." She picked up a biscuit, then let it drop back to the plate and brushed the crumbs from her fingers. "Your father thought we had all the time in the world to make the proper arrangements should anything ever happen to him. As it turned out, we had no time at all because of that horrible shipyard accident. If I had not done what I did when you were born, we would have been forced to rely on Lord Vander's generosity." She pressed her napkin to her mouth as though about to gag. "You know as well as I what would have happened had that come to pass."

"I realize that quite clearly, Mother."

"Do you believe yourself in love with that insufferably disagreeable duke who thinks of no one but himself? Are you not aware of what is said about him? I presume you researched him before your confrontation." The surprisingly genuine concern in her mother's tone kept Frannie from lashing out in defense of Alec, who was nothing of the sort.

"The time I have spent with him has shown him to be an incredibly kind and caring man who is terribly misunderstood. He is coming to dinner tonight. I would appreciate you giving him the chance he deserves." Frannie rose. "I am going upstairs now to see about a long, hot bath. Enjoy your tea, Mother."

"Do not be angry with me, Frannie. This is not my fault. Whenever you call me *Mother*, I know you are not happy and are struggling to be polite."

"I am simply struggling to *be*, Mother. As I have been for quite some time now." She left the drawing room before her mother responded. This particular conversation had left her even more ragged around the edges.

Sophie appeared as Frannie reached the top of the stairs, looking as though she wished for a complete report about both Alec and Mother.

Frannie held up a hand to silence her. "Not now, Sophie. But I would be very much in your debt if you arranged for a bath to be brought to my dressing room."

Sophie gave her a quick hug, then stepped back but kept hold of her shoulders. "Daisy and I already have it in the making. It should be nearly ready by now." She offered a sympathetic smile. "Are you all right, sister? Truly all right?"

Frannie shook her head. "I am not sure yet. I have an ominous feeling that something is about to go terribly wrong. Something of which I will never recover."

Sophie gently shook her, then pulled her into another hug. "I will not allow that, and neither will Celia. This will work out for the best, and you will finally have someone who loves you for you."

Frannie huffed a sad laugh. "At least until someone slips and he finds out the truth."

"Do not even say such a thing." Sophie followed Frannie into her rooms. "*Maman* says it is ill luck to speak of any bad that may happen. She says it becomes a self-fulfilling prophecy."

"Indeed." Frannie paused before entering her dressing room. "Well…Mother Ardsmere and I are now in full mourning. Let the madness begin."

Sophie squeaked and clapped her hands before belatedly tamping down her excitement. "Sorry." She cleared her throat. "Would you prefer we reschedule this evening's dinner?"

"No. Since it is quite intimate and doesn't require either Mother Ardsmere or myself to leave the house, it should satisfy the *ton*'s rules for mourning—should they ever happen to find out about it. Our maids may be hard-pressed to find appropriate garments as quickly as this evening, but I am sure something proper can be managed, since most of our clothing is winter wear due to the dreadful weather."

"My maids will help with whatever they need." Sophie squeezed Frannie's arm. "This is a new beginning. After a relaxing bath and a nap, you will be ready to embrace the future you deserve."

"I hope so." At the moment, Frannie wasn't so sure. She walked into the coziness of the attached dressing room and found Daisy waiting for her.

"Come, my lady," the maid said in a coddling tone. "I scented your bath with your favorite vanilla oil and lilac blooms. A good, long soak is what you need."

"I assume your impeccable hearing informed you of the latest news?" Frannie didn't mind Daisy eavesdropping because the maid always used the information for the greater good and kept Frannie informed about anything of importance. "The fictional Lord Ardsmere is dead, and I am now a widow."

"Good," Daisy said, then had the decency to look abashed. "Beg pardon, my lady, but you understand my meaning."

"I understand." Frannie turned so Daisy could undo the buttons of the pale yellow dress that would not be worn again for six months—at the very least. "I cannot imagine mourning for a year and a day for a pretend husband. Do you think the tongues will clack too loudly if I only do full mourning for three months and then half mourning for three more?"

"The tongues will clack if you marry the duke before the year is up." Daisy steadied Frannie as she stepped out of the dress, then crouched in front of her to help her remove her slippers and stockings. She glanced up with a grin. "But from what I gather, the duke doesn't give a fig about clacking tongues or Society."

"Be that as it may, I did not mention the duke, nor has he ever mentioned marriage." Frannie fixed the girl with a stern look before climbing into the steaming tub and sliding down into the water's fragrant, heated depths.

"Rest on this, my lady." Daisy slid a plump, folded square of linen behind Frannie's head. "Lady Sophie sent a cake of her favorite soap. It smells of lilacs. I'll leave it right here with a cloth. Call out when you are ready to wash your hair. I'll be looking for something proper for you to wear this evening. I know you don't have any black bombazine or crepe, but I think the dark velvet lavender and gray might do if I send out a girl to fetch some black gloves and a shawl. Finest she can find, of course. Would that be all right?"

Frannie closed her eyes and breathed in the soothing steam. "I trust you to prepare whatever you deem fitting." Daisy would take care of everything. She always did. But then again... "Daisy!"

"Surely you cannot be ready to wash your hair already. You just began your soak," Daisy called from the bedroom.

"I am not ready to wash my hair." Frannie lathered the washcloth until suds tumbled over her hands, then stretched out her arm and soaped it. "But I am wondering if I should ask Lady Sophie to consider rescheduling tonight's gathering." She ran the suds down her other arm, then submerged herself back to her chin. "After all, most would find a widow enjoying a dinner party on the very day she became a widow slightly..." The exact description escaped her, but it couldn't be anything flattering.

"You are staying here, my lady." Daisy's voice sounded muffled, leaving Frannie with the impression that the girl was digging in the wardrobe. "And you have to eat." The maid grunted and mumbled something under her breath that was likely one of the coarser words she only used whenever extremely frustrated. "And only Lady Sophie, your mother, and His Grace are going to be here. That's not really a party at all. Just a few people eating at the same time in the same dining room."

"Daisy, I believe you could justify Saint Peter allowing Lucifer back into heaven." Frannie smiled and worked her fingers through her hair, plucking out the pins to save the maid some time. One slipped from her grasp and bounced across the floor.

"I heard that, my lady! Leave those hairpins alone. I shall take them out when we wash your hair. I'd rather do that than have to crawl around looking for the ones you drop. Thank you very much."

"If you had eavesdropped for the realm, the war would have ended much sooner," Frannie called out while stubbornly removing the rest of the pins.

A loud knock on the outer door interrupted their banter.

Frannie strained to listen, wishing she possessed Daisy's exemplary hearing. Unfortunately, only the low hum of indistinct murmuring came to her.

"From His Grace, my lady," Daisy said from behind an enormous bouquet of deep red roses interspersed with ivy. "Flowers that symbolize passion, desire, commitment, devotion, and fidelity?" The maid peeped around the flowers and made a disapproving clucking noise. "Hardly the sort of bouquet a gentleman should send to a newly widowed woman." Her impish smile made a mockery of her scolding.

"He is not going to make this simple. Is he, Daisy?" Frannie stared at the lovely flowers while chewing on her bottom lip.

"Men rarely do, my lady. Nothing is simple when it comes to that lot."

CHAPTER EIGHT

"A RE YE CERTAIN about this?" Dunkeld asked. "The woman just received word that her husband not only died but is already buried."

"I have not received a cancellation. To the best of my knowledge, Lady Sophie's intimate dinner engagement is still in play." Alec lifted his chin so his man could properly tie his cravat. "It is a neckcloth, Winthorp, not a hangman's noose."

"Forgive me, Your Grace." Unfazed by the scolding, the stoic valet adjusted the knot. "Suitable now, Your Grace, or shall I fetch a fresh one?"

"This will do, Winthorp. Thank you." Alec turned and faced his friend's disapproving glower. "Do not look at me like that. If you were in my position, you would do the same."

"Hardly." Dun resettled his stance as though preparing to charge into battle. "I realize the *ton*'s opinion of ye is the least of your concerns, but think of the lady. She is a young widow and might very well have a difficult time of it, depending on whether or not appropriate provisions were made for her. Do ye wish the tongue waggers to make a spectacle of her? Ye should not make this trying time even more difficult for her and Lord Ardsmere's mother."

"Firstly…" Alec strode to the liquor cabinet and poured them both a glass of port. Mainly to irritate Dunkeld, because he knew the Scot preferred whisky. He couldn't resist a smirk as he offered the glass. "Lady Ardsmere is not one to fret about her standing in Polite Society either. She has no time for the ridiculous gossips. Secondly, as long as I live and breathe, that lady will not have a difficult time with anything."

Dun eyed the port with disgust, then ungraciously accepted it. "Ye speak like a man in love. Not a man merely seeking to set up another mistress."

"Mind your tongue," Alec warned. "I will tolerate not even the slightest slander of Lady Ardsmere."

Dun leveled his own warning glare in return. "Then do not behave in such a way as to stir any unsavory rumors against the lady. Red roses and ivy? On the first day of her full mourning? What the devil were ye thinking?"

"I had young MacGinnis cut them from my private garden and deliver them. No one knows but myself, my London butler, and Lady Ardsmere."

"And the Rydleshire servants." Dun shook his head. "Think, man! Ye know as well as I that the gossips depend on their servants to keep them informed."

"If you intend to lecture me for the remainder of the evening, you may decline the invitation and be on your way." Alec tugged on his gloves. He understood and appreciated Dun's intentions, but he had not felt this much anticipation and hope in ages. He would allow nothing to spoil it. "However, I thought you would surely wish to attend in order to help Vivvy. We must all plan carefully and ensure each of us knows our part in this venture."

"Ye know I would do anything to help Lady Violet." Dun flexed his fists while slowly shaking his head. "Such a bloody shame she fell to the wiles of such a heartless bastard."

"Vivvy has always longed to be loved." Alec ached for his poor little sister. He knew that terrible feeling well. Never in all his years had he ever met such a cold, unfeeling pair as their soulless parents. "I am sure she believed the man loved her."

"And what will happen if we canna find the devil? Or worse yet, if we are unable to make the fiend do right by her?"

Alec headed out of his chambers and down the stairs. "I have no idea, Dun. Vivvy knows I will protect her and provide for her and the child as best I can. I only want her happy—and of late, she has been nothing but miserable. I am not so sure my sister even knows what she wants."

"We will sort it, Lion. We will sort it." Dun clapped him on the back. "To the dinner party, aye?"

"To the dinner party."

As they walked outside and descended the front steps, Alec shot a glance up at the night sky. It was clear for a change, a dazzling expanse of blue-black velvet gleaming with pinpricks of light. The stars winked and sparkled like the finest diamonds. A good omen, perhaps? Whether or not it was, that was how he would take it.

The Rydleshire butler, Thornton, granted them entry with a staid bow and ushered them into the drawing room. A footman stepped forward with a tray of long-stemmed goblets glistening with a pale, effervescent liquid that could only be champagne.

"Forgive me, Your Grace." Lady Sophie flew into the room like a fiery-haired fairy trying to escape capture. "It was my understanding that the dowager countess was already down to greet our guests, but obviously I was mistaken." Irritation flashed in the lady's rich brown eyes that resembled the shade of finely polished mahogany. With a harried twitch, she offered a belated curtsy to both men.

"It is I who must beg forgiveness for arriving unfashionably early, my lady." Alec bowed, then turned and tipped a nod toward Dun. "Allow me to introduce Robert Galloway, the Viscount of Dunkeld. One of my few trusted friends. Dun, this is Lady Sophie, sister to the Earl of Rydleshire."

Lady Sophie smiled and offered another curtsy. "Welcome to Rydleshire House, Lord Dunkeld."

Dun bowed and lifted his glass as though toasting her. "Thank you for so graciously extending Lion's invitation to include me, my lady."

"Forgive me, Lady Sophie," said a plump matron swathed in layers of black as she swept through the door to join them. She touched a hand to the frothy cluster of black feathers sprouting from her bun of gray curls piled high on her head. "I had come down to help greet our guests, but the lace on my crepe veil insisted on behaving most uncomfortably by scratching my neck. I simply had to switch to my feathers." She aimed a strained smile first at Alec, then at Dun, then gave them each a dismissive curtsy. "Forgive me. Your Grace, is it? My lord? Is that what I heard from the hallway? As you can well imagine, it has been a most distressing day." She dramatically fluttered her black-gloved hand and released a heavy sigh. "I am the Dowager Marchioness of Ardsmere. I assume you are aware of my son's passing? Do find it in your hearts to be generous in your opinion of me."

Before Alec could respond, Lady Sophie cleared her throat, but it sounded more like a growl as she aimed a somewhat discreet yet irritated glare at the dowager. "Your Grace, milord, this is Lady Emmeline—to avoid any confusion between her and the newest dowager marchioness, Lady Ardsmere, of course." She angled a gentler look toward the men. "Lady Emmeline, this is His Grace, the Duke of Lionwraith, and this is his lordship, the Viscount of Dunkeld."

Both men bowed, and Alec tried not to smile. He rather liked Lady Sophie, and took note that she did not appreciate Lady Emmeline's ploys to gain attention.

"You have my utmost condolences," he told the matron who reminded him of a fussy, plump black hen. "And, of course, we will bear in mind your circumstances. You have no worries, my lady."

"Absolutely none, Lady Emmeline," Dun interjected with another bow. "It is a pleasure to meet ye, and may I also offer my heartfelt condolences."

Lady Emmeline fanned herself with a black fan. Alec wasn't quite sure where she had pulled it from, since she wasn't carrying a reticule. The woman must have kept it hidden in the layers of black crepe that enrobed her stout form.

Frannie appeared in the doorway, looking more breathtaking in a black shawl and dark lavender dress than any widow ever should. In one gloved hand, she carried several small, fuzzy black feathers and looked as though she wished she didn't. She confirmed this observation by hurrying to hide them behind her back.

He tried not to smile as he stepped forward to greet her. "Lady Ardsmere. I am grateful to see you chose to join us. Again, allow me to offer not only my condolences but the assurance that should you need assistance with anything, you have but to send for me."

With her hand still behind her back and her sapphire eyes filled with what he perceived as uneasiness, Frannie curtsied. "You are most kind, Your Grace."

"I believe you already know the Viscount of Dunkeld."

She curtsied again, but bobbled a bit with her arm still held behind her back. "My lord," she said, her tone flustered.

Mischief and curiosity in his smile, Dun bowed. "My lady, I extend my condolences as well."

"Excuse me," she told them both, then turned to Lady Emmeline. "Mother Ardsmere, perhaps you should excuse yourself for a moment?"

"Whatever for?" the lady said as she placed her empty glass on the tray and picked up another full one. "I am savoring some champagne before dinner. After all, we shan't be going out for quite some time to enjoy ourselves anywhere else."

Frannie tightened her jaw, took her hand out from behind her back, and held out the feathers. "You appear to be molting, Mother Ardsmere. I would not wish any feathers to fall into your glass and spoil your champagne."

Lady Emmeline's eyes flared wide, but she quickly recovered and snatched them out of Frannie's hand. "Rude child," she growled as she hurried from the room while taking care not to spill a drop of her drink.

Lady Sophie snorted, then clapped her hand over her mouth. "Oh dear. Excuse me." Still giggling, she gave an unabashed shrug, then turned to Frannie. "She deserved it, sister. She has been horrid all day."

Frannie shuddered with a soft groan. "Yes, she deserved it, but I will pay later. I promise you." She turned back to Dunkeld and curtsied again. "Forgive me, my lord. I do hope His Grace warned you about our company. I fear this evening will be nothing as sedate and proper as our past business dealings."

"I find the lot of ye refreshing, my lady," Dun said with enough interest that Alec considered jabbing the man in the ribs to remind him that Frannie was taken—or soon would be, if he had his way about it.

"Since we are only the four for dinner"—Lady Sophie cleared her throat and smiled—"at least for now, anyway, I see no reason for us to constrain ourselves to the rigid rules of etiquette's pomp and privilege for marching into the dining room. Please, let us merely go in and be seated. I hope you don't mind, Your Grace, since you are the highest-ranking peer among us."

"I do not mind at all," Alec said. Lady Sophie was indeed as delightful to be around as Frannie. He sidled a glance at Dun, wondering if the Scot would take notice. After all, the man needed to marry and produce an heir eventually.

His wondering was answered when Dunkeld stepped forward and offered Lady Sophie his arm. "Brilliant suggestion, my lady."

Alec leaned closer as Frannie took his proffered arm. "How are you?" he asked quietly as they trailed along behind Lady Sophie and the viscount.

"A bit harried, but I shall be fine as soon as I convince Mother Ardsmere that she would be more comfortable at the Ardsmere townhouse rather than here."

"Will you not accompany her?"

Frannie stared straight ahead with a slight frown. "I would prefer to stay here. Mother Ardsmere can be quite"—a despondent sigh escaped her—"distracting."

He would rather she stay here too. It was as close as she could get to him without residing under the same roof. "How close is Ardsmere House?"

"Quite close. A few houses down here on Curzon Street. Closer to the park."

"But not next door." He hoped she understood his meaning. A flash of her eyes in his direction assured him she did.

"No. Not next door. But nothing farther than an easy walk." She seemed uncharacteristically agitated, struggling to maintain her composure. "I prefer to stay here with Lady Sophie, so we might better join our forces to help your sister. But I am not quite certain how I could explain my not joining Mother Ardsmere at our home." Another sigh left her, making him wish he could take all her worries away. "And I also fear if Mother Ardsmere opens the house, that will surely alert our elusive man and make him flee." She squeezed his arm, sending a surge of protectiveness through him. "I fear we must act quickly. I pray we haven't already bungled any chance of finding him." She turned to him, tempting him to take her into his arms. "Please forgive me. I don't mean to unravel like a mindless ninny. There is just so much to balance at the moment."

He couldn't resist turning her toward him and taking hold of her shoulders. "Breathe, lovely lady. Take a breath and steady yourself. We will balance everything together. This is much like waging war. We shall plan our battles and conquer everything, I promise."

"Frannie, dearest. Whatever is wrong?" Lady Sophie asked as Dunkeld helped her seat herself at the head of the table.

"Everything," Frannie said. "Simply everything."

"Frannie, this isn't like you." Lady Sophie nodded at the other end of the intimate setting, and Alec hurried to pull out the chair for Frannie. "Calm yourself, dear sister." Lady Sophie offered a smile of encouragement. "There is nothing that cannot be managed." She swept her gaze across them all. "Just look at the forces we have amassed."

"That is absolutely right," Alec said as he seated himself to Lady Sophie's right.

"Aye," Dun chimed in as he settled in the chair across the table from Alec.

Frannie managed a half-hearted smile. "I know we are fierce, but I fear the target of our search may already know we are here in London." She jumped as though startled when a maid appeared in the open doorway closest to her. "What is it, Agnes?"

The older woman hurried in and whispered something Alec couldn't quite make out, try as he might. Whatever the maid said appeared to be good news, because Frannie smiled, and the set of her shoulders relaxed the slightest bit.

"Thank you, Agnes. Speak to Mrs. Thornton about sending up a tray." She nodded at them all. "Mother Ardsmere sends her apologies, but she will not be rejoining us."

"What a shame," Dunkeld said in a tone that made Lady Sophie snort another laugh.

"Indeed," Alec added, unable to keep from grinning. He lifted his glass to toast the woman, but a hard banging on the front door rattled through the quiet house and interrupted him.

"What on earth?" Lady Sophie stared at the doorway opening to the front hall.

The distinct murmur of deep male voices followed by the heavy clump of boots across the marble floor of the entryway made Alec rise. This might not be his home, but he would not have these ladies intruded upon. He stepped to the doorway. "What goes on here?" he demanded.

Thornton hurried to him and bowed. "Your Grace, Lady Ardsmere's Bow Street Runners are waiting in the parlor." He paused, angled his stance so that his back was to the ladies, and lowered his voice. "Forgive me for being so bold, but perhaps it would be better if you spoke to them. They informed me their news is quite dire."

"I shall deal with them, Thornton, and thank you for being so considerate of the ladies' sensibilities." Before Alec headed to the parlor, he tossed a meaningful glance back at Dun, who immediately rose to join him.

"This is my home," Lady Sophie said as she pushed back her chair and stood. "Who is here, Thornton, and what is going on?"

"I will speak to the visitors and report back, my lady," Alec promised before aiming a pointed look at Frannie. "Both of you, please wait here. It is my understanding that it is for the best. I shall not be long."

Frannie's frown darkened to a scowl, but she didn't argue. Lady Sophie shot him a glare that should have turned him to ash before she flounced back down into her chair with an irritated huff.

Somewhat confident they would stay put, Alec and Dun followed Thornton to the parlor. Before dismissing the butler, Alec said, "I know it is a tall task, but do your best to keep the ladies in the dining room, please."

"I shall, Your Grace." With a confident nod, Thornton hurried back down the hallway.

"Mr. Judson, Mr. Marcus, isn't it?" Alec recognized the men from their stay at Lionwraith. "What ill tidings have you brought to Rydleshire?"

Both men looked at each other as though dreading what they were about to say, and then Mr. Judson stepped forward. "We found the gentleman claiming to be Lord Ardsmere."

"Excellent." Alec shot a glance at Dun, inviting his friend to join him in convincing the devious cove to do right by his sister.

Dun grinned and flexed his fists.

"You do not understand, Your Grace," Judson said.

"How so?" Alec growled.

"The man claiming to be Lord Ardsmere is dead," Marcus said. "We took the liberty of securing the body should you or Lady Ardsmere wish to have it identified further. The murder was made to look like a smuggling deal gone sour, but Mr. Judson and I are not so sure about that. Something about the scene did not feel quite that way, by our reckoning."

Not only was this bad news for Alec's sister, but Frannie would not bear the news well either. She had lost a great deal of money because of that lying cheat. Alec could help her with that. But what would he tell Vivvy? "Are you aware that the real Lord Ardsmere recently died and that Lady Ardsmere just entered full mourning?"

Both men glanced at each other again and fidgeted with uneasiness. "No, Your Grace." Mr. Judson twisted his hat even tighter between his hands. "What would you have us do? We do not wish to upset her ladyship further during this trying time."

"Does the body match the description Lady Ardsmere and I gave you?"

"Without a doubt, Your Grace," Judson said. "And several on the dock confirmed the man called himself Lord Ardsmere."

"Then see that the man is properly buried."

"And why do ye believe the murder was *not* a smuggling deal gone bad?" Dunkeld asked.

Judson tipped a nod at Marcus.

"We have several informants on the docks," Marcus said. "They said the fake lord was brash and foolhardy, but liked enough by everyone he dealt with." The investigator puckered a dubious scowl. "They also said he was known to be a coward. Whenever anyone challenged him, he gave them whatever they wanted with no argument. No way could the man have been making any profit, what with everyone taking advantage of him."

"At that rate, you would think they would keep him alive," Alec said.

"How was he killed?" Dun asked.

"Blow to the back of his head," Judson said. "Somebody bashed him hard. Poor sod probably never knew what hit him and died quick as a doused candle."

"And what caused you to say that the scene was made to seem like a smuggling deal gone bad?" Alec asked.

"He was on the dock. Gun in his hand but not fired. The captain of his ship told us the lord had gone ashore to find out for himself where the brandy was to be unloaded," Marcus said. "Would you not think all that would be settled aforehand when they made the deal?"

"Especially since, after a bit of encouragement, the captain admitted to us that there was no brandy in the hold," Judson added. "Something about this smells of getting rid of the lord to keep him quiet."

"Damn." Alec rolled his shoulders, fighting the burning urge to rush down to the docks and speak to everyone himself. "Who bought the brandy that didn't exist? Were you able to get any of that out of the captain?"

"Even though we used considerable *encouragement*," Judson said, "the captain swore only Lord Ardsmere knew who was to receive the goods. Said the lord wouldn't tell him who, just which port to put in at and what and how much to have the men unload."

"And we are certain this man is the one?" Dunkeld asked with a meaningful slant of a fair brow.

"I cannot imagine more than one individual impersonating a peer. But, for the life of me, the man's actions make little sense. Why smuggle if not to turn a profit?" Alec slowly shook his head, trying to study the facts from every angle. "Unless someone was attempting to ruin West Belgium International. Frannie mentioned that problems with missing cargo were on the rise."

"That company is successful enough to be the envy of many," Dun said. "But surely there would be an easier way to ruin them. Pretending to be the owner and practically giving away the wares just to stir trouble when West Belgium charged full price for the next delivery? I mean—what the devil? Makes no sense. Pirating rather than smuggling, ye suppose?"

"None of this makes sense." Alec eyed the Bow Street Runners. "Is there anything else, gentlemen?"

"No, Your Grace." Judson offered a solemn bow. "If we discover anything more, we will report it to you. Please extend our condolences to Lady Ardsmere. She is a fair woman with a kind heart who deserves better than to be targeted by such unsavory business as all this."

"Aye to that," Marcus added. "Please give my sorrows and prayers to the lady as well."

"Thank you, gentlemen, and do be sure to report to me personally. Moving forward, I shall see to your payment. I do not wish any additional troubles added to the heavy load Lady Ardsmere already bears."

Alec dismissed them with a nod and saw them to the front door before turning back to Dunkeld. "What the deuce do you make of this?"

"The way I see it, someone hired the man to pose as Lord Ardsmere and then got rid of him either because he had served his purpose or they wished him silenced. Either way, the question remains—how do we go about discovering who set this strange game in motion?"

"And confirm their targets," Alec said. "Was their sole intent to ruin West Belgium International, or were they after the Ardsmere family as well? And are they done, or planning a different attack, since this one was discovered?"

Dun shot a fierce glance down the hallway toward the dining room. "And how did they find out their ploy was discovered? Who knew of this? Of Vivvy's fall from grace and Lady Ardsmere's intent to return fire when ye attacked her warehouse and ships?"

"But those two things were merely the end results of this wicked game. The counterfeit lord's smuggling had apparently been active for some time before he met my sister at the Twelfth Night Ball at Lionwraith. One cannot simply start a smuggling or pirating operation on a whim and get it up and running." Alec idly scrubbed his jaw. "Who the devil would do such a thing, and why?"

"What are ye going to tell the ladies?" Dun made a sideways tip of his head in that direction. "I doubt those two will stay in that dining room much longer."

"Fair point." Alec rolled his shoulders again. "I am afraid they must be told the truth. I do not tolerate lies and will not be a party to telling any." He strode back down the hallway, hating what he was about to do. Frannie did not need this additional problem.

As he entered the dining room, both ladies rose from their seats.

"What did they say?" Frannie asked. "Did they find him? Do they know where he is?"

Alec went to her and pulled out her chair. "Please sit, my lady." He looked up and nodded at Lady Sophie as Dunkeld held her chair for her. "Both of you."

"Oh heavens," Frannie groaned. "He discovered us in London and has already escaped."

"Sit," Alec repeated a little more curtly than he intended. "Please," he belatedly added, noting that the addition of the *please* only made Frannie's glare turn even flintier.

She unceremoniously dropped into her seat, folded her arms across the fullness of her delightful breasts, and pinned him with a hard scowl. "We are sitting. Proceed." Her eyes flashed with frustration and worry, as though she had read his mind and already discovered he bore unfavorable news.

"Mr. Judson and Mr. Marcus did indeed find the counterfeit Lord Ardsmere," he said as he seated himself and waited for Dun to do the same. "There is no gentle way to say this. The man is dead."

"They killed him?" Frannie planted her hands on the table as though to keep herself from toppling over.

"No." Alec covered her hand with his, not giving a damn what Lady Sophie or Dunkeld thought. "The information they uncovered led them to the man, and they found him dead. At the docks."

"At the docks," Lady Sophie repeated. "Murdered?"

"Yes, my lady," Dunkeld said. "We will not disclose the details. Ye shouldna be exposed to such things."

"Suffice it to say, the scene was made to appear as if it was a botched smuggling deal," Alec said.

"But you don't believe that." Frannie slid her hand out from under his and seemed to curl into herself as she leaned back in her chair.

He immediately missed her touch. "No. I do not believe that." He folded his hands and rested them on the table in front of him. "And neither do your Bow Street Runners. They are presently in the process of trying to discover more information."

She closed her eyes and started massaging her temples. Her sudden pallor concerned him.

"I think we could all use a drink," he gently suggested to Lady Sophie.

"Yes, indeed. Do forgive me." Lady Sophie rang the small bell beside her plate. When Thornton appeared, she fluttered a hand his way. "Wine, port, champagne—no, not champagne. That would be most inappropriate. We need drinks, Thornton. Gather what you think best, but please hurry."

The butler hurried back out, and a pair of footmen appeared in no time. One bore a tray of empty glasses, while the other carried a tray of decanters and a bottle of wine. They set the trays on the table, then looked to everyone, waiting to pour.

"That will be all," Alec said. "I shall pour. Thank you."

The servants hurried back out, leaving them to themselves.

Alec poured Frannie a glass of port rather than sherry. She needed the fortified wine's strength. "Drink this," he said as he placed it in front of her. "And then you shall have another."

"I am not worried about me." She frowned up at him as he passed the pouring duties to Dun. "What about Lady Violet? Whatever will she do now? How overwrought will she be when she discovers the man she loved is gone?"

"That, I cannot answer." Alec accepted a glass of port, took a long, slow sip, and then set it on the table. "Of greater concern to me is discovering who is behind this grand plan targeting West Belgium International or the Ardsmere family itself." He didn't wish to frighten her, but he had to keep her safe. "I can ensure that Vivvy and her child are well provided for. That was never a question. You are my worry now, Frannie. I will not have you harmed."

"Harmed? Me?" Disbelief filled her face. "Why on earth would anyone want to harm me?"

"That is what I intend to not only find out but prevent."

CHAPTER NINE

"YOU SHOULD STAY here," Sophie said. "At least until Lionwraith gets back from telling his poor sister the news. He should return any day now, and it will be far safer for you here than at Ardsmere House. Especially when Lord Vulture finds out you are not only in London but also in full mourning. The fiend who hatched the fake Ardsmere plot is not your only worry." She shook with a visible shudder as she peered out of Frannie's bedroom window. "It is as though that old vulture already circles us."

"We must stop referring to him like that or we shall surely end up calling him Lord Vulture to his face." Not that Frannie minded, but it might make moving out of Chanticlare a bit more pressing, to ensure the man didn't toss their personal belongings out the windows.

She stared down at the blank sheet of paper on the writing desk. She had decided to tell the odious man of the news. Better to end the nerve-racking wait for the proverbial ax to fall and let Vander's gloating begin. "I wonder if I should just congratulate him and inform him of the date and time of the reading of the will. I am certain that is all he cares about."

"I pray Elias is right that the will cannot be contested." Sophie settled herself on the amply padded bench at the foot of the bed. "As soon as Lord *Vander* discovers he is only to inherit Chanticlare, its small winery, and the title, he is sure to pop his buttons. Supposedly, the man froths at the mouth like a rabid dog whenever West Belgium International is mentioned."

"It is not a rumor. He sputtered like an overflowing teakettle the last time I witnessed it mentioned in front of him." Frannie turned and frowned at Sophie. "Do you think he might be behind the Ardsmere smuggler plot?"

Sophie snorted. "That toad is not intelligent enough to dream up such an endeavor." She shifted on the bench as though finding it uncomfortable. "I also had my contacts look into such a thing being a possibility, and they confirmed he is not. What he is," she said, "is dangerously indebted to several—so many, in fact, that he might be planning to leave England to escape those whom he owes money."

"Then he should be quite pleased to discover that my beloved Chanticlare, Belgium now belongs to him." Frannie hated abandoning the place of her birth and the wonderful people of the nearby village. But no amount of deviousness or creative lying would ever make it belong to her. Not when the Ardsmere patent insisted only sons were fit to be heirs.

She huffed a bitter laugh. And thanks to her mother, she wasn't even considered an Ardsmere daughter. Every church record attached to her name claimed her to be nothing more than the family's ward.

"Your mother is quite eager to settle back into Ardsmere House." Sophie leaned back against the bed and slowly swung her feet like a child with legs too short to reach the floor. "I am not quite sure I understand her hurry."

"Think about it, dear sister." Frannie shifted in her chair to make it more difficult to maintain the nervous jiggling of her knees. Her infernal twitching was even getting on *her* nerves today. "Mother Ardsmere can set herself up there in grand fashion, so she might receive visitors and gain their sympathy with her theatrics."

Sophie rolled her eyes. "Forgive me. I understand she is your mother, but she can be so unbearable."

"Where is *your* mother?" Frannie asked. "Lady Redwell is the only person I know able to keep Mother Ardsmere in line."

"She is toying with some noble in King Louis's court." Sophie frowned and shook her head. "I cannot, for the life of me, remember the man's name. But he is completely besotted with her, and she is torturing him like a cat does a mouse."

Frannie grinned. "I love your mother. She is so…"

"Exactly," Sophie said. "She is *so*."

A loud *thud* and a stream of unintelligible muttering came from beyond the open dressing room door. "Daisy? Are you quite all right?" Frannie called out.

"Yes, my lady," the maid said, her tone strained. "All the hatboxes fell, but I have them sorted now, and they'll not fall again. Now, all I have to organize are the new gowns, gloves, and stockings."

"See?" Sophie said. "You must remain here at least for a little while, or all of Daisy's hard work will be for naught."

A light knock on the sitting room door prevented Frannie from arguing. "I shall answer it, Daisy," she called out again. "Don't trouble yourself." She set down her quill, crossed through the sitting room, and opened the door. "Yes, Thornton?"

"His Grace, the Duke of Lionwraith, is here, my lady. Waiting in the drawing room."

Frannie drew a quick breath, finding herself awash in the surge of warm and nervous fluttering the man always caused. "Thank you, Thornton. I shall be down directly."

The butler nodded and hurried away.

"Will you join me?" she asked Sophie.

"Absolutely not. The man is not here to see me." Sophie winked and shooed her onward. "And I promise to keep your mother from joining you, even if I have to lock her in her rooms."

"If I hear a commotion, I shall realize an uprising has started and will come to the rescue." Frannie tugged on her black gloves but forwent the horrendous feathered turban of black and white striped crepe gauze with an attached veil that Mother Ardsmere had insisted she needed. The ostentatious thing, with its tall ostrich and heron feathers sprouting up from one side, was hideous. Mother Ardsmere could wear it. Frannie wore her black taffeta robe with a crepe handkerchief, a black petticoat, and simple jet earrings. That was quite enough.

Despite promising herself she would remain calm and in control, her heart leapt as soon as she stepped into the drawing room, and Alec rose from the settee with a warm smile just for her.

He closed the distance between them in two powerful strides and took her hands in his, thrilling her with his shunning of propriety and convention. "Forgive me, Frannie. I realize I am dusty from travel, but I had to see you as soon as I reached London." His hazel eyes were ablaze, sparking golden with emotions she dared not hope for. "I missed you, my lady. Very much so."

She held tightly to his hands, selfishly allowing herself the moment, even though she knew it could never be anything more. "I missed you as well, Your Grace." Reluctantly, she eased free of him and moved to the settee in front of the hearth. "Come. Tell me how Lady Violet took the news. I have been so worried about her."

He settled down beside her and took her hand again, as though he couldn't bear not touching her, even though her gloves provided a discreet barrier between them. His thoughtful expression gave her pause. Had his visit with Lady Violet gone well? She held her breath and forced herself to be patient.

"Vivvy surprised me." He stared off into space with a faint smile that reminded her of his achingly delicious kisses. A soft laugh escaped him. "She seemed almost relieved when I told her the man was dead. I didn't understand her reaction in the least. Still don't."

But Frannie understood Lady Violet's reaction completely. "With the permanence of death silencing him, he can never reject or scorn her. He can never spoil what they shared during the best of their days together."

"I suppose I never thought of it that way." He settled a more penetrating gaze on her until she felt the need to squirm. It took every ounce of control she possessed to remain still.

"What is it?" she asked, primly pulling her hands away from him and folding them in her lap. She tried not to notice his faint frown of disappointment.

He sat straighter, then shook his head. "My mind was merely wandering. How were you while I was gone? Dunkeld reported all seemed quiet, and our Bow Street investigators echoed the same."

"I foresee all remaining quiet until tomorrow."

"What happens tomorrow?"

"The death announcement will not only be published in the papers but will also be posted at all West Belgium International offices. I took the liberty of arranging for word to be sent to our customers as well." She dreaded the response, and wondered how many clients they stood to lose when the results of the will became public knowledge and she was no longer merely standing in for an ailing husband but replacing him. "I also intended to post a letter to Lord Vander with the date and time of the reading of the will." She involuntarily shuddered. "That will be most unpleasant, I am sure. He will not be pleased when he discovers he gains nothing more than the title and Chanticlare." She swallowed hard, almost choking on the lie she was about to tell. "Even though there was no true affection between myself and my husband, he ensured I would want for nothing if he passed before I did. He even left West Belgium International to me. To run as I see fit."

Alec stared at her, slowly narrowing his eyes, his expression unreadable. Or perhaps she merely didn't wish to read it.

"West Belgium International will not lose the business of Lionwraith, I hope?" she asked.

"Of course not. What sort of question is that?"

"There will be those who refuse to deal with a business that has a woman permanently at the helm." She twitched a halfhearted shrug. "It is one thing for them to tolerate me as a temporary replacement. Quite another for them to be stuck with me forever."

"Do you wish to be stuck in that business forever?" he asked quietly. "Once, when I asked if you had children, you seemed quite sad to say no. Do you never wish to have a family? Never wish to try marriage again?"

She forced a light laugh that sounded false even to her. "Surely even the mighty Lion of Lionwraith would not be so audacious as to ask for the hand of a new widow in full mourning?"

He reached out and touched her cheek, preventing her from looking away. "What if I am?"

"Do not, Alec," she softly pleaded. "It cannot be."

"Why can it not be?" He leaned in and nibbled a slow kiss across her mouth. "Tell me, Frannie," he rasped softly. "Tell me why it cannot be."

Praying that her waning composure would hold out a little longer, Frannie pushed away and stumbled to her feet. Before he pulled her close again, she made her way to the front window and stared out at another cold, dreary day. The drizzling grayness muting the vibrant colors of summer laughed at her, showing her how gloomy her future without Alec would be. "Do not toy with me. It is too soon. Even after a marriage as loveless as mine was, it is much too soon. Not only for propriety's sake, or for Society's opinion, but because I have entirely too much to overcome at the moment." He had no idea about her battles with logic and her aching need to be loved. She would give anything to fall into his arms and never leave them again. But not before she figured out a way to make it work—a way to make it safe and lasting. She risked turning and looking at him, silently pleading for him to understand.

He joined her at the window, yanked the heavy damask draperies closed, then took her into his arms and held her tight. "I will wait for you a little while as long as you remember you are mine," he whispered against her cheek. "I need you, Frannie. Not as a mistress. Not as a casual conquest. But as the one I wake up to every morning and hold in my arms every night. The one I make love to until we both collapse into a spent and breathless heap."

He tipped her head back, framing her face with his hands and trapping her in his unrelenting gaze. "I see an ache, a longing for the very same thing reflected in your eyes. Tell me I am wrong, and I will never trouble you again."

That was one lie she would never say, no matter how hard she tried. "You are not wrong," she breathed more than whispered, fearing she was making a terrible mistake she would someday regret.

He bent his head and accepted her revelation with a fierce kiss.

She wrapped her arms around his neck and melted into his muscular embrace, returning his ferocity with every ounce of yearning within her. Surely they would burst into flames, and Mayfair would soon be swallowed in the inferno they ignited.

Before she realized what he meant to do, he swept her up into his arms, carried her to the plump, overstuffed sofa tucked into an alcove at the far end of the room, and lowered them both onto it. She found herself wonderfully sunk into the pillowy backrest, embraced and shielded from the rest of the world. Were anyone to walk in, they would realize he was in a compromising position with a woman—just not which woman.

His scent, the heat of him, and the way he touched her—it all worked together like a powerful spell that made it impossible for her to think of anything other than enjoying the bliss of his embrace. Her heart pounded until she could barely breathe, and her body burned, aching for more. She had to stop him. Be the voice of reason.

With a gentle but firm push, she made him pause and lift his head. "This drawing room could become quite busy at this time of day. After all, it is receiving hours. We must not—"

"I will make them go away," he growled, then nuzzled searing kisses along her throat.

"Alec." She fought to maintain a grip on her slipping self-control. "We cannot do this. Not here." She dug her fingers into his unruly black mane, held on tight, and kissed him hard before forcing herself to say, "I cannot be the only one of us who is strong here. Help me, Alec. Please see sense."

A throaty groan escaped him, and he pressed his forehead to hers. "Of course you are right. But damn it all—"

"Damn it all indeed," she said, feeling quite naughty for using such language.

He sat back from her and raked a hand through his hair, making it even wilder. His eyes smoldered with yearning, possessiveness, and a hunger that thrilled her. Never had a man looked at her that way before, and she reveled in it.

"Tomorrow, I will be by your side. For the reading of the will."

"What an odd shift in subject," she said, still somewhat dazed and breathless.

His expression turned seductive, even more smoldering than earlier, if such a thing was possible. "Shall we return to what we were doing, then?"

"No, we shall not." She scooted away while straightening and tucking her black crepe fichu back in place. "Is my hair as messy as yours?"

"My hair is not messy."

"It is." She couldn't resist grinning as she eyed his wild, disheveled waves.

He ran both hands through it, raking it back with his fingers. "Better?"

"Beautiful."

He snorted and rose to his feet, keeping himself turned away from her.

"Did I make you angry?"

"No, my lady, you have left me..." He walked over to the

window but didn't bother opening the draperies. After tossing a wicked smile back at her, he added, "I am struggling for composure." He appeared to be attempting to adjust his falls or something to do with the front of his pantaloons. She couldn't quite tell for sure.

"Forgive me," she said, not really understanding what he meant by *struggling for composure*. She slid her hands across the floral cushions of the sofa in search of at least three hairpins.

After a few moments by the window, he returned to her. "As I said, tomorrow, I will be by your side. Will the reading of the will be here or at Ardsmere House?"

Frannie found two of the three hairpins and tucked them back in place. "Here. I have yet to open Ardsmere House." The admission stirred her uneasiness about what would happen when it became widely known that she was now a widow. "Unwise of me, I know. But Sophie thought it better that I stay here until you returned." She found the final hairpin and secured yet another errant curl. "She is not comfortable that we have made no headway in discovering the mastermind of the fake Lord Ardsmere scheme, and with the death notice in the papers tomorrow, she also fears Lord Vulture's appearance to devour Mother Ardsmere and me."

"Lord Vulture?"

Frannie shook herself. "Mother of heaven! No, not Lord Vulture—Lord *Vander*. If I call the man Lord Vulture to his face, there is sure to be an unpleasant scene with the toad before the will is even read."

Alec ducked his head, but Frannie could tell he was smiling. "There is nothing humorous about this, Alec."

He cleared his throat and squared his shoulders, but mirth still danced in his eyes. "Quite right, my lady. Forgive me. And what time is the will to be read tomorrow?"

"Half past three."

"That gives Lord Vander little time to react to the notice in the paper. How is he to know about the reading of the will?"

"I was about to write to him when you arrived." She really should bid Alec farewell and see to it, but she just didn't have the willpower to shoo him away—not after his being gone for so many days. She had truly missed him. "But this visit with you seemed much more important."

"Shirking your duties, my lady?" His slow, lazy smile made her believe he had actually read her mind.

"It appears I not only shirk my duties but also my moral proprieties whenever you are around. You are an exceedingly bad influence, Your Grace."

"I endeavor to be an even worse influence. Dine with me tonight. In my home." His tone and the look in his eyes left no doubt that a simple dinner would not be the only thing on the evening's menu.

She rose, brushed the wrinkles from her gown, and straightened the infuriating fichu that refused to remain where she tucked it. "No."

"No?" He towered over her, working his effortless magic to distract her. "Why not?"

"I am a widow in full mourning. It simply is not done." She licked her lips, which still throbbed from his wondrous kisses. "Now do forgive me, Your Grace, but I must get to that correspondence I mentioned."

"On one condition, my lady." He jutted his chin higher, waiting for her to be foolish enough to take his dare.

She eased a step away from him, determined to manage a more effective means of self-control than she had so far. Meeting his challenge, she tipped her chin to just as defiant an angle as his. "Which is?"

"Be my guest at Lionwraith Estates for the remainder of the summer. As soon as possible. Before too many know you are here in London. Not only will you be safer there until we discover the miscreant behind the smuggling scheme, but distance from the *ton* during this time could only work in your favor. And Vivvy feels terrible about her behavior during your last visit and wishes to make amends." He resettled his stance and calmly folded his hands in front of him. "She needs the distraction of guests now more than ever—and Wellington and I need you there too."

She opened her mouth to decline, but he cut her off.

"Do not say no. Bring Lady Sophie and your mother along for company and for the safety of your beloved propriety. Dunkeld is coming too, so I shan't be too badly outnumbered by females. We shall all have a grand time and survive this dreary, cold summer together." He took her hand and pressed a lingering kiss to it, then pinned her with his gaze. "Please say yes, Frannie. Please?"

"But there is so much to do. I have to open Ardsmere House, and I have only just written to my housekeeper at Chanticlare to oversee the packing of Mother Ardsmere's and my things and have them sent here to London. And then there is Celia. She is just now out of her confinement and so starved for company."

She opened her mouth to say more, but he pulled her into his arms and silenced her with another kiss. Unable to fight such delicious persuasion, she slid her hands up his broad chest, then wrapped her arms around his neck, pressing close enough to discover a particular *firmness* that explained what he had meant earlier by *struggling for composure*. His hard length pressed against her as if no clothing dared stand between them. How could a mere kiss make her so powerless? And, heaven help her, how helpless would she become if she risked allowing him to introduce her to even more of the pleasures she had no doubt he could provide?

He finally lifted his head just as she was about to become boneless and unable to stand on her own. The smug certainty on his face as he smiled down at her helped restore her resolve.

"It...it is not possible, Alec," she said. "I must stay here."

His dark brows twitched to a more determined angle. "Your Celia and her family are invited as well. As you well know, there is plenty of room." He added a curt nod. "Besides, it might do Vivvy good to see how a truly loving mother is with her child, since she and I never knew that with ours."

"But—"

He stopped her with a finger across her lips. "I have people who can fetch your things from your Chanticlare residence and deliver them to Ardsmere House. They can also oversee the opening of your home here in London and guard it from Lord Vulture. All you need do is give them a list and also let them know if there are any servants you wish moved here as well." He took his finger away and brushed the lightest of kisses across the seam of her mouth. "I will not take no for an answer, my lady," he whispered. "You made me realize that in spite of it all, I do still possess a heart. Please, Frannie. Do not make me drop to my knees and beg."

A despondent sigh escaped her—while at the same time, a bubbling rush of excitement started deep in her core and effervesced through her. "I will have to speak to both Sophie and Celia," she said. "I cannot possibly commit them without their permission."

"Of course. I would expect nothing less."

"And you understand I am still in full mourning?"

He gave a serious nod. "Absolutely."

"And we still must discover who is behind the attack on West Belgium International, and who murdered the father of Lady Violet's baby."

"That is an ongoing investigation I fully intend to see resolved." He kissed her on the forehead. "I want you safe, and until we capture the villain responsible, I will not rest."

"Do not look so pleased with yourself, or I will not go."

"I am not pleased with myself." But his lofty expression didn't hide the victory flashing in his eyes. "I am pleased with you for being such an intelligent woman who is willing to listen to reason."

"Do not be smug and overplay your hand with flummery, Your Grace, lest your victory become tenuous."

He threw back his head and laughed. "Noted, my lady." Eyes

dancing but attempting to contain his happiness, he tenderly cupped her cheek in his hand. "You fill me with light and joy, Frannie. I never thought that possible."

His words both elated and worried her. She swallowed hard against the ache of wanting to cry. If he ever found out the truth about her, would he love her enough to shoo it all away, or would he hate her for the deception?

Still touching her cheek, he leaned closer, his mirth shifting to concern. "Frannie? What is it?"

She managed to twitch a nervous shrug and avoided his gaze, dropping her focus to his chest. "I am afraid to be happy, I suppose. Afraid something will happen to make it all go wrong."

He pulled her closer and cradled her to his chest. "Nothing will go wrong, my sweetling. I swear it."

She hugged him just as tightly, praying he was right. And now, with the course set, she would battle with all her might to make it a success.

With a great deal of reluctance, she forced herself to move out of his embrace. "Well then, Your Grace, I have much to do to confirm the guestlist to Lionwraith Estate as well as tie up what few loose ends remain—such as a list for your magical people who, according to you, are able to handle anything."

His victorious smugness returned, and he made no attempt to hide it. But now, she didn't care. "You will see, my lady," he assured her. "We will sort everything to your liking." He scooped up her hand and kissed it. "I shall take my leave now. When I return for the reading of the will, you may inform me of your progress."

"Good day, Your Grace. Until tomorrow."

A wistful sigh escaped her as he left the drawing room, and the thud of the front door told her he was gone. If she had walked him out, she couldn't guarantee that one or the other of them might not surrender to one last passionate kiss and be discovered by the servants. Of course, the servants probably already knew. But no sense in giving them more fodder for gossip.

Frannie pulled in a deep breath and slowly exhaled. Time for a new chapter in her life. Sadly, a new deception. But she hoped, with everything in her being, that with time, the deception could fade away and only a life of love, happiness, and no lies would emerge and win the day.

Chapter Ten

"**T**HE VULTURE IS here," Celia announced as she swept into Frannie's dressing room. "He brought a solicitor with him too, and guess who it is?"

Frannie noted Celia's outrage. "With that stormy look, it must be Parkerton."

"How can that vulture afford a solicitor?" Sophie asked as she handed Daisy a somber, feathered headpiece of black with an attached black veil that would fall to Frannie's waist. "We discovered him to be so deeply in debt, it's a wonder he has avoided prison."

As Daisy settled the hat and veil in place, Frannie huffed the silky fabric away from her nose. The breeziness of the gossamer cloth triggered a fiendish tickle, making her sneeze and dislodge the topper before the maid had it fully secured. "Sorry, Daisy."

"My lady!" The maid set it back in place and added extra pins. "If you feel another sneeze while downstairs, you must scratch your nose to halt it—and remember to sniff so they believe you are weeping for your dearly departed husband."

Frannie chose not to comment on that sage advice. Instead, she turned to address Sophie. "I would imagine Lord *Vander* is under the impression that he is about to inherit a solution to his dire straits." She reached under the veil and rubbed her nose without adding the convincing subterfuge of a sniff. "Trust me, once Parkerton discovers the poor odds of his ever receiving payment, he will excuse himself as fast as he can make his exit."

"Elias will sort it," Celia said. Her beaming smile did not quite fit with the seriousness of the occasion. "And your duke is already here as well, glowering at Parkerton and the Vulture. I doubt very much if either of them are brave enough to challenge His Grace."

"If I call Vander *Lord Vulture* and set him off, it will be the fault of both of you," Frannie told Celia and Sophie.

Sophie erupted into a cacophony of snorting giggles. "Oh, please do call him that, Frannie," she said. "I want to see his face."

"Well, I do not," Frannie said. "All I want is to get through this afternoon, so we might all look forward to our summer at Lionwraith." After donning her long black gloves, she caught hold of Celia and Sophie's hands. "Thank you both so much for agreeing to come. I don't think I could have braved it alone with Mother Ardsmere. Not with her current level of petulance."

"I hate my Elias isn't coming," Celia said with a sigh. "He feels he must remain in London in case the settling of the will is attacked." She squeezed Frannie's hand. "But Oliver and I shall enjoy the trip immensely."

"I wouldn't miss it for the world," Sophie said. "Without you and Celia here in London, I've no reason to stay and rattle around in this townhouse."

"Well, I am thrilled you are both coming. It eases my mind immensely." Frannie turned back to Daisy. "Might I have a sip of water? I promise not to spill on the bombazine." Her nerves felt ragged as a frayed rope, and her mouth dry as dust.

Daisy offered an encouraging smile as she poured a glass and handed it to her. "Take heart, my lady. With your black skirts, a bit of spilled water would never show. Hold fast—you will make it through this day."

"I sincerely hope so." Frannie sipped the water, wishing it was something a great deal stronger.

"We should go down now." Celia carefully eased the glass out of Frannie's hold and set it on the table.

"Chin up." Sophie looped her arm through Frannie's. "You are not in this alone."

Frannie nodded. "Thank heavens for you both, my dearest sisters." After a deep breath, she charged forward, determined to get the unpleasantness of an encounter with Lord Vander behind her. As she, Celia, and Sophie descended the stairs, Mother Ardsmere's maid hurried to catch up with them and brought them to a sudden halt.

"Agnes—what is it?" Frannie caught hold of the older woman's trembling hands, disturbed that the maid who had served her mother for as long as she could remember was so overwrought. "What is wrong?"

The matron's mouth tightened as she glanced first at Sophie, then Celia, then returned her fretting scowl to Frannie. "Her ladyship is drunk as a wheelbarrow. She'll soon be casting up her accounts."

Frannie cringed and shook her head. "Well, isn't that a lovely predicament?" She squeezed the maid's hands and gave her a consoling smile. "Just keep her in her rooms, even if you have to block the door with a chair. With any luck, she'll be sleeping it off before she makes a horrible mess."

"I have never seen her like this, my lady." The maid gave a worried shake of her head as she turned to start back up the stairs. "Never in all the days I have served her has she ever been like this."

"I know, Agnes. I have never seen her like this either. Just try to keep her from hurting herself."

Agnes tipped a harried nod, then rushed back up to her mistress's rooms.

"What has gotten into your mother?" Celia asked quietly as she watched the maid return to the second floor.

"Mother Ardsmere was not ready for her chapter of the game to end." Frannie held tightly to the banister as she continued her descent to the first floor. Not so much to steady her steps as to brace herself for what lay ahead. If her mother's latest antic was an omen, this afternoon would not go well at all.

As she entered the drawing room, Elias and Alec stepped forward to meet her.

"Steady on, my lady," Elias said quietly, then took his place behind a small table bearing several pages of paper.

Alec offered her his arm while glowering at the back of the room, where Lord Vander stood with Mr. Parkerton at his side. "I will personally escort that man out if given just cause," he quietly assured her as he led her to the row of chairs closest to the table.

"Do not touch him unless you have to," she said softly.

"And why not?"

"Because I am sure the stench of the man does not wash off easily." Once seated, she ran her hand up under her veil to scratch her itching nose again. She remembered to sniff to make it appear that she wept for her loss. Daisy would be so proud of her.

Seated beside her, Alec leaned close enough so that his shoulder brushed against hers. "Have courage, my lady," he whispered. "All will be well."

"If everyone would be good enough to take a seat," Elias said, his tone curt and authoritative. "We will begin."

"I shall remain standing," Lord Vander announced.

Frannie almost gagged at the repugnant man's shrill voice that dripped with greed and condescension. She wagered that before the afternoon ended, his tone would hit the highest pitch his vocal range could reach.

"Mr. Parkerton," Elias said, "did you review the copy of the will given to you upon your arrival?"

"I have not, my lord. Since you drew up the document well before taking over the Ardsmere account, I felt sure all was in order." Mr. Parkerton cleared his throat and hacked as though about to spit—a nervous habit he had always possessed that irritated Frannie to no end.

"Your new client, Lord Vander, might very well disagree." Elias picked up the sheaf of papers from the table and shuffled through to what appeared to be the last page. "Might I direct you to the last page, clause 5b? Just above the dated seal and the signatures."

Frannie didn't turn. Instead, she tensed, ready to leap to her feet and defend herself from what would, at the very least, be a verbal attack. Behind her, the soft shushing of the pages stopped, warning her the time was nigh.

"That is not possible," Lord Vander squeaked. "They have cheated me! This is pure, unadulterated heresy!"

Alec shot to his feet and faced the man. Elias stepped out from behind the table and stood beside him.

She rose and cast a leery look back at Lord Vander and the wide-eyed Mr. Parkerton, who was rapidly flipping back through the pages of the will while shaking his head.

"It all appears to be in order, my lord," the solicitor told Vander.

"It cannot be!" Vander squealed like an enraged pig. "The entirety of the Ardsmere holdings are mine by right, by the patent that explicitly sets the rights of primogeniture through the males of the line." He pointed a shaking finger at her. "She gave him no heir. No son! Everything belongs to me!"

Although it was a struggle, she remained silent. It would be far better for Elias to handle this.

"I will challenge this!" Vander plowed toward her, knocking chairs and tables out of his way. "I will have it all, you classless chit! You are nothing more than a light-skirted ward who trapped my cousin. You cannot steal what is rightfully mine."

Alec blocked Vander just as he toppled over the last chair in front of her. "You will leave now, Vander, or I shall take great pleasure in tossing your mewling arse back out into the gutter where you belong."

"Gutter?" the lord sputtered. "*Gutter?*" Again, he jabbed a finger at her. "She is the one from the gutter, Your Grace. She is nothing more than a conniving whore trying to steal my fortune!"

Alec slammed both hands onto Vander's chest, grabbed him

by the waistcoat, and forcibly backed him out of the room before she could utter another word.

The loud slamming of the front door silenced Vander's high-pitched screams of blubbering profanity. After several long, tense minutes, the door slammed again, and shortly thereafter Alec calmly entered the drawing room while staring down at his hands in disgust.

"Thornton!" he bellowed.

The butler appeared as though stepping out of thin air. "Yes, Your Grace?"

"Hot water and the strongest soap this household possesses, if you please. My hands are soiled with a powerful stench."

The stoic Thornton actually cracked a smile. "Right away, Your Grace." Then he disappeared to do Alec's bidding.

"You are next," Elias said to Mr. Parkerton. "That is, if you are unable to see reason?"

Mr. Parkerton surrendered with a shake of his head. "Absolutely not, my lord. The will appears to not only be in order, but I also noted its date was well before Lord Ardsmere purportedly fell ill. It appears unquestionably solid."

"You realize your client is headed for debtor's prison unless he leaves England," Frannie said, unable to remain quiet any longer. "I would advise you to cut your losses, Mr. Parkerton, and cease your association with him."

The solicitor nodded. "I will indeed, my lady. And please accept my condolences for your loss. Even though you are the most independent lady I have ever met, I know this new situation cannot be easy for you."

The man's sincerity touched her heart, enabling her to forgive him a multitude of sins. "Thank you, Mr. Parkerton. You have my best wishes for your future endeavors. It is my hope you achieve the greatest of success."

He accepted her words with a polite bow. "Good day, my lady." He bowed again to Alec and Elias. "Your Grace. My lord."

The men nodded at the solicitor. Elias followed him out.

Sophie and Celia rushed into the room and hugged Frannie.

"You are shaking," Celia said.

"Thornton! Wine for Lady Ardsmere." Sophie righted a chair and helped Frannie into it. "Oh dear, I forgot he's gone to fetch soap and water. Watch her," she ordered Alec as she rushed out to find a servant to do her bidding.

Alec crouched beside Frannie, then gently lifted her veil and folded it back as though she were his bride. "It is over, sweetling," he said softly. "The demon is slayed."

"No." She allowed herself a resigned sigh. "I fear the demon is merely wounded and now angrier than ever. He will endeavor to do whatever possible to get revenge."

"Without money, the man can do very little."

"Yes," she agreed, "but he has the *promise* of money to convince some unsuspecting soul to help him. Such a promise enabled him to secure a solicitor—at least for a short time."

"Lord Raines and I shall see to it that nothing happens." He touched her cheek with a tender caress. "Do not concern yourself further about that worthless toad. You will be safe at Lionwraith, and my men here in London will ensure nothing happens at Ardsmere House other than the delivery of your belongings from Chanticlare."

"What would I do without my courageous lion?" She caught her breath as soon as the words slipped out. She should not have said that.

He gave her the seductively possessive smile that always sent a surge of heat through her veins. "I intend to see you never have to find out." He pulled up a chair and took her hand in his and simply held it as though loath to let her go.

Sophie hurried back into the drawing room with a pair of footmen following close behind. Each of the servants bore a tray filled with glasses bubbling with pale champagne.

"Well played," Celia said as she helped herself to a glass.

"Sophie—champagne? Really?" Frannie hoped her friends' celebratory air wouldn't strike Alec as cold and unfeeling.

"To celebrate the ousting of Lord Vulture, my sister," Sophie said. "Not the passing of Lord Ardsmere."

"The Irish celebrate their dead," Celia said. "I believe they call it a 'wake,' and they consider it a way to remember and celebrate the life of their dearly departed."

"We are not Irish." Frannie worried what Alec might think. His expression gave away nothing, but the slightest glint in his eyes made her hope he understood and didn't find their behavior off-putting. "You will not be bored with us as your guests at Lionwraith," she told him.

The bold smile he flashed helped her relax. "I can say with all honesty that this is the first house full of guests I have ever looked forward to receiving."

Elias returned and lifted a glass in a silent toast. "I shall hate to miss this visit." He wrapped an arm around Celia's waist and kissed her cheek. "And I shall also miss my family terribly. But I would be remiss if I failed to remain in London to ensure the will was properly and without a doubt settled."

"Thank you, Elias." Frannie hoped he understood how much she appreciated his assistance. It made her thankful that she and Sophie had conspired to ensure that he and Celia fell in love and married.

"Do forgive us for leaving after only one glass of champagne," Celia said. "But we must get home to Oliver and enjoy some family time before I leave poor Elias on his own."

Elias grinned. "Never fear, dearest. Monty has promised to keep me company."

"That is what I fear most. Your brother is wonderfully incorrigible." Celia looped her arm through his, and the couple took their leave amid laughter.

"And I must go upstairs to check on Mother Ardsmere," Sophie said. She gave Frannie a sly look, then disappeared into the hallway.

"Are they always this obvious?" Alec took Frannie's empty glass and swapped it with a full one off the tray left beside the door.

"Obvious about what?" She knew exactly what he meant, but after the way the day had gone, she didn't wish to assume anything.

He arched an incredulous brow. "Leaving us alone in the drawing room with two trays of glasses filled with champagne."

"You will find that Celia and Sophie are as incorrigible as Elias's brother. They are most certainly not your average ladies of the *ton*."

"Good. I have very little tolerance for most ladies of Polite Society." He returned to the chair beside her, then flinched as his gaze settled on the top of her head. "I fear the feathers of your hat are quite beyond repair. It appears I broke them when I smoothed your veil back. My apologies, sweetling."

She reached up, started removing the black hatpins, and handed them to him. "No apology necessary. I hate this dreadful thing. The veil tickles my nose and makes me sneeze." She swept it off and tossed it onto a nearby chair.

"At Lionwraith, you need not worry with such frippery." He carefully placed the hatpins on the table.

Frannie tried to tame her hair, fluffing her curls back in place. "Thank heavens for that." She paused and locked eyes with him. "But my wardrobe will still be full mourning for several months. Out of respect, you understand."

"Neither the colors nor the fabric of your wardrobe concern me, my lady." He kissed her hand and gave her a wicked look. "Separating you from your gowns is my focus."

"Your Grace!" The quickening beat of her heart made her swallow hard.

His deep, rumbling chuckle as he leaned in close and nibbled a trail of kisses along her jawline sent such a surge of heat through her that she gasped.

"Frannie," he said, "I cannot keep the truth of my wants, nor my hands and lips, from you. You taste divine—the sweetest I have ever devoured." He paused and trapped her in his gaze.

"And I do mean to devour you completely when we have our privacy at Lionwraith, dear lady. Make no mistake about that."

She had no idea what to say. And here she was supposed to portray an experienced married woman. She wished she had paid more attention to those unmentionable books with illicit lovers that her mother had always tried to keep hidden from her.

All mirth and sultry wickedness faded from Alec. "Pray tell me I have not offended you." His worried frown tugged at her heart. "Today has been horrible for you—forgive me if I have upset you. It appears my rudeness knows no bounds, and even though you are accustomed to my careless behavior, I have shocked you."

"You have not shocked me." Belatedly, she realized that might be misunderstood. "What I mean is—you have not offended me. I am simply not used to such overt attention."

"Was your husband blind?" He clamped his mouth shut. "Damn and blast! Forgive me again. One should never speak ill of the dead."

She couldn't help but laugh. "I told you my marriage held no emotion or love. It was more of a contractual agreement. Remember?"

"Even so—"

She silenced him with a hard shake of her head. "There was never an *even so* between myself and Frank." She forced a smile, determined to get the conversation on to a safer topic. "Might we speak of something else? Did you write Lady Violet and warn her we were all about to descend upon her?"

"I did, and I know she will be thrilled."

"I hope the letter reaches her before we do. Should we wait a few days rather than leave tomorrow?" Frannie didn't want Lady Violet upset. Not in her condition. It could very well be unhealthy, and she would never forgive herself if they caused something terrible to happen to Lady Violet or her baby.

"I posted it with one of my most trusted men."

"About your trusted men…" She had been meaning to speak

with him ever since his offer to help her settle her affairs and also further investigate the Ardsmere smuggling plot with his *men.* "Are these the same gentlemen who gave you the wrong information and cost me two ships and a warehouse?"

"Those gentlemen are no longer in my employ." He set his chin to a sullen angle that tempted her to smile.

She had hurt his feelings by reminding him of the mistake. "Alec."

"What?" He avoided her gaze and downed a full glass of champagne in one gulp.

"I know you are not a man who makes it a habit of erring, but you are human. For all you knew, the information they gave you was accurate. It could happen to anyone."

"Not me." His jaw flexed as he glared off into the distance. "I take the greatest of care with where I place my trust. Mistakes about my confidence and trust in an individual are unforgivable." He frowned and leaned toward her. "Frannie, sweetling? Are you unwell? You have gone quite pale."

His sentiments regarding trust had hit her like a slap in the face, but she couldn't very well tell him that. She pulled her handkerchief from her sleeve and dabbed it against her throat. "Forgive me, but I fear today's excitement is catching up with me. Perhaps I should retire upstairs for a bit of a rest."

"Of course." He jumped to his feet and helped her stand, then wrapped an arm around her waist and supported her against his side. "I shall escort you. As pale as you are, I will not allow you to attempt the stairs without my assistance."

She couldn't bear to meet his gaze, so she bowed her head and kept her handkerchief pressed to her mouth. Ever so carefully, they made their way upstairs. "This door is mine. Thank you so much, Alec. For everything."

He didn't answer, nor take his arm from around her—just opened the door and escorted her into her private sitting room. "What is your maid's name?"

"Daisy."

"Daisy!" he bellowed loudly enough to be heard clear to Scotland.

The bedroom door flew open, and the maid's eyes went wide. She immediately rushed to Frannie's side. "My lady. Let us get you abed. You do not seem well at all."

"Have Lady Sophie message me later this evening," Alec told the maid. "I want to know how Lady Ardsmere is faring and will not be pleased if I am forced to wait until morning for an update. Am I understood?"

Daisy paled a little herself and curtsied. "Yes, Your Grace. I will see to it. I swear."

He kissed Frannie's cheek. "Rest, sweetling. And please be well."

"I am sure I'll be fine." She caught his hand as he stepped away from her and gave it a squeeze. "Thank you for everything. Today would have been unbearable without you."

"I will always be here for you, my lady. Always."

She didn't trust herself to speak, just gave him a quick nod and hurried into the bedroom with Daisy at her side. As soon as she heard the sitting room door click shut, she dove face first onto the bed. "Oh, Daisy. What am I to do?"

Daisy clambered up onto the bed and started unlacing Frannie's gown. "You grab hold of that fine man and never let him go. He is a duke, mind you. And quite taken with you, if I do say so myself." She gently tugged on Frannie's arm. "Sit up now, my lady, and let me get you undone down to your shift so you might rest more comfortably."

Frannie righted herself and peeled off her long black gloves. "If he finds out the truth, though—"

"Make him love you so hard that it won't matter." Daisy tucked Frannie's slippers into one of her apron's deep pockets, then rolled up the gloves and stuffed them into another pocket. "Stand up now so you can step out of this dress." She frowned. "Where did you leave your hat and veil?"

"In the drawing room. Alec fears he broke the feathers."

Frannie rubbed her forehead, hoping to massage away the subtle pounding that warned a terrible aching was on the way. "I hope he did ruin it. I hate that thing."

"You have to at least wear the veil whenever out. 'Tis only proper." Daisy shook out the dress and returned it to the wardrobe.

"Only a proper way to perpetuate the lie." Finally down to her shift, Frannie flopped back onto the bed and dropped her head into her hands. "He is going to find out, and he is going to hate me. I just know it. He abhors deception, and that is all I have ever been."

"No, my lady." Daisy removed Frannie's stockings and then plumped the pillows behind her. "You are not an abhorrent deception. You are a kind and caring mistress who has saved many from dying in the streets. You gave them back their pride by giving them an opportunity to show they can take care of themselves if only given the chance. Lay yourself back now, while I fetch something for your head."

Frannie sank into the pillows, rolled over onto her side, and curled into a ball. "I don't think what good I have done will matter to him, Daisy."

"Then he is a bloody fool, and it was never meant to be." Daisy pulled the covers up and tucked Frannie in as if she were a child. "Rest, my lady. I'll be back shortly with an herbal for your head."

"Thank you, Daisy. I could never get through this without you."

Daisy gave her a proud tip of her head. "Of course you couldn't. But don't you worry none—I am not going anywhere. I am wise enough to know my mistress is the best in all the realm."

As Daisy left the room, Frannie pulled the pillow over her eyes to block out all the light. Wouldn't it be lovely to possess a lion's share of wisdom?

The coincidence of the idiom *lion's share* only made her head hurt worse.

CHAPTER ELEVEN

F RANNIE'S LIGHTHEARTED LAUGH echoed throughout the vast marble atrium. "Oh my heart, look how baby Oliver is taking everything in. He heartily approves of Lionwraith."

Alec glanced over at the little one tucked into a cradle-like basket carefully carried by a footman and watched over by Celia and the nanny. The infant squirmed on his pillow, turning his tiny head from left to right, looking all around with eyes wide and alert. Unable to keep from smiling, Alec gave the baby boy a polite nod. "Why, thank you, Your Grace. I am pleased you like it here."

Celia beamed with pride at her child. "Even at this tender age, my young duke recognizes exquisiteness."

"And thank you as well, Your Grace." Alec bowed to Celia. He recalled when Parliament had voted to amend the Hasterton dukedom patent. At the time, it had meant little to him. But now that he knew Celia and Elias, he was glad he had voted in favor of it.

"It *is* quite beautiful here," Sophie said, "but are we certain our precious Oliver's interest isn't because he is finally out of that dark, stuffy carriage? This atrium is airiness and light itself."

Alec allowed himself a rumbling laugh. He couldn't remember the last time he had actually enjoyed guests invading his home. "It is entirely possible, Lady Sophie."

"And where is that fine Scottish wife of yours?" Dunkeld

asked MacGinnis as he handed the butler his hat and gloves.

"Inspecting the rooms, my lord," MacGinnis replied with the barest twitch of a bushy white eyebrow. "'Tis our honor and pleasure to serve His Grace's guests."

"What he means," Alec said, "is that they are not accustomed to my inviting guests for the summer—or any time, for that matter."

"Then it is we who are honored." Frannie cast a sweet smile at the butler. "I hope you have been well, MacGinnis."

The man bowed, remaining staid as ever. "Quite well, my lady, thank ye. And might I be so forward as to extend the heartfelt condolences of all the servants here at Lionwraith?"

"Thank you, MacGinnis. That is very kind."

Alec tucked her hand into the crook of his arm. "Lady Ardsmere was quite the bully to my staff during her last visit," he announced to the group. "I believe they all still fear her."

"Your Grace!" Frannie swatted his shoulder. Then a bright blush flooded her cheeks as she realized what she had done.

Alec couldn't help but laugh, but before he could tease her even more, Mrs. MacGinnis scurried down the stairs with four maids and a pair of footmen struggling to keep up with her.

Her plump face was shining with the exertion as she dropped a series of graceful curtsies along with polite nods and a beaming smile. "Your Grace, I beg ye to forgive my tardiness. I felt the need to make one last inspection, and your arrival caught me unawares."

"Mrs. MacGinnis!" Catching the matron up in an extraordinarily unconventional hug, Dunkeld kissed her on the cheek. "And how is the bonniest housekeeper who ever escaped Scotland?"

"Welcome back, Lord Dunkeld." With her cheeks flaring to an even brighter red, Mrs. MacGinnis hugged him as though he were her long-lost son. "Ye've not had any more trouble with that terrible ague in your lungs, have ye?"

"I have not, thanks to ye and your remedies, my dear woman." Dunkeld stepped back and gazed at her with the adoration of a child.

Alec noted not only Frannie's surprise but also that of the other ladies. "Mrs. MacGinnis snatched Dun away from death's door when we first returned from the war. If not for her, the Dunkeld line would have been nothing more than a memory."

The housekeeper shuddered, then took on the seriousness of a war general. She turned to the footmen and maids and clapped her hands with a sharp pop. "What are ye waiting for? Show our guests to their rooms. Would ye have them stand here in the atrium all day?"

Alec kept Frannie by his side as everyone else followed the servants up the stairs. Lady Emmeline and her maid, Agnes, dragged along at the back of the group. He had the distinct impression that the elder dowager marchioness did not wish to be here.

"I will show you to your rooms," he told Frannie. "I thought it might be nice to have a bit of quiet away from the others first. Do you mind?"

"Not at all." A peacefulness seemed to settle across her as her gaze followed Dunkeld and the ladies in their ambling up the gentle curve of the marble staircase. She pulled in a deep breath and blew it out. "They are all dear to me, but nearly four days in the closeness of carriages and inns has made me remember why we live in separate homes and, most of the time, separate countries. Celia in London, Sophie in France, and Mother Ardsmere and me in Belgium." She shuddered. "Familiarity does indeed breed contempt." She cast a dubious glance his way. "Are you quite certain you wish for us to stay here as long as a month or more?"

He pulled her close and tipped her face up to his. "If it means I get to have you in my arms, they can stay here forever." Then he took her mouth, returning to the sweetness he had hungered for ever since their last kiss. She was in his home, his secluded sanctuary from Polite Society's self-proclaimed elite. "We belong here together, you and I," he whispered across the velvety softness of her lips. "You need not fear the *ton* and its gossipmongers here."

Ever so subtly, she eased away with something akin to worry or leeriness tightening her features. "One can never escape the *ton*, Your Grace. Not ever." Then something seemed to shift within her, and the genuineness of a smile that reached her eyes enabled him to breathe easier. "While I usually try my best to follow Society's strict etiquette," she said, "I fear I have already breached it by coming here while in full mourning. I should be burrowed away in the darkness at Ardsmere House rather than spending the summer at the country estate of London's most eligible duke. But I cannot say I am not glad to be here, and I thank you for offering your home as a lovely refuge."

"You know why I offered it, Frannie." He would not pretend otherwise. Honesty counted for much more, in his opinion, than lying to give a pretense of gallantry. "We can be together here, however we want. Whenever we want. The choice is always yours, my lady."

"Brother! Lady Ardsmere!" Violet hurried toward them from the direction of the library. "MacGinnis didn't tell me you had arrived. I shall have his ear."

"Vivvy." Alec strode forward and welcomed her with a kiss on the cheek. He caught hold of her hands and gently turned her back and forth. "I believe you are rounder than the last time I saw you."

"Your Grace!" Frannie stepped in and took Violet's hands from him. "Ignore your brother. You are even more beautiful than before. Loveliness itself."

"I am so glad you agreed to return, Lady Ardsmere. I was a horrid little wretch the last time you were here. Please forgive me." Violet cast a wily glance at Alec.

He braced himself. Since he had banished their mother to the wilds of Scotland, Vivvy's personality had blossomed into a powerful and uncontrollable force all its own. "Sister—I have no idea what you are about to say, but I beg you to think twice before saying it."

She smiled and arched a dark brow, as though accepting the challenge. "I was merely about to say that I cannot remember when I last saw you this happy to have a house filled with summer guests."

"I doubt that," Alec said. "Not the statement, but the fact that those were the words you were about to say."

"Leave her alone," Frannie scolded in an affectionate tone. "I am truly happy to see you, and I know you will love Sophie, Celia, and sweet baby Oliver. Dunkeld is here too."

"You do not think she will enjoy meeting the dowager?" Alec teased.

"I am the dowager now—dowager the younger, I suppose." Frannie shot him a curt look, then turned to Violet in a much more amiable manner. "And no, you will not enjoy meeting Mother Ardsmere. Her current frame of mind is…"

"Unpalatable?" he offered, unable to resist a wicked grin.

Frannie nodded. "Most definitely."

"Well, I must go upstairs to welcome them," Violet said. "As the lady of the house"—she paused and cast a sly smile in Frannie's direction—"at least for the time being, it is my duty to ensure our guests settle in nicely and do not fail to let us know if there is anything they should need." Partway up the staircase, she paused and cast a mischievous smirk back at her brother. "And by the way, Alec, the workers finished the new duchess's chambers two days ago. They are ready for your inspection."

"Minx! You never could resist spoiling a surprise." He huffed a growl he didn't mean, feeling his heart lighten even more at his sister's much happier spirits. As he turned back and beheld Frannie's expression, a sense that he had overstepped his bounds twisted within him.

Tightly clutching her hands in front of her, she seemed… He couldn't put his finger on it, but she did not look happy.

"Frannie?"

"Alec—I…" She caught her lovely, full bottom lip between her teeth. "You know I am… I feel…"

"Shh, sweetling. I never want you to do anything or say anything that you do not wish to say or do, my lady." While he yearned for her with a fury, he also needed her to come to him because she wanted him just as badly—not because she felt obligated or pressured into doing so. He placed her hand back into the crook of his arm. "Let us walk for a bit and see if we can find Wellington. Vivvy has given him the run of the estate since he became a father."

"Became a father? Wellington?"

Alec nodded. "Apparently, the old boy found his lady love and brought her here to have their babies. Sir Henry discovered the mother and her kittens in the conservatory's storage room." He laughed. "Wellington's wife is a sleek little thing, lovely and black as a wild panther from the jungle. However, all three of her kittens are the spitting image of their father. Fluffy little ginger cats that become quite loud when they decide their mother isn't giving them enough attention."

"Well done for Wellington." She squeezed his arm. "Please, may we go see them?" But then she paused. "Are they old enough for visitors? I wouldn't wish to upset the mother cat and have her move them somewhere else."

"Move them?"

"Yes—a mother cat will move her kittens if she considers them no longer safe wherever she has them."

"Indeed." Alec opened the dining room door for Frannie so they might follow the covered walkway to the conservatory. "Are there any cats at Chanticlare that need to be relocated to Ardsmere House? I would not wish them to find themselves under the rule of Lord Vander."

"Thankfully, no. No pets whatsoever. I wish we could relocate the kindly folk of the town most likely to incur his wrath, though. Unfortunately, we cannot." Her steps slowed, and she cast a sad, almost tearful gaze up at him. "I fear I have done them ill by casting them off to that odious toad. All these years I kept them safe, and now I failed them."

"Entailments can tie up lands for generations, sweetling. There is nothing more you could do." He hugged her closer to his side. "As the next male in line, Vander has all rights to it."

"I just pray the people of Chanticlare can find a way to forgive me when that horrid little man makes their lives miserable." She stepped up into the conservatory, but her unhappy focus remained on the floor rather than the beauty all around her.

He gently pulled her to a stop and curled her into his embrace. "There are ways to convince horrid people not to be so horrid. Rest easy, sweetling. I shall do what I can to help the people of Chanticlare. They will not suffer. Mark my words."

She leaned back, eyeing him with a faint smile. "That sounds rather ominous, Your Grace. Remind me never to displease you."

"I am only ominous to those who deserve it." After giving her a tender, reassuring kiss, he added, "And you, my lady, could never displease me."

Three demanding, yet squeaky, meows, followed by a deep, somehow vibrating *purrrrp purrrrp*, warned they were no longer alone.

Frannie turned out of his arms and wiggled like an excited child. "There they are," she whispered. "The entire family. Wellington looks so proud."

Wellington looked bored and sorely put upon, but Alec wasn't about to spoil Frannie's happiness. The one-eared, three-legged, long-haired ginger cat was stretched across the top of a wooden crate, well out of reach of the three fluffy kittens trying to snag hold of his slowly flipping tail. Mother cat sat close by, systematically catching her young ones, one at a time, and holding them down to wash them from the tips of their tiny tails to their little pink noses.

"I am so glad you gave Wellington a home. Just look at that familial bliss." She rewarded Alec with a hug that made him decide that none of the cats would ever be given away. They had found their permanent home.

"Wellington earned it." He kissed her hand before tucking it back into the crook of his arm. "After all, he is a war hero."

"Indeed, he is." She leaned her head against his shoulder, filling him with the feeling that all had finally become right with his world. She shifted against him with a soft sigh.

"Was that contentment or weariness, sweetling?"

"A little of both, I fear. It's as if everything from the past few weeks has suddenly caught up with me."

"Then let me show you to your rooms so you can rest. We can visit more with the Wellingtons later."

"What did your sister mean by the *new* duchess's chambers?" Frannie's careful tone revealed that Vivvy's announcement had both worried and intrigued her.

Even though he knew he would eventually have to tell Frannie about his first wife, he hated to spoil this pleasant time by dredging up the past. He remained silent, trying to choose his words carefully.

As they made it to the end of the covered walkway and he reached for the dining room door, she stopped him. "Alec? What is wrong? Why won't you tell me what your sister meant?"

He stared down into her eyes, drowning in their sapphire depths. "When I came home from the war, I had my dressing room enlarged and fitted with a permanent bathtub. My chambers also now include another small library where I keep my favorite collections of books. My first wife's rooms were no longer needed, so I did away with them with that expansion." He tensed, bracing himself for her reaction. "You must think me vain and selfish."

"Absolutely not," she said with a caring softness that made him ache to pull her into his arms and take refuge in her warmth. "Your wife's rooms had to have distressed you. I understand she died in childbirth while you were away at war. I am so sorry for your loss."

"My loss." He didn't curb a bitter laugh as he yanked open

the dining room door and waited for her to step inside. "I lost her when she took a lover while I was at the front—not when she died giving birth to that man's child."

"Oh, Alec." Frannie halted again and stared up at him. Shock filled her wide-eyed expression. "Forgive me for…"

He caught her hand and kissed it. "Do not apologize, my lady. I intended to tell you eventually. No time like the present, I suppose." He pulled in a deep breath, then forced it out, determined to resurrect the pleasantness of earlier. "There are many rooms here at Lionwraith, but I wished for yours to be closest to mine whenever you returned for a visit. I wanted our suites connected for when you choose to…" He kissed her hand again while keeping his gaze locked with hers. "I had them done with you in mind. I hope you find them pleasing."

"I am certain they will be lovely."

The shyness of her smile surprised him. He found it both refreshing and perplexing that a married woman could seem so *virginal*, for lack of a better word. Perhaps she'd had no experience with men other than her husband. Surely, during her coming out, she'd had any number of suitors and admirers with which to hone her flirting—and her curbing of advances.

"Come. To your rooms, my lady." He escorted her through the dining room, down the long hallway, and up a private set of stairs rather than the main staircases in the atrium. "Our rooms take up the entirety of the east wing's top floor. This stairway is not only more private, but also more practical."

"Your home is breathtaking, Your Grace."

"Because of its beauty, or the expansiveness that requires so much walking?"

She laughed. "Both. Thankfully, I have always enjoyed a hearty constitution and nice, long walks." She came to a sudden stop, closed her eyes, and tipped her nose higher. "Lilacs. This entire floor smells of lilacs."

"Well, of course it does. Is that not our favorite flower?"

She eyed him with a coy tilting of her head. "You are trying entirely too hard, Your Grace."

He brushed the backs of his fingers across the soft curve of her cheek and treated himself to another taste of her lips. "I want you, Frannie," he whispered. "In my bed. In my life. Always at my side. That is why I am trying so hard."

She gazed up at him and barely shook her head. "I want you too. More than I could ever say. But…"

"But what?"

She touched his face and caught her bottom lip between her teeth. With a faint shrug, she almost cringed. "I guess I am afraid."

"Afraid of what?"

"That once you have me—" Rather than finish speaking, she blew out a frustrated huff and turned away. She hurried farther down the hall and nodded at the first door she came to. "This must be your room?"

He caught up with her and took her back into his arms. "I will not tire of you once I have you. Is that what you were about to say? You are not a conquest, sweetling. You are…" She was so many things. A simple word would never suffice.

"I am what?" She fixed him with a guarded look, angling her chin to a defensive tilt.

"Light. Love. Hope." He shook his head. "You are all those things and more. You are everything, Frannie."

Her guarded demeanor turned dubious. "You are setting up quite the challenge for me, Your Grace. How am I to live up to such sentiments?"

"It is no challenge, sweetling, because you already are those sentiments."

She ducked her head, but not in time to hide her smile.

"I am quite serious," he said.

"Forgive me." She glanced up at him, merriment twinkling in her eyes. "But I remember your opinion of me was quite different the last time I was here at Lionwraith."

"Only at first." He pulled her close and nuzzled her throat

while breathing in her warm, alluring scent—lilacs, vanilla, and aroused woman. "It did not take you long to cast your spell on me." He couldn't help but chuckle. "I believe the turning point was when you set your skirts on fire."

She leaned tighter against him as he tickled the tip of his tongue across the silky spot beneath her ear. "A gentleman would not remind a lady of such," she faintly scolded him.

"I have never been accused of being a gentleman." He caught her earlobe between his teeth, then gently suckled it. "Shall we proceed to your room, where I will be happy to prove why I have never been labeled as such?"

"Indeed, Your Grace," she agreed in a breathless whisper.

He swept her up into his arms and strode to the next door down as if meaning to carry her over the threshold as his bride. *Perhaps one day,* he promised himself. If all went well between them, as he planned. "You will have to open the door, sweetling." He treated her to his wickedest grin. "My hands are full—delightfully so, I might add." The deeper blush across her lovely cheeks rewarded him nicely and made him want her all the more.

"Angle me so I might reach it, Your Grace," she said with a coy toss of her head. Before she touched the latch, the door opened wide.

"Oh dear." Daisy backed away, looking ready to bolt but not knowing which way to run. She belatedly dropped a curtsy. "Forgive me, Your Grace. I thought it was another footman banging on the door with the last of Lady Ardsmere's trunks."

As much as he hated to, Alec lowered Frannie's feet to the floor but kept her tucked to his side. "All the trunks should have been brought up by now, Daisy. Do you need to go downstairs and box my footmen's ears?"

Daisy curtsied again while keeping her gaze locked on the floor. Her freckled cheeks flamed to a brilliant red. "I wouldn't think of doing such, Your Grace. There were many trunks to bring up. I am sure they're just busy sorting them to the proper rooms."

Determined to get Frannie all to himself, he turned to her. "Your weariness concerns me, my lady. I do not wish you to become ill and unable to enjoy all that Lionwraith has to offer. Since it seems your maid still has much to do to settle your rooms, might I offer you my chambers to rest in—at least until yours are sorted?"

"Uhm…" Frannie stood there with her luscious lips barely parted and her cheeks rivaling the bright red hue of her maid's face. She fluttered her hands as if not knowing what to do with them. "I… Uhm…"

"You became quite weak in the conservatory. Remember how you leaned against me so you could catch your breath?"

She snapped her mouth shut and ratcheted both her fair brows higher, eyeing him in disbelief.

Perhaps he was pulling the longbow a bit much with this story. "You did lean against my shoulder and sigh with weariness."

"I did, Your Grace. You are quite correct about that."

Daisy curtsied again, then edged past them and stepped out into the hallway. "Perhaps I will run down and check on that last trunk, my lady. You go rest. I shall get everything sorted and fine as five pence before you know it."

As the maid disappeared, Frannie folded her arms across her chest and glared at him. "That was ridiculously horrid."

"Indeed, it was." He reached for her, but she stepped back and appeared rooted to the spot. "Now, Frannie, don't be fractious. A lady's maid knows everything, and an exemplary lady's maid always keeps her mistress's secrets. Are you telling me Daisy is lacking?"

"Daisy is not lacking." She huffed an impressive yet ladylike snort. "And neither is she a fool. Your silly exaggerations were not necessary."

He doubted very much that she would appreciate his telling her maid as bluntly and boldly as possible that he intended to enjoy her mistress's charms the remainder of the afternoon. He also sensed he better tread carefully here, or any possibility of said enjoyment would soon disappear. "You are absolutely right, my lady." He offered his arm. "Come and let me show you the door that connects our suites."

"By the way," she said, her tone somewhat contrite. "This sitting room is very lovely. All the shades of lavender, the pale blues, and soft whites mixed with every range of delicate green imaginable. It reminds me of the lilacs in your conservatory or a perpetual spring garden. So very peaceful and relaxing."

"As I said earlier, I prepared these rooms with you in mind." He led her into the disheveled bedroom filled with open trunks, hatboxes, and gowns draped over the backs of chairs. "It appears your Daisy still has much to do."

"We have only just arrived. I assure you, she will have all this sorted and perfectly organized in no time at all." Frannie tilted her chin to that defiant angle he loved. "She merely needs time and *all* the trunks, I might add."

"Of course, my lady." He chuckled to himself as they crossed the room, then he paused and opened the drawer of a small, round table holding a vase overflowing with deep lavender lilacs. With hope and anticipation stirring in his chest, he withdrew a key. "This key either locks or unlocks this door between our rooms." He nodded at the door in front of them. "It is my hope that the door will remain unlocked." He placed the key in her hand and closed her fingers around it. "But that, my lady, is entirely up to you. Always."

She opened her hand and eyed the long bronze key with the elaborate filigree heart serving as its bow. "And do you have a key, Your Grace?" she asked without looking up at him.

"I do not." He slid a finger under her chin and gently tilted her gaze up to his. "And please let that be the last time you address me as *Your Grace*. I am and ever will be your Alec." He brushed his lips across the velvety softness of hers as he whispered, "Or your Lion, my love. Whichever you prefer."

CHAPTER TWELVE

H E HAD ADDRESSED her as *my love*. Her heart lodged in her throat and almost strangled her. Frannie eased back a step while rubbing the key until it warmed between her trembling fingers. She wanted this with Alec more than anything, but once it was done, nothing would ever be the same between them.

She inwardly shook herself, determined that he not witness her as the quaking, inexperienced ninny she truly was until after they had talked. "Is the door presently unlocked?"

"It is, my love."

Oh my, he said it again. She carefully opened the table's tiny drawer and dropped the key back into it. "Let us leave this here for now."

"As you wish." He opened the door and held it for her. His sultry gaze was ravenous as it raked across her.

She had no idea what she had envisioned a man's bedchamber would be like, but this room fit him perfectly. It smelled of fine leather, sandalwood, and citrus, along with an unmistakable note of a man who feared nothing—Alec's familiar scent. The richness of the gold-corded draperies to the matching counterpane of the large, canopied bed, and the lush Turkish rugs, perfectly mirrored his courageous personality in deep, passionate burgundies, regal indigos, and burnished golds. The dark woodwork of the walls made the vast room almost cavelike. This truly was a lion's lair made for siring the mighty beast's heirs.

She swallowed hard and made her way deeper into the room, trying to calm herself enough to speak above the erratic pounding of her heart. At the rate it was drumming, he wouldn't be able to hear her speak. And hear her he must. They needed to talk before she entered his bed. If she attempted what would hopefully be the last deception between them without setting the stage first, the necessary lie would surely fail and snatch away her one hope for true and lasting happiness with him.

"Might we ring for some wine?" She worked her mouth, finding it parched as dust. "There are things that must be said before we…" She caught the corner of her lip between her teeth again, unable to say anything further.

"Are you all right, dear one?" His immediate concern made her swallow hard again. He moved closer and frowned when she backed up. "What is it? If you have changed your mind, my love, say so. I would never force myself upon you. This will always be your choice."

She lifted her hands to fend off that notion while struggling to embrace and conquer the situation. "It is not that. I want this. I do. But might we please have some wine? I find myself sorely in need of a bit of false courage to sustain me through the conversation I fear we must have before…before we do anything else."

He arched a dark brow. "You worry me when you speak of *false courage* and *fear* while standing in my bedchamber."

"I promise all will be made clear." She prayed her falsehood would be accepted as the truth and not become the hammer that shattered this precious bond growing between them. She tipped a hopeful shrug. "But it will be easier with wine."

"I keep brandy here in the room. Would that do, or is it too strong? I shall be happy to call for sherry or madeira if you prefer."

"Brandy would be lovely." She tried to lighten the mood she had so unfortunately weighed down with her request. "And you keep it here in your room? Do you entertain here often, Your Grace?"

"I do not think it appropriate for me to answer that, my lady." He cast her a narrow-eyed glance from where he stood in front of a mahogany cabinet, pouring brandy into a pair of glasses. "Why do you insist on formalities between us, Frannie? Is it your desire to push me away?" His expression had become guarded, almost stormy, as he closed the distance between them and handed her a glass.

"Forgive me. It is nothing more than the etiquette ingrained in me since birth. Like a reflex. I assure you it is nothing more than my nervousness." She sipped the brandy and breathed in its bouquet while holding it on her tongue. The exemplary flavor and warmth strengthened her resolve. "This is lovely and exactly what I needed. Thank you."

He lifted his glass in a silent toast, took a sip, then eyed her while tilting his head. "Talk to me, my sweetling. Allay my fears. Tell me I have not misread what I thought was an undeniable attraction between us. A bond that promises to only grow stronger. Pray tell me it is not one-sided."

"It is not one-sided. I promise you." She pulled in a deep breath and sent up yet another silent prayer that he would believe her. "But there is something you need to know about me. Something of an intimate nature."

His guarded expression darkened to a thunderous scowl. "Did your husband misuse you?"

She hurried to shake her head. "No. Nothing like that." She took another drink, a deep gulp that emptied the glass so quickly it made a very rude, slurping squeak. Heaven help her. She was handling this so badly. She swallowed hard again. The burning trail of brandy pooling in her middle did nothing to douse the nervous fluttering that threatened to send the drink back out. "I can think of no delicate way of saying this, so I shall simply say it." She squared her shoulders, lifted her chin, and looked him square in the eyes. "I am a virgin."

"What?" Looking bewildered, he tilted his head. "What did you say?"

"I am—" She coughed, almost choking on the confession and the continued burn from the large swallow of brandy. "I am a virgin, Alec. Completely inexperienced in what goes on between a man and a woman in…" She cast a glance over at his massive bed. "I have never been with a man in that way."

"You are telling me that during your marriage of—How long did you say?"

"A little over six years," she whispered. "Closer to seven, actually." More brandy would be so helpful right now. She held tight to her empty glass.

"Your marriage of almost seven years was never consummated by Lord Ardsmere?" He stared at her as though she was some strange, exotic animal he had never seen before.

"That is correct. My marriage was never consummated." At least everything she had said so far was the truth. She took some solace in that.

Still appearing dazed, he slowly shook his head, then took her glass as well as his and refilled them both. "Forgive me for being vulgar or indelicate—but why not?" He returned to her and held out the fresh drink. "Was the man…?" He didn't finish, just snorted and shook his head again.

"Unable," she supplied while lowering her gaze to the floor. For the first time in her life, the lie caught in her throat, making it impossible to look Alec in the eye. "It wasn't possible." She twitched a shrug. "I remained untouched."

"You could have annulled the marriage," he said quietly.

Still staring at the floor, she shook her head. "It did not seem right to do so." She took another deep sip, thankful that the drink was finally causing the tingly calm she so badly needed at the moment. "He was not unkind to me." Technically, that was true as well. Lord Ardsmere was not unkind because he did not exist.

Staring down at the floor while he slowly paced back and forth, Alec raked his hand through his dark hair while sipping his brandy. He halted and eyed her. "And you were never tempted to take a lover?"

"Tempted? Of course. But I never did." She couldn't take a lover. If she had, the secret of the real Lord Ardsmere might have been revealed, just as she was trying to keep it from being revealed at this very moment. She found herself fidgeting beneath the intensity of his gaze. "Must you stare? It is as if I am a bug beneath a quizzing glass. Surely you have met a virgin before."

"I have, my lady. But a virgin I expected, not one hidden behind a marriage in name only."

She drew herself up, fighting to hold the charade together. "I did not think it appropriate to mention my *condition* until now." She retreated to the door that separated their chambers. Without looking back, she pushed down on the latch and barely opened it. "I am sorry, Alec. Truly, I am." And she meant that more than he would ever know.

He crossed the room and thumped the door shut before she could slip through it. "Forgive me, Frannie. My words were not an accusation."

She couldn't face him—not yet. So she stared at her hand still clutching the golden handle of the latch. "This is why I wished to speak with you before…well, before. I did not want you wondering why I had no idea what to do to please you."

Ever so gently, he turned her to face him and tilted her face up so she had no choice but to look him in the eyes. "Your being here at this very moment pleases me. Your allowing me to touch you, to kiss you, pleases me." He slid his fingers along her jawline and up into her hair, loosening her braided chignon. "You please me more than you will ever know," he whispered, then sealed his mouth over hers.

His other kisses had tasted of a raw, untamed urgency. This kiss claimed her with a raging possessiveness that made it difficult for her to remain standing. She wrapped her arms around his neck, holding tightly to keep from melting down to the floor.

He broke the connection, swept her up into his arms, and carried her to the bed. As he eased them both down onto it, he gently laid her back among the multitude of satin pillows piled against the headboard. "Allow me to help you with your boots and stockings, my lady."

Thrilled and a tiny bit too fearful to speak, she managed a hesitant nod as she sank into the soft, cool nest of satin. The ease with which he unfastened her boots, slipped them off, and tossed them aside made her wonder if he had done the same for other women. But this time, she wouldn't ask. She didn't want to know about his other women. She wanted to imagine him only behaving this way with her.

Her breath caught and her heart pounded harder as his warm mouth pressed a kiss to the inside of her ankle while he slid his hands up to her thigh. With an expert tug, he untied the ribbon garter holding up her silk stockings.

"Oh my," she said, though she never meant to say it aloud.

He cast a devilish glance up at her as he bared her other leg. "Oh my, indeed, my love."

An embarrassing squeak escaped her as he hooked one of her legs over his shoulder and leaned in to nibble and kiss his way up the inside of her thigh, sending a series of shivers cascading through her.

"Forgive me," she said while finding it impossible not to squirm. She so badly wanted—what? She had no idea, but was certain Alec would provide *it*.

"Forgive me," she squeaked again.

"Forgive you for what?" he asked, while shoving her skirts higher.

"For making such ridiculous noises. I sound like a cornered mouse."

He chuckled deeply and stretched up to treat her to a slow, deep kiss that made her press her body up against his hard length. He lifted his head and smiled down at her. "It is my hope to cause you to make a great many noises this afternoon." He kissed her again while tugging her fichu out from around her neckline and tossing it aside. "But perhaps I was getting a bit ahead of myself. All these layers between us must go."

He helped her sit up and backed off the bed, gently pulling her along with him.

"I hope you do not expect me to stand. Not after you have turned my bones to jelly."

He grinned and tugged her into his arms. "I shan't let you fall, my love." While supporting her in the crook of his arm, he undid the tiny buttons running up the back of her gown. The dreadful black thing sagged loose, and he worked it down her body until it lay in a crumpled heap of bombazine and crepe around her ankles.

"My goodness. You are quite the expert." She didn't know whether to be impressed or upset, but when he kissed a burning trail across her exposed shoulder as he unlaced her stays and pushed them down to join her gown on the floor, she forgot all about it. All she wanted was to experience everything he offered. And suddenly, she was very bare, and his warm, calloused hands caressed her in the most delicious ways imaginable.

"And now you," she whispered, wantonness conquering her shyness.

"I would see you in my bed first with your glorious golden hair fanned across my pillows." He stripped back the counterpane, then scooped her up and laid her down among the bed linens. "Undo your hair, my love, while I rid myself of these trappings."

She meant to undo her hair as he asked. Really, she did. But instead, she found herself transfixed by the first real man—no, the first wondrously made Greek god—she had ever seen in the nude. His bulging muscles rippled and gleamed by the light of the candle she didn't remember him lighting. Her gaze dipped lower, and she bit her lip. His *appendage* was indeed a great deal larger than any statue's *accoutrement* she had ever observed.

He climbed into the bed beside her and eyed her with a mock scowl. "Hairpins, my lady? Still in your hair and soon to be scattered in our bed?"

"*Our* bed?" Hands trembling, she shoved her fingers into her hair, plucked out hairpins, and flung them off onto the floor.

Pulling her into his arms, he smiled, then bent to the task of nibbling the ridge of her collarbone in such a manner that sparks hotter than any fiery ember shot through her. "Yes, sweetling. Our bed. For I want you here forever."

Her breath came faster as he worked his way lower, nibbling, kissing, closing his lips around the buds of her nipples, and sucking until she arched against him and cried out. Heaven help her. She'd never dreamed such unbelievable sensations existed. And she no longer cared about making embarrassing noises. Apparently, he found them acceptable, because he growled in return, and the sound of his throaty purring thrilled her to no end. A startled squeak exploded free of her as he touched where no man had ever touched her before.

"We will go slowly, my love," he promised quietly as he gently stroked, then kissed his way down to the juncture of her thighs and used his mouth along with his tantalizing fingers to torment her even more wonderfully.

She buried her hands in his hair and clutched him harder against her while bucking beneath his ministrations. A ravenous, pounding ache, an incredible pressure begging to be released, stormed within her like a building tempest. And then the sensations exploded, raging through her with wave after wave of more bliss than she ever knew existed. She screamed, or groaned, or maybe growled like a feral beast. She didn't know, and nor did she care. All she knew was that she had never experienced anything like this.

"Oh, Alec," she gasped. "Lion…my lion."

"My love," he said in a rasping whisper as he rose over her then settled his hips between her thighs. With slow, tender kisses, he eased into her. "Relax," he breathed across her mouth as he pushed the hardness she so badly needed deeper inside her. "Relax."

"I cannot relax because you have made me want more." She ran her hands up and down the smooth hardness of his muscular back. The rigid fullness of their joining made the tempest within her build again. She hungered to return to the blissful waves that had left her breathless. "More, my lion. More."

With a rumbling groan, he gave a sudden thrust and completed the bond, body to body, united by the wonderful link within. And then he stilled and lifted his head to stare down at her. The candlelight danced across his face, revealing such caring and concern that tears sprang into her eyes.

His eyes widened with horror. "Forgive me, dear one. Is the pain unbearable? Would you have me leave you?"

"If you leave me now," she warned as she wrapped her legs tighter around him, "I will never forgive you." She held his face between her hands and smiled. "It was a mere sting. My tears are from what I saw in your eyes. No one has ever cared for me like that before."

"I love you, Frannie," he growled. He buried his face in the curve of her neck and started rocking in and out, building force with every thrust. "I love you," he groaned louder as he increased to a hard, pounding rhythm.

She arched and met him, storming into the ancient dance with the raging hunger he created within her. Then the glorious waves of ecstasy returned, making her thrash and shudder as she cried out her pleasure.

He roared with his own release, joining his cries with hers. He collapsed but caught himself on his elbows before he crushed her.

She reached up and pulled him down, needing the feel of him on top of her, skin against skin, their heartbeats pounding against each other. She held him tight, struggling not to release the tears of pure joy burning in her eyes.

"Are you all right, my love?" he whispered against her ear.

"I am better than all right, my wonderful lion. Except for one thing."

He tensed in her embrace, hardening his muscles to stone. "And that one thing is?"

"I fear I love you, Alec. More than I ever thought it possible to love anyone."

He slid his arms around her and hugged her tight as he rolled to his side and took her with him. "We must work on this habit of yours of frightening me when you are about to tell me something that is not frightful at all." He kissed the tip of her nose, then frowned at her. "It is quite cruel, sweetling."

She couldn't resist a smile. "I shall strive to do better."

"Thank you. That would be most appreciated."

She combed her fingers through his unruly hair, brushing it back from his face. "Is it always like this?"

He studied her for a long moment. "The loving?"

"Yes."

"No, my sweetling. Not always. But it will be between us."

She thought about that, not fully understanding what he meant. "Why is it not always this way between lovers, and how do you know it will be forever between us?"

After a deep, sighing groan, he rolled to his back and tucked her against his side. "Many make the mistake of thinking the physical act without an attachment of the heart is more than enough." He cleared his throat, and she sensed he was embarrassed with himself. "I was guilty of such. I found release, but not the unexplainable contentment and joy I feel right now."

She snuggled closer and hugged her leg across him. "I feel boneless with happiness." Then a belated sigh escaped her before she could stop it. She cringed, praying he hadn't noticed.

Alec gently rubbed her arm. "Tell me what troubles you so I might slay that dragon, my lady."

She couldn't tell him. All she could do was make up another half-truth to distract him. She nestled her head more comfortably into the dip of his shoulder. "I worry that something will happen to end this happiness between us. Now that I know love—I am greedy to protect it and fear losing it."

He nudged a kiss to her forehead and hugged her tighter. "We will protect it together. Nurture it and see that it grows. I swear it, my love."

"I am glad," she whispered while tickling the wonderful dusting of tight curls across his chest. She traced his muscles, outlining the firm broadness upon which she rested her head, noting how his waist narrowed with impressively hard, ridged muscles that were almost like the rungs of a ladder leading down to his glorious *appendage*. "God sculpted you so nicely."

"Not as nicely as He sculpted you." Alec slipped his hand underneath her arm and cupped her breast.

While nibbling kisses across his chest, she slid to where she was more on top of him than beside him. With her breasts delightfully squeezed between them, she wiggled in place and hugged him between her legs. Stoking her courage, she lifted her head and looked him in the eyes. "Is it terrible of me to want you again so soon?"

He filled his hands with her buttocks and held fast as he leaned up to kiss her. "I would be sorely disappointed if you did not, my love."

She wiggled again, delighting in the feel of him beneath her as she nibbled along his jawline. She paused and smiled down at him again. "You are so nice and bristly."

"I have heard it said a man's beard grows faster when his lady makes him lusty." He squeezed her bottom again, then ran his hands up her back and around to cup both her breasts.

She couldn't help but laugh as she gently ran her fingers across his day's growth of stubble. "I shall have to remember that should you ever suddenly appear with a beard."

"Indeed." Wrapping his arms around her, he rose and treated her breasts to his full attention.

Astraddle him and hugging his head to her chest, she wriggled and rubbed against the hard length of him rising between them rather than inside her, where it belonged. "Alec," she gasped as she burned for more. "We must remedy this position."

With one of her nipples sucked wonderfully deep into his mouth, he lifted her hips, set his weaponry where it belonged, and seated her on it nicely with a fine, tilting thrust, all while shifting deeper into the pillows and leaning back against the headboard.

"Now we are properly secured," he said with a husky groan against her breasts.

"Yes, we are, my lion." She hoped he didn't find her too wanton, but this was so… A breathy groan escaped her as she took hold of his shoulders and rocked harder.

"That's it, my love." He threw back his head and arched upward while clutching her waist with his hands and helping her move. "Yes," he hissed.

"Oh, yes," she echoed, riding harder, charging ever deeper into the ecstasy building toward the explosion of pure bliss. She reached the pinnacle with a throaty scream, shuddering while the delicious sensations crashed through her.

Alec roared and arched higher again, holding her hard in place as he found his release and spilled within her. Then he slowly eased back down and pulled her closer, kissing her while trying to catch his breath.

She sagged against him, nestling her face into the crook of his neck to savor the salty sweetness of his skin. She couldn't hold back a lazy giggle at the silliness that just popped into her head.

"And what is so amusing, my love?"

"If anyone had ever told me I would someday love the taste of a man dampened with sweat from passion, I would have thought them a noddy."

He rumbled beneath her with a chuckle of his own. "As long as it is only *this* man."

"Of course." She sat up and ran her fingers through his hair. A sudden surge of emotions filled her as she smoothed her thumb across one of his sleek, dark eyebrows. Fear, uncertainty, and worry took over, strangely battling with her hopefulness, joy, and love for him. She didn't know whether to laugh or cry, and somehow felt the need to do both.

His focus on her sharpened. It was as though he looked inside her and peered into the deepest corners of her tormented soul. "Frannie?"

"I find it amazing how you can say my name in a tone that asks so many unspoken questions."

"Then answer them, my love. Do not make me say them aloud."

"I worry. About this…this predicament we are in. I am honor bound to observe full mourning for at least six months." She shifted to sit beside him while gathering up the bed linens to cover her nakedness. A heavy sigh left her as she leaned back against the headboard. "If I were a proper widow, full mourning would be for at least a year and a day." She shrugged. "I have never worried about what Proper Society thought of me. But *this* is quite bold even for me." She pulled up her knees, balling up as she leaned her head against his shoulder. "Even coming here rather than remaining in London is sure to be headlined in the gossip sheets."

He took her hand and laced his fingers through hers. "Let them be damned, my love. They do not matter."

"They do if it risks West Belgium International." She squeezed his hand. "And I do not wish to bring ruin to Lionwraith Shipping, either. Our businesses provide for many families. It is not just our reputations we risk but those people's livelihoods. And we have yet to find the devil who tried to pit our two companies against each other."

He kissed her hand. "What are you saying? Do you wish to return to Ardsmere House and cloister yourself for a year and a day?" He stared at her, unblinking. "I hope not, because I do not believe I could bear it. Not after today."

"I could not bear it either." She hissed out another heavy sigh. "No. I will not return to Ardsmere House nor bend to the gossips. But we must take care of all we say or do whenever outside of Lionwraith." She curled tighter against him. Surely they were safe here. His staff was devoted, as were the maids and the nanny she and her sisters had brought. She was just being silly and emotional.

But there was so much more than mere gossip to worry about. What if someone from Chanticlare finally spoke up after finding themselves tossed to the likes of Lord Vulture? She shuddered that thought away. No. It would not happen. The villagers had kept the secret safe since her birth. Surely they would not turn on her now.

"Forgive me for being such a worrier," she whispered. "I did not intend to ruin our time together."

"You could never ruin what we just shared, Frannie," he said just as softly. "I understand how you find yourself overset about everything. Especially in light of what you shared about your marriage." He kissed her hand again, then hugged it to his chest. "I love you, Frannie. We shall think this out and form a plan. A plan for us. Our businesses. The devil who campaigned against us. Everything. Together—we will sort it all and emerge victorious."

I hope so. But she didn't say that out loud. She curled tighter against him and pulled his arm around her. "I love you, Alec. More than anything."

He slid them both down into the bed while hugging her closer. "And I love you more. Rest now, dear one. I shall keep the dragons away while you sleep."

CHAPTER THIRTEEN

Alec and Dunkeld sat in the shade of a mighty oak that had supposedly been planted by Alec's grandfather several generations back. At least three, if memory served him correctly. The day had turned out to be a rare, warm, sunny gift that begged to be fully embraced. To honor that gift, Alec had ordered a luxurious picnic set up outside, complete with comfortable chairs and an enormous banquet table groaning with enough refreshments to last them until well past sunset.

"Does a picnic not require us to sit on the ground?" Dun leaned back in his chair and stretched out his long legs, crossing them at the ankles as he lifted a tankard of cider.

"Last night's heavy rains would cause today's wet arses," Alec said while admiring Frannie's competitiveness as she took part in a lively game of shuttlecock with Sophie, Celia, and Violet. It was quite obvious that his lady did not like to lose. The others appeared just as competitive, and he wondered if the four would eventually come to blows. "Were we to wager, I would place my money on Frannie."

Dunkeld shook his head. "Shame on ye betting against your sister." With a knowing nod, he winked at the shrieking women scurrying around to keep the shuttlecock from hitting the ground. "Dinna underestimate my Vivvy."

"*Your* Vivvy?" Alec set a sharp look on his friend. "Since when do you address my sister in such a manner?"

Dun flashed a self-assured smile. "Since she granted me permission to do so. Do ye mind?"

Alec shot him a warning look. "As long as you are aware that if you hurt her, I shall be forced to kill you."

Dun raised his tankard in a toast. "I would expect nothing less of ye, Lion." He nodded at the women again, but this time, he eyed them with an almost pained scowl. "Should she really be hopping about in such a way? What with her condition and all. Do ye think it wise?"

"I do not, but Mrs. MacGinnis informed me to leave her alone and allow her to do whatever she feels capable of doing." Alec shook his head. "Vivvy seems happy and hearty enough. I pray Mrs. MacGinnis is right."

"That wise old hen saved my life," Dunkeld reminded him. "I would trust her to keep Vivvy and her bairn safe."

A sudden urgency to know the extent of his friend's interest in his sister gnawed at Alec. Dun was Vivvy's senior by a good ten years, and the two had always been amiable enough, but no interest had ever sparked between them. Why would it spark now? "What are your intentions with *my* Vivvy?"

Dun shifted in his chair, squared his shoulders, and sat taller. His troubled gaze remained locked on the women playing on the lawn as he set his tankard on the table. "She needs a father for the babe. A good husband and a protector." He turned and leveled a narrow-eyed glare on Alec. "A man who would never throw her unfortunate choices back in her face and make her consider herself a fallen woman."

"You are not bothered by the fact that she carries another man's child?"

Dun's expression turned incredulous. "I am not a virgin. Why does she need to be?"

"And you would treat her child as your own?"

"The bairn would be mine. Blood doesna guarantee a loving family. Ye should know that well enough."

"Truer words were never spoken." Alec offered his friend a

heartfelt smile. "You are already my brother because of all we endured before, after, and during the war. I would be honored to accept you as a brother *legally* by your marrying Vivvy."

"Thank ye, Lion. I hoped ye would feel that way." Dun tipped his head toward the women, who were now clustered in a laughing circle with the poor shuttlecock and rackets tossed to the ground. "And might I suggest ye get to marrying that fine widow of yours before she finds herself in the same condition as my Vivvy?"

"And have her demonized by the *ton* when word gets out that she remarried a little over a month after her husband's death?" He wished Frannie *would* agree to go on and marry him. After all, Gretna Green was but an easy ride from Lionwraith. "Not to mention the haranguing Lady Emmeline would give her. I understand the woman lost her son, but when she's not drunk as David's sow, she is a mean-spirited old cat. You experienced her claws at dinner the other night."

"Where is she, by the way?" Dun sat taller and looked all around. "I have yet to see that old cow today."

"With any luck"—Alec glanced in the direction of the house—"she's already properly foxed and on her way to sleeping it off."

"Frannie won," Sophie announced as the ladies rejoined them.

"She cheated," Celia accused as she strolled over to where the nanny sat beside her babe's basket, watching over little Oliver as he slept. "I suppose my sweet young duke has enjoyed enough fresh air," she said as she motioned for a footman to come carry the basket. She frowned and pressed a hand to her heart as she watched the nanny and the footman take the baby back inside. "I suppose it is not usual, but I simply hate it when he's not with me."

"I think it is absolutely lovely," Frannie said. "Oliver is your child, and you love him." She returned to her seat beside Alec and helped herself to more lemonade. "And I did not cheat. Violet and

I simply understand the benefit of cooperation. You and Sophie do not." She lifted her glass in a toast. "Next time, I shall see that Violet wins."

With a dramatic huff, Sophie rolled her eyes. "Such collusion!"

Dunkeld rose to his feet and held up his tankard. "I am obliged to toast this fine day, make a verra special announcement, and invite all of ye to join me in a wee excursion." He held out a hand to Violet and smiled.

Alec had a fair idea what the announcement was, but Dun's inference to a *wee excursion* left him baffled. He cast a knowing glance at Frannie and wondered if Dun and Violet's decision to unite might entice her to toss propriety to the winds and agree to marry him now. He noted with interest that a delightful blush rose on Frannie's cheeks. Apparently, the women had been discussing Violet's choices amongst themselves.

Dun took Violet's hand and kissed it. "It pleases me to share that Lady Violet and I are to be married."

Alec allowed himself a quiet smile as the three women cheered. Yes—they had been discussing the subject among themselves. He wondered if Frannie had hinted about going against Polite Society and marrying him.

"As a matter of fact," Dun continued, "if ye will join us for a wee jaunt up the road, the two of us shall marry this very day at Gretna Green, and the lot of ye can be our witnesses."

While Sophie and Celia clapped and cheered again, Alec noticed Frannie remained quiet. He studied her with a surreptitious gaze while the others busied themselves with congratulations, toasts, and deciding what Vivvy would wear. His dear one's smile was forced, her pleased expression locked in place, as though she struggled to maintain it.

He straightened in his chair and leaned toward her, keeping his voice low. "Frannie?"

Without so much as a fluttering of an eyelash, she slid her gaze to him. "Alec?"

He rose and held out his hand. "Come." Once she took it and stood by his side, he turned to the others and said, "Do excuse us for a moment, if you please."

With his arm around Violet's waist, Dun offered a knowing nod. "We willna leave without ye, Lion."

Alec tucked Frannie's hand into the crook of his arm. "It is time, Frannie," he said quietly as he led her down the gently sloping hillside toward the peacefulness of the estate's private lake.

"Time?"

Rather than answer, he continued walking in silence. She understood what he meant. He felt it clear to his bones. But it was her choice to summon the courage to take hold of their future and do what they wanted to do rather than continue to conform—at least *somewhat* conform—to what Society expected of them. By the time they reached the water's edge, her carefully controlled expression had turned into a pained scowl.

"I thought you said the choice was always mine." She glared at the mirrorlike surface of the lake as though ready to spit in it.

"The choice is and ever will be yours, my love."

"And yet you said, 'It is time.'"

"I want you in my life permanently. Not as a mistress. Not as a nightly warmer of my bed. But as the beloved wife I find myself loving more with each passing day. I do not give a damn about the rules of etiquette, and neither should you. Why should you lose a year of your life mourning a marriage that was never real?" He turned her to face him and held her there so she couldn't turn away. "And what if you already carry my child?"

She bit her lip and stared up at him.

He couldn't resist allowing himself a faint smile. "I see you fear the same, my lady."

"You and I could not possibly be…be expecting this soon. Celia and Elias were married for six months before little Oliver was on the way." She smoothed her hands down the flatness of her trim waist. "I am merely overset about all that has happened over the past few months. Attacks on my ships and warehouses. Discovery of an enemy I didn't know I had." Her eyes gleamed with unshed tears as she fought to stop her bottom lip from quivering. "Then I met you. And then this!" She swatted at the folds of her black dress. "And then the murder of my enemy…or at least, the murder of my enemy's weapon." She jutted her chin upward. "I am not with child. Not a possibility."

"I am not saying you are, my love." He reached out and caressed her cheek. "But I have enjoyed the indescribable delights of having you in my bed every morning and then again every night since we arrived here at Lionwraith almost a month ago." He moved in and gentled her with an imploring kiss. "Marry me, Frannie. Today. At Gretna Green. Not because you might carry my child, but because I love you, and you love me."

She puckered with the loveliest pout he had ever seen. "I refuse to marry you while wearing widow's weeds."

"Borrow a gown from Sophie or Celia," he said. "Or wrap yourself in a bed linen. I do not care, as long it means you become my wife. Today."

Her sapphire eyes flared wide. "Wrap myself in a bed linen? Indeed! How could you say such a thing?"

He pulled her into his arms and held her tight against his chest. "Easily. I want you as my wife. Today." He kissed her forehead and breathed in the familiar and intoxicating scent of her—lilacs and vanilla. The same mouth-watering fragrance she left behind in his bed and on his skin every morning when she rose and returned to her rooms. "Make the choice, Frannie. I am not a man accustomed to not having control, but in this, I do not. It is your choice, but I implore you to choose with your heart."

"I promise to consider it—with my heart."

Her soulful gaze made his chest ache as though she had ripped out his heart and cast it aside. What held her back? "Polite Society can stand on its ear for all I care. Do you really hold the opinion of the *ton* in such high regard?"

"No. That is not what gives me pause." She bowed her head,

burying her face against him with a heavy exhale.

Could she be worried about her company? In their weeks together, he had quickly come to realize that she tended to it as if it were her child. "Before we leave for Gretna Green, I shall write up a paper that states every material thing you bring into this marriage—your company, your homes, your stocks and funds— remains yours alone. None of it will ever become my property. It shall all be set aside for you and our children. Dunkeld and the ladies can sign as witnesses. It will be our marriage contract. I want only you, Frannie. I care not about your possessions or your wealth."

She stared up at him as though insulted. "I do not think you a greedy man, Alec. That is not what concerns me."

"And there you are wrong. I am a greedy man when it comes to you. I want to possess you fully—body, mind, heart, and soul. And until you are my wife, I will not rest."

She shifted in his embrace until she stood with her cheek nestled against his chest, and wrapped her arms around him in a tight hug. "I love you, Alec. I merely worry about disappointing you." She leaned back and looked up at him again. "You know very little about me."

"I know everything I need to know. I see it when I look into your eyes." She was wearing down. About to agree. He could sense it. "Say you will, Frannie. My heart is ready to leap for joy."

With a dubious look, she reached up and held his face between her hands. "I will, Alec. This very day, I will marry you."

"Yes!" Alec threw back his head and roared, then grabbed her up by the waist and spun her around in circles.

Dunkeld, Violet, Sophie, and Celia scurried toward them, alarm filling their faces until they drew closer and saw nothing amiss.

"I take it there will be a double ceremony at Gretna Green today?" Dun asked.

"There will." Alec settled Frannie back on her feet, then kissed her soundly. "It is a joyous day of celebration here at

Lionwraith."

"Dear heavens! We must get you into a proper gown," Celia said as she caught hold of Frannie's arm and tugged her away.

"You cannot possibly get married in black bombazine and crepe!" Sophie said as she latched hold of Frannie's other arm.

"We shall let you know when we are ready to leave," Violet called back to Alec and Dun as she scurried along behind the ladies. She paused and shook a finger at Alec. "For heaven's sake, do something about your hair. It is quite wild and unruly. Get cleaned up before you see to the carriage, or there will be no elopement for any of us."

"We haven't even married them yet, and they are already giving us orders," Alec said.

Dunkeld clapped him on the back. "We best be about it then."

"Your Grace!" Giving the cluster of laughing women a wide berth, MacGinnis hurried toward Alec, his lanky form reminiscent of the gawky tattie-bogles of Scotland or the scarecrows dotting his own fields and gardens. The butler waved a white paper of some sort, as though attempting to flag them down. "Your Grace!"

"It must be urgent. The man has lost all decorum," Dunkeld said.

"Calm down, MacGinnis, before you make yourself ill." Alec hurried to meet the older man to prevent him from running any farther. "What is so urgent?" An alarming thought tensed him as effectively as a call to war. "Mother has not escaped Douglas Manor, has she?"

MacGinnis shook his head. "No, Your Grace. A messenger from your men in London just delivered this and said it is quite urgent." He held out the folded and sealed parchment. "He implored me to give it to you without delay, and he waits in the blue parlor in case you would like to send an immediate reply."

Every muscle tensed, Alec glanced at the seal and recognized it as that of Fitch, his best investigator, a young man who was determined to be better than the best Bow Street Runner because they had not accepted him as one of their own. Sliding his finger under the wax, he slowly unfolded the message and squinted at the messy scrawl, deciphering it as best he could. A single paragraph jumped out at him, its meaning, unfortunately, clear as day:

The dead man who posed as the Marquess of Ardsmere was Baron Warren Sandilands. Confirmed by the man's wife, who begged the Bow Street Runners to find him. She used the last of her money to take his body back to their parish in Cumbria for burial. His widow is as poor as a church mouse due to the man's gambling debts.

Alec slowly refolded the paper. "By all the saints in heaven."

"What is it?" Dun asked.

"The man who posed as Lord Ardsmere and stirred trouble for West Belgium International was none other than Lord Sandilands." Alec bowed his head and slowly shook it. "My distant cousin, whom I only met once when the old demoness tried to force his sister upon me for a match that, in her opinion, would keep the Lionwraith line more pure rather than marrying outside the family."

"*He* is the man who pitted Lionwraith Shipping against West Belgium International?" Dun resettled his stance as though unable to believe it. "I met that cove once. The man was a complete bird-wit. Had no sense about him at all."

"Someone had to have put him up to it." Alec struggled to imagine who would do such a thing, and why. "I remember him now, and you are correct. He was as flighty and foolish as a drunkard—even when sober."

"Do you wish to send a reply, or shall I tell the man to go?" MacGinnis asked, as though uncomfortable at being privy to the discussion.

"I have a very simple reply," Alec said, "one that need not be written down. Tell the messenger to inform Fitch I want the person behind this plot found. The one who hired Lord Sandilands."

MacGinnis accepted the order with a nod and turned to go.

"And MacGinnis," Alec called out. "Have Fordson ready a bath and set out my best. Lady Ardsmere and I are marrying today at Gretna Green, as are Lord Dunkeld and Lady Violet."

A rare smile tugged at the corners of the old butler's mouth, and his eyes sparkled beneath his bushy white eyebrows. "Very good, Your Grace. I shall see to it immediately." He took off toward the house at the same speed as when he delivered the message.

"I have never seen that man smile before," Dun said with a cringing frown. "Quite fearsome. Like the gargoyles at Rosslyn Chapel."

Alec agreed. He could only remember a handful of times when old MacGinnis had smiled.

He refolded the message and tucked it inside his waistcoat, determined to set the information aside and not allow it to taint the rest of what he knew in his heart would be a very wonderful day. The day Frannie became his wife.

"SHOULD I TELL him before we leave?" Frannie couldn't rid herself of the quiver in her voice. In fact, she trembled all over and was once again stricken with the need to laugh and cry at the same time. She was thrilled, terrified, and determined to make sure she never lost Alec. He was her heart and soul. But the fear of losing him because of her lifetime of lies made her ready to drop to her knees and weep. "I do have to tell him—don't I? Would it not be wrong to marry him without telling him the truth about my life? Tell him about the Sisterhood and try to make him see reason?"

"Frannie—stop!" Sophie caught her by the shoulders and gave her a gentle shake. "Do not tell him anything. Your past is resolved and sealed quite nicely by that very fine headstone in Chanticlare. Do not meddle with it and stir up any old ghosts."

"Sophie is absolutely right," Celia agreed as she held one of her gowns up to Frannie, then shook her head and tossed it aside. "Your *origin* was not nearly as complicated to resolve as mine, and there are no loose ends that might cause you future issue. For once in your life, leave well enough alone and embrace what destiny has seen fit to gift you."

"But there *are* loose ends." Frannie stood with her arms extended so Daisy could strip her out of her drab mourning garb, stays, and chemise and help her take a hastily prepared bath. "What if the villagers resent having Lord Vulture set over them? What if they seek revenge? The entire town of Chanticlare helped Mother Ardsmere carry out her complicated creation of the fake Marquess of Ardsmere. They *are privy to* everything."

"Did you not say Alec promised to protect them?" Sophie held up a lovely white gown with green trim and a matching vibrant green spencer. "As a matter of fact, did you not receive a letter from the Fredlingtons that was positively effusive with gratitude for all the duke has already done to protect everyone from Lord Vulture's threatened *enhancements* to the village?"

Frannie stepped out of the circle of discarded black clothing piled around her ankles and sat on the bench at the end of the bed to remove her slippers and stockings. "Then what about Mother Ardsmere?"

Both Sophie and Celia halted as though frozen in time and stared at her.

"Surely she wouldn't," Celia said quietly.

Sophie made a face as though she'd just tasted something foul. "I am not so sure. Lady Emmeline has become increasingly more difficult to be around. Her drinking has honed her tongue to an unbearable sharpness."

Celia shook her head. "I do not understand why she is so bitter. She understood this day would someday come. I remember her saying so herself at one of our private teas years ago. And now that you are to be wed to a duke, what has she to fear?"

"She fears descending into social oblivion." Frannie shook out her stockings and draped them across the bench. "The last will and testament Elias devised provides her with an ample allowance, but she has become obsessed with being perceived as irrelevant and inconsequential amongst the *ton*."

"But her daughter is marrying a duke, becoming a duchess. How does that make her *less*?" Celia placed a straw bonnet next to the pile of clothing on the bed. The beribboned hat was dyed to match the spencer's shade of green perfectly.

"But the *ton* does not know me as her daughter. Remember?" Frannie lowered herself into the tub of steaming water scented with her favorite essence of lilacs. She breathed in the refreshing floral sweetness, hoping it would bring her a sense of calm. "She proclaimed me a ward of the family because she needed a *son* to keep from losing everything to Lord Vulture. I am merely the woman who married her creation and was later widowed by her fabrication's death."

"But you *are* her daughter," Sophie argued. "Why would she do anything to ruin your happiness?"

Frannie closed her eyes and leaned back against the folded towel cushioning the end of the tub. "My happiness has never been a priority to Mother Ardsmere. Her happiness is her primary concern." She roused herself out of her bitter melancholy and started scrubbing. This was not the time for a lazy soak in self-pity and, hopefully, senseless worry. She was about to marry the most incredible man she had ever known.

An uncomfortable silence settled over the room, and she turned to discover Sophie, Celia, and Daisy staring at her as though she were an abandoned kitten found starving in an alley. "Do not look at me like that. Mother Ardsmere has never been openly cruel. She is simply—"

"A cold-hearted wretch," Daisy said, then popped a hand over her mouth. She belatedly curtsied, then hurried to the tub with the drying linen and bowed her head. "Beg pardon, my lady. I should not have said that. Hurry now. I feel sure His Grace and Lord Dunkeld are ready to get this lovely journey on its way."

Frannie allowed herself a sad smile as she stepped out of the tub and into the drying linen. Daisy efficiently wrapped it around her, then shook out a smaller cloth and started drying the tips of Frannie's curls that had escaped the pins and gotten wet.

Frannie turned to Sophie and Celia. "You truly think I'll be safe just moving forward and forgetting about my past? I have told you how Alec abhors deception. If he ever finds out, I will surely lose him."

"You will not lose him," Celia said, her jaw set to a determined angle.

"We will not allow it," Sophie agreed with a curt nod.

"All will be well," Daisy quietly added as she helped scrub Frannie dry and got her into a fresh chemise. "You and His Grace are meant to be. I just know it."

Frannie held tight to the bedpost as Daisy yanked on the laces of her stays to pull the corset extra tight. "I hope all of you are right." She glanced over at Celia. "Since you now live in London for more months during the year than you stay in Germany, you do realize you could very well be caught up in the scandalous gossip I am about to unleash."

Celia laughed and gave a nonchalant toss of her shoulder. "I am quite certain the gossip already started by our coming here for the summer." She threw her hands up. "Who cares? If we three shared our mothers' concerns regarding Society's opinion, we would all be bitter, dried-up spinsters—would we not?" She stormed forward as though speaking on the floor of Parliament. "But we discovered that the satisfaction of wielding power and finding love far outweighs the *ton's* easily lost approval. As long as we are loved, happy, and able to keep our families comfortable, who gives a fig if we get invited to elite parties?" She stamped her foot and smiled. "We shall give our own parties and make them beg for invites from us."

Celia's speech lifted Frannie's heart and her hopes. "You are right." She leaned forward so Daisy could slip the delightful white muslin gown with green trim and tiny embroidered leaves over her head. "This is so lovely, Sophie, and I know it is your favorite. Thank you so much for allowing me to borrow it."

Sophie beamed at her. "Perhaps your wearing it to Gretna Green will bring me luck in finding my own knight in shining armor to sweep me away."

"Your knight will come, Sophie," Frannie promised. Her sweet friend was too lovely and passionate to end up as the bitter, dried-up spinster Celia had described.

Celia patted Frannie's arm. "I am going to peek in on little Oliver before we leave. It eases my heart to ensure he's content." She smiled at Sophie and Daisy. "You are in excellent hands here. When I finish giving my little duke a few extra cuddles, I shall look in on Lady Violet and see if she is ready to join us. Hurry now. We must not keep your avid groom waiting."

Sophie kissed Frannie on the cheek. "I am going to ensure that your mother is already sleeping off her morning tipples and instruct poor Agnes to be sure to keep her well oiled and oblivious while we are gone."

"Thank you, Sophie." And Frannie meant that more than her friend would ever know. Attempting to reason with Mother Ardsmere in her current state bordered on the impossible. Frannie couldn't remember her mother ever maintaining such a prolonged state of drunken mindlessness, nor being so openly hostile to anyone who dared speak to her about it or anything else.

"Come, my lady," Daisy gently urged as she helped Frannie slip on the lovely silk spencer. "Today is a day of celebration." As the maid fastened the silk-covered buttons of the short jacket, she gave a pleased wiggle. "I cannot, for the life of me, remember when I have ever seen you as happy as you are with His Grace. I am so pleased for you, my lady. Happy as happy can be."

"Thank you, Daisy, and you are so right. I mustn't let anything spoil this day."

Daisy wiggled again, reminding Frannie of an excited puppy. "Just think, my lady. When next I see you, you will be the Duchess of Lionwraith."

"Oh my." Frannie pulled in a deep breath and slowly let it out. "Indeed, I will."

Chapter Fourteen

H ER INSIDES FLUTTERED and churned with every sway and bounce of the carriage. Not because of the roadway's bumps but because of the destination. Frannie stared out the window at the quaint village of Springfield in the infamous parish of Gretna Green. The whitewashed walls of the Bard's Inn up ahead gleamed like a wishing star waiting to grant all her dreams and hopes. She was about to marry Alec, the man who filled her heart with unbelievable happiness.

She took the brilliance of the clear blue sky and the warm sun smiling down upon them as a sign that her union would be blessed. This glorious day, a rarity during this season's strangely cold, dismal weather, had to be a good omen. Even if it wasn't, she would take it as one.

"Are you as nervous as I am?" Violet whispered to Frannie, even though everyone would still hear her in the close quarters of the overstuffed carriage meant to carry four in comfort but was now laughingly called upon to hold all six of them.

"I am," Frannie whispered back while doing her best to ignore Alec where he sat across from her, smugly grinning. Sophie and Celia had insisted the brides not sit beside their future husbands. So Frannie, Violet, and Celia occupied the seat facing the front, and Sophie, Dunkeld, and Alec sat across from them in the seat behind the driver.

The carriage rumbled to a stop, making Frannie swallow

hard. Violet must have felt the same, because she grabbed her hand and squeezed. Frannie tried to comfort the dear lady with a reassuring return squeeze. Violet's situation was a great deal different from hers. Frannie prayed it would end in a happily ever after for the sweet lady.

Alec exited first, then reached up to help Frannie. As she stepped down, he smiled up at her, love and certainty flashing in his eyes. "Do not be nervous, my love," he said quietly. "We are meant to be."

"I know," she said, determined to let no misgivings ruin their day. The village of Chanticlare was far away, Polite Society hadn't learned about their scandalous behavior as yet, and Mother Ardsmere was so deep in her cups, she had not bothered dressing—simply remained in her bed. As Alec said, this day, this wedding, was meant to be.

The elderly lady sweeping the front step of the inn looked at them with an avaricious gleam in her pale, watery eyes. "Be any of ye looking to marry?" she asked with an arch of her wispy white eyebrows.

"Indeed we are, my good woman," Alec said as he placed Frannie's hand on his arm.

"Aye, that we are," Dunkeld added with a smiling glance at Violet. "And we even brought our own witnesses."

With a merry cackle, the matron set her broom aside and waved for them to follow her inside. "Welcome to the Bard's Inn and the Springfield forge. Single ye might be for now, but not for long!" As they stepped through the door, she clapped her hands. "Step lively with ye, Mr. Morrison! We have two pairs of lovers to unite!"

"I be coming, Mrs. Morrison." A cheery gentleman with a round face and bright red cheeks hurried out from a side room, wiping sweat from his face and brushing off his blacksmith's apron. "Welcome! Welcome! Pass right through to the forging room, if married ye wish to be."

"Just a wee moment," his wife said, while blocking the door

with her ample body. "Pardon me for being so bold, but business first, if ye dinna mind." She held out a hand and wiggled knobby fingers bent with age.

Alec pulled a drawstring pouch from an inside pocket of his jacket and dropped it into her hand. "Will that cover two ceremonies for today, my good lady?"

With the tip of her tongue peeking out between her thin lips, the old woman frowned as she worked the money bag open and peered inside. A gasp escaped her, then she poured the gold coins out into her hand. "Ten guineas? I reckon that'll do quite nicely indeed, good sir." She stepped inside the room and directed them to a large, ragged journal open on a small table. "We keep our own registry of sorts here. Would ye be so good as to sign your names?" She held out the quill and nodded at the pot of ink beside the book.

Frannie and Violet signed their names first, and Dun and Alec signed beside them.

The innkeeper's wife squinted down at the pages, then hurried to offer a curtsy. "Happy to be of service to ye, Your Grace." She gave another curtsy to Dun. "And to ye as well, my lord. And may I be the first to bless ye both with good wishes on this wonderful day?"

"Thank you, Mrs. Morrison." Alec hugged Frannie closer as if fearing she would change her mind.

"I promise I am not about to run," she whispered as they made their way up the short aisle between two rows of chairs to the head of the room, where a large black anvil with a hammer resting upon it awaited them.

"Good. I would hate to have to chase you down and bring you back thrown over my shoulder," he teased.

Mr. Morrison chuckled. "Aye, we had that happen not so long ago with a lady who decided she didna wish to share her money or lands with her newly found man." He leaned forward and winked first at Frannie and then Violet. "But dinna ye fret none, gentle ladies. If ye dinna wish to marry these fine men, all ye need do is say so. Not only be I the blacksmith and innkeeper here in Springfield, but I also do my part to keep ne'er-do-wells in line."

"That be right," Mrs. Morrison chimed in from the back of the room. "Mr. Morrison and I will have no part in forcing a lady to do anything against her wishes."

"I appreciate that, thank you." Frannie couldn't remember ever being happier. She glanced over at Violet's sudden pallor and worried that Alec's sister did not feel the same. "Violet? Do you need to sit and rest a bit first?"

Her smile trembling at the corners, Violet shook her head and edged closer to Dunkeld's side. "No. I want this." She cast a thankful look up at him. "I could not ask for a better man to marry."

"I swear to always do my best to make ye happy, lass," Dun promised.

Sniffling from the back of the room warned Frannie that Sophie was already crying. Her dear sister always wept on joyous occasions.

Alec cleared his throat and resettled his stance. "Might we get on with it, Mr. Morrison? As you can imagine, we are most eager to make these lovely ladies our wives."

"Aye, Your Grace." Mr. Morrison nodded at Alec. "Do ye hereby claim…" He paused, pointed a look at Frannie, and leaned forward a bit as if waiting.

"Francis Isabella Marie Croyden," she said, hoping her name was what the man sought.

It was. The innkeeper bobbed his head. "Aye, then. Do ye hereby claim Francis Isabella Marie Croyden to be your wife in sickness and health, hard times and good, and protect her with your name, your body, and your heart?"

"I do," Alec said without hesitation.

The innkeeper looked at Frannie again. "And do ye claim…" He looked at Alec and waited.

"Alec Douglas, Duke of Lionwraith."

"Aye, do ye take His Grace, Alec Douglas, Duke of Lionwraith, to be your husband? Promise to honor and obey, love and care for him in sickness and in health, when times are good and when they're not, and protect him and his name all your life?"

"I do," Frannie said, trying not to cringe when it came out as a nervous squeak.

"Then as God and Scotland and all gathered in this room are witnesses, I now pronounce ye man and wife." He smiled. "Ye may kiss, and if ye have a ring, Your Grace, ye might want to put it on her finger now." He lifted the hammer and brought it down hard upon the anvil, making the metal ring out that their lives had been forged into one.

As Alec's lips touched hers, Frannie's heart leapt, and her joy almost bubbled free in a heartfelt cry. She was married to this amazing man, actually married. A happy sob escaped her as he lifted his head. She covered her mouth as tears broke free. "I am not sad! I promise."

"I am glad to hear it." He reached into his pocket and brought forth a band of gold filigree inset with pale lavender stones that formed a circle around a large, rose-cut diamond. "Your hand, my duchess?"

Speechless, her tears streaming ever faster, Frannie ripped off her glove and held out her hand. Another joyous sob escaped her as Alec slid the beautiful ring onto her finger. It fit perfectly—another prosperous omen. "It is too lovely," she whispered, then hopped up onto her tiptoes, wrapped her arms around his neck, and kissed him soundly.

Everyone in the room clapped, and then Dun said, "Now, Mr. Morrison, get on with doing the same for myself and my lady, if ye please."

"Happy to, my lord!"

Frannie tried to be polite and pay attention to Dunkeld and Violet's vows, but all she was truly aware of was Alec standing beside her and the way he held tightly to her hand. This had to be a dream, and she never wanted to awaken. He was now her husband. She jumped and belatedly clapped as the anvil rang out again and everyone cheered.

Alec brushed a kiss to her cheek, then lingered near her ear. "And where had your mind wandered to, my lovely wife?"

"Whatever do you mean, my darling husband?"

He chuckled and nibbled a trail of suggestive kisses along the tender skin just beneath her ear. "I rather like the sound of that."

"And now to the dining room to toast happy lives, happy wives, and houses full of healthy bairns," announced Mr. Morrison.

"Hear, hear!" Alec curled a possessive arm around her waist. She noticed that Dunkeld did the same with Violet as they all moved into the much larger dining room. It gladdened her heart. Violet was such a sweet soul. She prayed they would both be very happy together.

Sophie and Celia bounced up to her and hugged her so tightly that poor Alec had to back away in self-defense.

"You can have her back in a moment," Sophie promised, then dropped a coy curtsy Frannie's way. "Congratulations, Duchess Lionwraith."

Celia playfully pushed in and hugged Frannie again. "I am so happy for you. Now hurry and get your own little duke on the way, so my Oliver has someone to play with whenever we visit."

"Celia!" Frannie's cheeks flared hot, and grew even hotter when Alec threw back his head and laughed.

Celia smiled and coyly batted her eyelashes. "See? His Grace will be more than happy to comply."

"More than happy," he announced as he pulled her back into his arms.

"Lady Ardsmere?"

The vaguely familiar voice filled with judgmental shock and malicious disapproval made Frannie's blood run cold. She slowly turned and faced the table nearest the door and swallowed hard. The Marchioness of Bournebridge sat with the two women who always served as her lapdogs, taking every step she did and bowing to her every word—the Countess of Essendon and the

Marchioness of Mardlebon. Polite Society would be abuzz with Frannie's scandalous behavior as fast as the trio could make it back to London. "Lady Bournebridge, Lady Essendon, Lady Mardlebon, what a surprise to find you all here!"

"Obviously," Lady Bournebridge drawled with a gleefully snide inspection of Frannie's apparel. "Forgive me, my lady, but I was under the assumption that you were in full mourning." She gave a lazy flip of her hand. "If memory serves, was it not but a few short months ago that your husband finally died from his strangely lingering illness?"

"I *was* in mourning." Frannie lifted her chin, daring the old crone or her followers to think her a coward. "But as I have just happily married the Duke of Lionwraith, I am sure you understand that my mourning has now ended." She allowed herself a wicked smile. "And might I ask what brings the three of you to the lovely parish of Gretna Green? The wedding of one of your daughters, perhaps?" She couldn't resist the not-so-subtle jab. Not after Lady Bournebridge's behavior.

The trio of women drew themselves up and rose from the table as one, turned their backs on her, and marched out of the establishment without another word.

"Scabby old hens," Alec growled. "How dare they give you the cut direct. I shall have a word with those two-faced—"

She caught him by the arm before he dashed after them. "No. They are not worth it." She pulled in a deep breath and released it, discovering she wasn't as upset about falling from Polite Society as she had expected. "I have you. I have our friends. What more do I need?"

"Are you sure, my love? I have no problem whatsoever giving them the dressing down they deserve." His gaze was filled with more love and concern than she had ever known existed. Her heart swelled, and it became difficult to breathe.

"I am positive." She touched his face, so very thankful that this handsome Adonis with the courage and protectiveness of the fiercest lion had chosen her. "Now that we are one, I have everything I need."

"Well, I intend to find out what those three old fussocks are doing in Gretna Green," Sophie declared. She narrowed her eyes, and they took on a wicked glint. "As you said, they all three have daughters. Perhaps they are trying to avoid a scandal of their own."

"Leave them be," Frannie said. "They are not worth the effort."

"Indeed, they are," Sophie said. "Save me a seat. This should not take long." She hurried out of the room.

"Should I fear Lady Sophie?" Alec asked as he fixed a mock look of fear upon the door the lady had just exited.

"With all your heart and soul," Frannie advised. "Sophie and her twin brother were born after her father, a renowned spy for the Crown, was assassinated. Her mother ensured that both Sophie and her brother were trained in the arts of subterfuge and defending oneself without so much as a dinner spoon to foil an attacker. She is quite able. I promise you."

"I am glad she is on our side."

"You should be."

As they joined the others at the table, Violet reached out and took Frannie's hand. "Are you all right? I saw what those deplorable women did."

"I believe I am quite a bit better than all right," Frannie said, and she meant it. "Thanks to your brother and my loving friends Sophie and Celia—and you, of course—I have everything I need: a loving husband, a wonderful sister, and dear friends." She shifted her smile to Dun. "As well as a fine new brother and a new little niece or nephew that I cannot wait to meet. The *ton* is fickle. My friends and family are a constant joy that will not waver."

Violet's eyes filled with tears. "I so wish I could be as brave as you."

"You do not have to be," Frannie assured her. "All you need do is to be yourself, the Vivvy we all love."

"I agree," Celia said, lifting her glass with a wink that assured Frannie she was doing her best to lift the mood. "A toast to family and friends and the joy with which they fill our hearts."

Sophie came flouncing back into the room with a smug look of victory. She took her seat, lifted her glass, and announced, "A toast to the health and happiness of Lady Bournebridge's daughter, Lady Temperance, and her new husband, the head groom from her mother's London stables."

"To Lady Temperance and her new husband," Frannie echoed with satisfaction, then sipped the wine that had never tasted so sweet.

"And ye will be having a meal to celebrate, of course," Mrs. Morrison announced as she and a young girl set platters of venison, guinea fowl, and stewed vegetables on the table. "Bread and turtle soup are coming too. Daren't ye worry."

"What a magnificent feast," Alec said. "And please bring your best bottle of port, good lady."

"Port?" Dun repeated. "Not just port. Bring us your best whisky for a proper toast, madam. We Scots know how to kick off a marriage."

Mrs. Morrison cackled with delight. "That we do, my lord!" She hurried off to do their bidding, shooing the young maid ahead of her as though herding an errant lamb. "On wi' ye, lass. Fetch the bread and soup!"

The diamond in Frannie's ring caught the sunlight and splintered it into a rainbow of stars dancing across the walls and ceiling, making everyone smile. "You have truly spoiled me, Your Grace," she said. Guilt filled her over such lavishness. "A simple gold band would have done just as well. After all, now I have you."

"You are the light that ended my darkness." He kissed her hand and said so much more with his expressive eyes. "Nothing simple will ever do for you, my love," he whispered, as though no one other than them existed in the world.

She blinked back more happy tears. Good heavens, this wonderful day had made her so weepy. She squeezed his hand and nodded at the steaming bowl Mrs. Morrison had just placed in front of him. "Eat, dear husband. Turtle soup is best enjoyed piping hot."

He smiled, released her hand, and started enjoying his soup.

She tried to take part in the lovely meal, but just couldn't bring herself to eat more than a few bites. She sipped her wine and enjoyed the lighthearted conversations for a while but found herself fidgety and unable to sit still. More than once, Sophie furtively nudged her under the table to make her stop jiggling her leg.

Why she couldn't calm herself and enjoy the day was a mystery even to her. Perhaps if she took some air and walked around outside for a bit, that would rid her of the annoying nervousness putting her on edge and making her feel as if something was about to happen that would end all this happiness. She pushed back from the table and rose from her chair. "I need to step outside for a stroll. Please continue on without me. I merely need some air."

Alec set down his glass and stood. "I shall accompany you, my lady."

Dunkeld also rose and stood ready as if waiting to see if Alec needed him to come along too.

"No. Both of you stay here and continue your meal. I simply need a bit of a walk and some deep breaths of fresh air. Today has been beyond wonderful but also a little overwhelming." She waved them both away. "I will be fine. Springfield appears to be a nice, quiet village." She slanted a hard look Dunkeld's way. "And you should stay here with your wife, my lord."

Although he seemed torn, Dun took his seat and protectively covered Violet's hand with his.

"I do not like you walking alone in a strange place," Alec said while offering his arm. "It simply is not safe—no matter how peaceful the area seems." His dark eyebrows slanted to the stubborn angle they always took whenever he refused to budge on a subject. "I am sure Dun will happily keep everyone entertained while you and I step outside and walk off your fidgety jiggles before you topple every vessel on the table."

"Do not be rude."

"I am always rude, but with you, lovingly so." He kissed her on the cheek then drew her arm through his and rested her hand in the crook of his elbow. "I protect those I love with a vengeance, and you know I already trust no one. Cede this battle to me, my love. I am certain you will be the victor in plenty of our future disagreements."

She rolled her eyes but kept her arm hooked in his. "Fine. But I cede nothing. This was not a battle—just a minor skirmish."

He grinned and offered a smug nod to those remaining at the table. "We shall return soon. Do not drink all the port, Dun."

Dunkeld snorted. "Why would I drink all the port when I have this fine whisky?"

"Are you coming or not?" She tugged on Alec's arm. If he insisted on accompanying her, he needed to get a move on.

"Yes, my love," he answered in a tone that made her huff. "Do not be fractious. After all, this is our wedding day."

She didn't answer, just pulled in a deep breath of the clean, crisp air as they stepped outside. She adored country air and despised the stinking Thames. It was time to clear her mind and make plans for the future. Perhaps that was why she felt so fidgety. She had always been a planner and liked to know what was coming at her. "Do you think I should sell Ardsmere House in London?"

"I think you should give it to Mother Ardsmere." Alec steered them down a wide path of tramped-down grass that cut through the lush green meadow behind the inn. He chuckled. "As a wedding gift, so she might accept the news of our union without soiling the air with her drunken, abusive opinion of everyone's behavior but her own." He snorted out a laugh. "Or we could always send Mother Ardsmere to Scotland to live with my mother and see which one emerges from Douglas Manor alive."

"That would be a cruel thing to do to Scotland and your servants at Douglas Manor." She pulled in another deep breath of the sweet air and nodded. "But I do agree. Mother Ardsmere belongs in London. I shall send a letter to Elias to transfer the house and servants to her." Although she hated doing that to the servants at Ardsmere House and hoped they would somehow find it in their hearts to forgive her.

The farther they walked, the more Frannie realized she was required to step higher and higher because the grassy field had swallowed up the path. "I think we should turn back now. When I said I wished to walk, I meant on the village roadway, not the cows' avenue across the hillside."

"Forgive me, sweetling. I thought this would be more private." He halted and frowned down at her, as though finding it difficult to put his thoughts into words.

She swallowed hard, fearing the worst. Had he somehow discovered the truth about her past? "Private? Do you require privacy? I merely wished for some fresh air and exercise."

He kept his gaze locked on the ground and shuffled his feet like a naughty lad caught picking pockets. "I should have told you earlier but didn't wish to tarnish our day. Yet now, I am weighed down with guilt for not sharing the news I received." He glanced at her, clearly at war with himself. "I never want there to be anything but truth and openness between us, Frannie. I never wish to disappoint you."

The burden of guilt he cast upon her threatened to crush her. He wanted only truth and openness. And what had she given him? Everything but. She reached up and framed his face with her hands. "You could never disappoint me. What is troubling you?"

"I received word about the identity of the man who posed as Lord Ardsmere."

She backed up a step, unsure what to say.

He gave her a troubled shake of his head. "It shames me to say that the man is my own distant cousin, Baron Warren Sandilands. His identity was confirmed by his widow when she found him with the help of the Bow Street Runners. He left her ruined and penniless because of his gambling debts."

Frannie blinked, trying to see the plot or the scheme that Sandilands intended to complete. "Did he do it to cover his debts?" That didn't seem feasible because of the report that many took advantage of the man and obtained the goods he bartered for so low a price that it had to have put him in the red.

Alec shook his head again. "I believe the man was a pawn. Dunkeld and I both knew him. He did not have the intelligence to put together such an undertaking on his own."

"So, we still know nothing." Relief flooded her that Alec's need for privacy was not because of her secret, but what he *had* shared was troublesome as well. "We have no idea of who hired him or who killed him."

"No. We do not." He gently took her hands in his. "But my men are doing their best to discover the identity of the person responsible. I do not intend to let this despicable plot rest. No one who threatens you will ever escape my wrath." He pulled her into his arms and hugged her. "I love you, Frannie—with a vengeance I find almost frightening."

She closed her eyes and tightened her hold on him. "I love you more, Alec. More than you could ever know."

"You know," he whispered into her hair, "the grass is quite tall and thick here. We could lie down in it and consummate our union without anyone seeing."

His suggestion both shocked and thrilled her, making her immediately ache for him to take her then and there.

She peeked up at him. "You cannot be serious."

"I assure you, wife, I am quite serious." He cupped her bottom in his hands and pressed her against his hardness as if to prove his point. "I want you. Here. Now." He gave her a sultry look. "After all, we have to get a little one started for Oliver to befriend. Remember?"

She looked all around, noting they were quite alone. Then she plopped back into the nearest hillock of cushiony grass and tugged him down with her. "Thank goodness the ground appears to be dry," she said as his weight on top of her sank her deeper into the nest of green.

He rucked his hand up under her skirts and slipped it between her legs. A satisfied groan escaped him as he slid a finger inside her. "You, my lovely wife, are not dry at all."

As his expert touch teased her ever closer to crying out with bliss, he rained kisses across the swell of her bosoms rising above her neckline. "So delicious," he murmured between nibbling tastes while plunging his fingers in and out ever faster.

"I must have you, husband," she demanded in a breathless whisper. Open-air loving behind an inn appeared to add a layer of excitement all its own. "Take me, Alec. Now. I beg you."

"Happily, my love." He undid his falls, then filled her exactly the way she needed.

"Yes," she groaned, struggling to keep as quiet as possible. She wrapped her legs around him and met him thrust for thrust.

He pounded harder, gaining momentum and shoving her deeper into the grass. As she shuddered into ecstasy, he covered her mouth with his and swallowed her cries, then kept the kiss strong and intact to muffle his groans when his release came, and he spilled inside her.

Breathing hard as she held him tight and stared up into the cloudless sky, Frannie was suddenly stricken with a case of the giggles.

Alec rose on his elbows and tried to scowl but failed miserably. "What is so funny, my beloved wife?"

"If you have grass stains on the knees of your pantaloons and I have grass stains on the backside of my gown, people will surely know that we were out here consummating our union."

He rumbled with a deep laugh that shook him delightfully both against and inside her. "A matter of course, my love. After all, we must make the union as undeniably legal as possible. A consummated marriage is a strong marriage."

She smiled up at him. "I love you, my lion."

"And I love you, my lioness."

CHAPTER FIFTEEN

THE TENSION MELTED from Alec's shoulders as the carriages bearing Mother Ardsmere, Lady Sophie, Lady Celia, baby Oliver, and all their servants rumbled out of sight. It wasn't that he hadn't enjoyed his guests, but he was ready for Frannie and himself to find and settle into their own routine at Lionwraith, making their home as it would be for years to come—God willing.

Of course, Vivvy and Dun were still with them, since Dunkeld's country manor was currently under massive renovation and, understandably, Vivvy didn't wish to go to his residence in London. But the newlyweds kept to themselves, nurturing their newfound bond and more than a little amiable companionship. If the two weren't already in love, they would be soon, and that pleased Alec immensely.

Frannie's deep sigh pulled him from his thoughts. He pulled her closer and pressed a kiss to her temple. "Do you feel abandoned, my love?"

Another sigh escaped her. "No. I understand Celia's longing to return to Elias, and Sophie needs to get back to her mother." She managed a weak smile. "It is always difficult when it's time to bid them farewell. They are the sisters I never had."

"I noticed you did not comment on Mother Ardsmere's departure?"

"She was oddly quiet this morning. Do you not think so?"

Frannie kept her worried frown fixed on the turn in the lane where the carriages had rolled out of view.

"She appeared to be quite sober. Perhaps that was the change in her." He glanced up at the dreary gray flannel of the sky and turned them toward the door. "Come. Let us continue this conversation inside by the fire. There is a chill in the air today." No matter how much Frannie denied it, he felt certain she carried their child and needed coddling. After all, they had shared a bed for a little over two months now, and not once had she refused him because of being troubled with her womanly time.

"It is colder today." She gathered her shawl closer. "It's as if we have only enjoyed a few days of summer this year. I worry for the farmers. How will they survive? And many of my suppliers have already expressed fears they will have far fewer goods to export in the coming months because of an expected poor harvest."

"We shall have to ensure those working our lands do not go wanting." He refused to have the people tending his fields during this dismal growing season starve to death in the coming months while his residences overflowed with abundance.

She turned and flung her arms around him, catching him in a tight hug.

He tipped up her chin and found himself unable to keep from smiling down at her. "Not that I am complaining, but what was that for?"

"Because I love that you are not a greedy man intent on increasing your riches despite the suffering of others." She took hold of his hand and pulled him down the hallway and into the room that had once been an extra parlor. After a pleased look around at the overflowing desk, bookshelves, cabinets, and bins, she turned and hugged him again. "And because you do not mind that I remain quite active in West Belgium International. I love my office. It is absolutely perfect for my needs. You are a gem for making it so."

"It appears I should have commissioned a larger desk, more

cabinets, and perhaps hired an assistant to keep your correspondence and files in order. Did a windstorm strike in here?"

"Says the man whose library is like a cave with piles and piles of books sprouting up from the floor like stalagmites."

A familiar *ahem* interrupted them. He turned to the open door. "Yes, MacGinnis?"

The butler didn't speak, merely held out an envelope and revealed the ominous black seal on its flap.

"Bloody hell." Alec snatched it from the man but hesitated to rip it open. This was the first letter from Mother since her banishment to Scotland. Whatever the missive held, it could not be good. Unless she was dead. Of course, if that was the case, it was doubtful her maid would have used the old demoness's seal. He ripped it open and stared at the single sentence scrawled across the middle of the page.

I have news of which you must be made aware.

"What is it?" Frannie eased closer, trying to peer at the page without his noticing.

He handed it to her. "From my mother. Who knows what cruel game she plays at this time?"

Frannie visibly paled and handed it back to him without a word. With a hand to her chest, she stumbled sideways.

"Frannie!" He caught her close and helped her to the settee in front of the fireplace. "What is it, sweetling?" He prayed she would finally admit they had a little one on the way, and her condition was making her a bit unsteady. At least, he hoped that explained her sudden weakness. He couldn't bear it if some disease or illness had stricken her.

"Might I have a sip of something? And perhaps send for a cool cloth?" She leaned back into the pillows, closed her eyes, and appeared to be going to great lengths to take in deep breaths.

"MacGinnis!" he roared. To hell with ringing the bell and waiting—he dashed into the hall to find the man. "MacGinnis!"

"Yes, Your Grace?" The spindly-legged butler careened

around the turn in the hallway, rushing toward him at full speed.

"Fetch Mrs. MacGinnis, some sherry, and a cool cloth to Her Grace's office. She is not well."

"At once, Your Grace." The elderly man took off at an impressive lope.

Alec rushed back to Frannie and eased down beside her. "All will be well, my love. Never fear."

Mrs. MacGinnis hurried into the room, followed by a maid bearing a tray with a glass of sherry, a bowl of water, and a cloth. A footman strode behind them, carrying a large basin and a pitcher.

"Here now, Your Grace," the housekeeper said to Frannie as she held the sherry to her lips. "Wee sips, now." After Frannie swallowed a bit of the drink, Mrs. MacGinnis set the glass aside, dampened the cloth, then folded it and gently draped it over Frannie's eyes. "Hold that there now, Your Grace. I put mint in the water to help settle ye. Breathe it in, if ye can. We have a basin here should ye need it. Be that any better?"

"Thank you, Mrs. MacGinnis. It helps a great deal." Frannie took in another deep breath, then slowly blew it out while holding the cloth against her eyes. "My hot chocolate and toast suddenly threatened to come back up. I have no idea why."

The housekeeper puffed up with a delighted grin and cut a gleeful look at Alec.

He took that to mean she believed a new little lion cub for Lionwraith was on the way as well. Excitement swelled within him. It was a wonder the buttons didn't pop off his waistcoat. "Shall I carry you upstairs, my love? Would you be more comfortable in bed?"

Without uncovering her eyes, Frannie waved his suggestion away. "Here is fine. I am sure it will pass. In fact, I am already doing much better."

"Well, if this continues, I insist on sending for the physician." He kissed her hand, then pressed his cheek to it. "I will not have you ignoring your health."

An echo of the *ahem* from earlier came from the doorway again. He tore his gaze away from Frannie and glared at the butler. "Momentarily, MacGinnis. Am I quite clear?"

"As the purest water, Your Grace." The butler disappeared.

"I shall talk to that fool man about his harrumphing at the doorway, Your Grace." Mrs. MacGinnis smiled down at Frannie, then shifted another pleased look to Alec. "If Her Grace wishes to rest here, then dinna move her. 'Tis far better that she keep her breakfast where it belongs. I shall give the two of ye your privacy now, in case she has something to tell ye." The housekeeper winked and wiggled like an excited child, then left the room after shooing the maid and the footman out ahead of her.

"Go see what MacGinnis wants," Frannie said, while settling deeper into the pillows Alec placed behind her.

"MacGinnis can wait. You are my priority." He took her hand in his and held it, praying she would tell him the words he longed to hear. "Besides, Mrs. MacGinnis seems to believe you have something to tell me, and that woman is rarely wrong. I believe in Scotland they call her gift *second sight*, or something to that effect."

Frannie lifted the cloth off her eyes and glared at him. "I believe they call it *meddling* everywhere else in the world."

He laughed. He couldn't help it. "Tell me, Frannie. Please—I beg you."

Her delicate nostrils flared with a frustrated snort. "I am not certain. It could simply be a matter of all the excitement of the past few weeks. That happens to a woman sometimes, and it is not something we generally speak about with gentlemen."

"I am not a gentleman. I am your husband."

"You know what I mean."

A sobering thought occurred to him. "Do you not wish to have children?"

"Well, of course I want children." She jerked upright and glared at him. "Why on earth would you even suggest such a silly thing?"

"Because you seem most determined to deny the obvious." He leaned closer. "How long has it been?"

"Since what?" she snapped.

He arched a brow. "Are you really going to make me ask you in detail?"

She narrowed her eyes at him. He delighted in their flashing more brilliantly than the finest sapphires.

"Eight weeks or so since my last *time*," she forced through clenched teeth.

"Perhaps you should consider consulting Dr. Tramadorn, Vivvy's physician. Even though he was here only last week, I am certain the man would not mind coming by today or tomorrow at the latest. Shall I send for him?"

She folded her arms and glared straight ahead. "That will not be necessary."

"Indeed, it is necessary. Clearly you are unwell if your womanly times are not coming as usual, and yet you insist you are not with child. If you were one of my horses or cows having such issues, a professional would have already been called."

"I *am* with child, damn you." Tears spilled down her cheeks, and she fixed him with a quivering frown. "And I do not appreciate your comparing me to a horse or a cow. Thank you very much."

He stared at her, both overjoyed and frighteningly confused. "This is wonderful news, my love. Why would you not wish to share it? Do you not wish it to be so?"

She stared down at her hands in her lap, wringing the damp cloth until it dribbled water all over her gown. "Well, isn't that just lovely?" She tossed it at the bowl of water on the table beside the settee but missed. Instead, she hit the bowl's edge and spilled its contents. "Damn! Damn! Damn!"

"Frannie." He gathered her into his arms, gently rocking to soothe her.

She tucked her face into the crook of his neck and sobbed. "If you do not stop rocking, I am going to cover you in poorly digested hot chocolate and toast."

"Sorry, my love." He pressed a kiss into her hair and held her still, reeling fear raged within him. Why did she not want their child? He had to ask, had to know, but bloody hell, he was so afraid. "Frannie?"

"What?" She sniffled.

"Why do you not wish to have our baby?"

Her high-pitched wail cut through the room. "I want this baby more than anything," she cried. "How could you ask me something so absolutely cruel?"

He blew out the breath he hadn't realized he held. At least she wanted their baby. That was a positive start. "Forgive me, my love. It's just that I am very confused why you didn't wish for me to know—just yet."

"Everything between us has happened so very fast," she whispered. "I have hardly had a chance to catch my breath. Things keep happening. Boom. Boom. Boom." With each *boom*, she thumped her fist against his chest. "At first, I was afraid my *condition* wasn't real. That it resulted from nerves—because of all the events of the past few months." She twitched with a shrug. "And now I am just afraid. I know nothing about being a good mother." She shuddered and let out a weepy sigh. "And so much good has happened to us so quickly. I fear we are very much due for something bad to take place."

"Since when are you so superstitious? Have you been spending too much time with Dun and Vivvy?" He pulled away so he could look into her eyes. "You are the first good thing that has happened to me in well over six years, and dare I say, rather boldly and with copious amounts of bragging, that this is the first time you have known a *real* marriage in every sense of the word. We are due some goodness, my precious sweetling. In fact, we two are overdue."

"I suppose so." She hitched in another sniff, then pulled a handkerchief out from her cleavage and dabbed it to the end of her nose.

He couldn't resist teasing her. "What a wonderful place to be tucked. Never in all my life did I ever imagine I would be jealous of a handkerchief."

She glared at him, obviously still overset.

"I love you, Frannie." He leaned forward and brushed a tender kiss across her lips.

She graced him with a somewhat kinder glare, then managed a sheepish smile. "I love you, my lion, and I suppose I should apologize for being so silly."

"You are not silly." He cradled her cheek in his hand. "You are my wife and the mother of our child, and I adore you."

The distinct sound of footsteps crossing back and forth in front of the hallway door abruptly interrupted them, making Alec straighten and peer over the back of the sofa at the open door. "MacGinnis! I have ordered men shot for less."

Silence fell, and the butler did not appear in the doorway again.

"You should find out what is wrong," Frannie quietly advised. "MacGinnis isn't one to overreact." She blew out a heavy sigh. "Unlike your wife."

"You do not overreact," he said. She sometimes thought too hard about things, but under no circumstances would he tell her about that now. He kissed her again, took the handkerchief from her, and gently dried her eyes. "I shall be right back once I get MacGinnis sorted."

She nodded. "I shall sit here by the fire with my sherry and have a long, serious conversation with myself about behaving like a complete ninny."

He shook a finger at her as he rose and headed to the door. "Not another disparaging word about yourself, or I shall be sorely displeased." He stepped into the hallway and forced himself not to unleash his irritation. "What is it, MacGinnis?"

"Your Mr. Fitch is *here*, Your Grace. In the blue parlor."

No wonder the butler had nearly paced a hole into the floor. Alec stormed down the hallway, into the parlor, and closed the door behind him. "A visit and not a message, Mr. Fitch? Is the news that dire?"

Nervously running the brim of his hat round and round through his hands, the young man bowed. "I fear you will see it as such, Your Grace."

"Out with it, then."

The investigator reached behind his back, under his jacket, and pulled out a small packet wrapped in cloth. Multiple knotted strands of twine kept the stained brown cloth snug around whatever was inside. "The captain of the ship Lord Sandilands used while smuggling under the name of Lord Ardsmere passed these along to us—for a fair bit of blunt, I might add."

"You will be reimbursed, of course, as long as you notated the cost in your report."

"I did, Your Grace." He pulled a knife from his boot and held it out. "To cut the ropes so you can get to the proof inside."

"Proof?"

Mr. Fitch offered a somber nod. "Me and the lads found the person who put Sandilands up to the scheme, and who I believe eventually had him killed."

"Did you have the devil arrested?" Alec cut through the parcel's twine and tore the cloth aside. A handful of letters spilled out onto the table in front of him. He started to pick one of them up, then a surge of rage locked him in place. He knew that handwriting. "No," he growled, then flipped the letter over and revealed the unmistakable black seal on each piece of correspondence in the bundle.

"We did not have the Dowager Duchess of Lionwraith arrested, Your Grace," Mr. Fitch said quietly. "I felt you would rather deal with this in your own manner."

"Quite right." Alec clenched his teeth to keep from roaring. He stiffly moved to the velvet pull hanging beside the entrance and rang the bell.

MacGinnis opened the door immediately. "Yes, Your Grace?"

"Take Mr. Fitch to the library and pay him whatever he says

he is owed. I trust him. Leave his report on my desk."

The butler nodded, then motioned for the investigator to follow him out.

"I am sorry, Your Grace," Mr. Fitch offered with a curt nod.

"Do not apologize," Alec said. "She is what she is." He forced himself to stare straight ahead and not react until he heard the door click shut behind him and knew he was alone. Then he picked up the table and threw it at the wall, splintering it into bits.

"Was this your news I needed to know, Mother dearest?" he bellowed as he snatched up the scattered letters and tore them open one by one. After reading each of them, not a doubt remained that Henrietta Douglas, Dowager Duchess of Lionwraith, was behind the fake Lord Ardsmere scheme. Her ultimate goal appeared to be the ruin of West Belgium International. The why of it, he didn't know. But each of the letters in his mother's hand laid out clear and concise instructions regarding meeting places, contacts, and goods to be stolen from West Belgium International's warehouses and then resold. If for a profit, excellent. If not, she hadn't seemed to care. He noticed the stolen goods always came from the same four warehouses. Apparently, Frannie had a few unscrupulous managers of which she was not aware. They had covered up the thefts by falsifying records. In one letter, the old demoness ordered them paid for their silence.

He would go to Douglas Manor today. It was only a day's ride. If the woman wanted a meeting to tell him lies in an attempt to hide her vile actions, then by heavens, he would meet with her and condemn her to her face with the proof he held in his hands. He bundled the letters into a neat stack, secured them with the original twine, and shoved them inside his waistcoat.

"Alec?" Frannie's soft call made it to him through the blinding red haze of his fury.

He slowly turned and faced her. "You promised to rest in your office, my love. I told you I would return."

"I heard you shout and wanted to make certain you were all right."

The loving concern in her eyes helped loosen the fiery knot in his chest. He had her, and they had their child on the way. The old demoness was no longer relevant. He would deal with that hateful, conniving crone one last time and be done with her.

"I am fine, my love." He gently turned Frannie back toward the hallway, but not before she saw what was left of the table he had destroyed.

She pursed her lips and gave him a dubious look. "Fine, you say? I believe that pile of finely polished mahogany kindling says otherwise."

"Let us return to your office and your sherry, and then I will explain."

Suspicion glinted in her narrow-eyed gaze. She remained rooted to the spot and yanked on the bellpull beside the door.

MacGinnis appeared within moments, slightly out of breath. His attention jerked back and forth between Alec and Frannie. "Yes, Your Grace…es?"

"Might we have tea in my office, please?" Frannie asked. "And be sure to include a bottle of His Grace's favorite brandy."

MacGinnis gave her a weary bow, then hurried away.

"This past hour appears to have been exceedingly difficult not only for the table in the parlor but also for MacGinnis," she observed. "What has happened?"

Alec gently but firmly took her by the arm and walked her back down the hall to the settee in her office. "Sit down, my love. You will need to."

"Is it that dire?"

"It is." He paced back and forth in front of her, trying to choose the best way to tell her. With a hard shake of his head, he finally decided there was no *best* way. "My mother was the one behind the Lord Ardsmere smuggling scheme."

She stared up at him, her lips barely parted, and her confusion settling into a full-blown scowl. "What?"

"My investigator from London, Mr. Fitch, was the one who sent MacGinnis into such a stir because he delivered the news personally rather than by messenger."

She resettled herself, fidgeting on the settee as though the news stung, and it did. He hated having to admit that his own mother had attacked the woman he loved. Or rather, attacked Frannie's business, which meant the world to her. He pulled the letters from his waistcoat. "Here is the proof. In my mother's own hand. Orders to *relieve* four of your warehouses of their inventory innumerable times and fence the goods as though it was your husband stealing from himself to do business with more nefarious channels rather than your clients covered by contracts."

"That is ridiculous." She fixed him with an incredulous stare. "Why would any businessman in his right mind do such a thing? To what end? What would be the profit or benefit?" She inched forward, sitting on the edge of the cushions. Her skirts twitched with her nervous jiggling, which meant she was deep into solving the strange riddle. She bounced faster, making the entire sofa tremble. "Unless she hoped for word to spread that Lord Ardsmere was not of sound mind and could not be relied upon or trusted in business matters."

She hopped up and started pacing. "But why would she target West Belgium International? We might be one of the more successful dealers of imports and exports, but we are not the largest. We are small competition compared to the likes of the East India Trading Company." She suddenly halted and pointed at Alec. "That's it. Lionwraith Shipping."

"What about it?" He didn't see her point. "We are not competition because we do not deal in the same inventory. Your company handles exotic food, drink, spices, and dress goods. Mine deals with imported woods, stone, and metals—construction materials."

"Different materials and clientele, maybe, but both our companies require prime warehouse space and places to load and unload. I remember seeing reports of delays because of ports short on spaces to dock."

He struggled with that logic. "A few inconveniences at ports made my mother decide to launch such an elaborate and expensive scheme? Utterly ridiculous. What a foolhardy course to take. I thought her wiser than that."

"I am not saying that is her reasoning," Frannie said. "But I thought it could be. It is the only reason I can think of."

"Well, I shall soon find out. I am going to Douglas Manor to confront her."

Just as she opened her mouth to say what he absolutely did not wish to hear, he silenced her with a long, deep kiss that stirred him dangerously close to sweeping her up into his arms and carrying her up to their bedroom. Either that or lock the door of her office.

When he lifted his head, he struggled to regain his composure. "I can travel faster alone on my horse rather than in a carriage. Stay here, my love. I cannot possibly imagine that it would be good for either you or our child to be anywhere near that cruel woman."

"But I don't want you going alone."

The look in her eyes, the worry on her face, the concerned pleading in her tone—all made his heart overflow. No one in his life had ever cared about him and his well-being like Frannie did. He pulled her close and cradled her against his chest. "Your love will protect me. It surrounds me and keeps me safe and warm."

"You have become quite the poet, my lion." She snuggled against him, burrowing her face close enough to torture him with loving kisses along his throat. A lilting giggle escaped her, reminding him of frothy bubbles. "You were so rude and roaring at our first meeting. But now I know it was merely a disguise for your sensitive soul."

"Or perhaps you tamed me."

"Perhaps."

He eased back and gave her a knowing look. "You are still staying here, my sly little wife. I am going to Douglas Manor alone."

She rolled her eyes. "Fine. You can at least have tea before you go. MacGinnis will be here with it at any moment."

"Or you could lock the door and send me on my way properly. That is—if you are feeling better. Has your turmoil passed?"

"I daresay my *turmoil* shall never pass here at Lionwraith." With a coy toss of her head, she sashayed over to the door and secured the latch's lock. "You know how it oversets MacGinnis and Mrs. MacGinnis when we lock the doors. They know very well what we are doing."

He swept her up into his arms and settled on the settee with her in his lap. As she straddled him, he rucked up her gown and filled his hands with her delightful behind. "I am sure they will forgive us when Lionwraith is filled with the laughter of our children."

"Indeed, my lion," she said as she arched her back and pressed the overflowing swell of her breasts closer to his mouth. As she slid her hand down his chest and swiftly unbuttoned his falls, she asked, "Will you be home tonight?"

"It is a day's ride there, my love." A groan escaped him as she unleashed his cock from his pantaloons, then buried it in her hot wetness.

"A ride," she repeated as she held tight to his shoulders and rocked her hips, settling herself with such brilliant expertise that he nearly lost control. "What a lovely idea."

"Yes, my love. A long, hard ride." He squeezed her buttocks as she leaned in and worked her hips, rocking faster.

"Long, hard rides are the best," she advised with a purring groan.

"Indeed, they are, my love. Indeed, they are."

Chapter Sixteen

EVEN THOUGH IT was late summer, the steady downpour made Alec thankful for his wool surtout. The multiple capes of the black greatcoat kept him warm and dry in the unseasonably cold, wet weather. Thank heavens Frannie hadn't gotten too fractious about staying behind. She didn't need to be out in this bone-chilling mess.

A contented smile warmed him. He hated arguing with her about anything, but the way they made up afterward made it almost too tempting to resist.

As the rain fell harder, he pulled his hat lower over his eyes. The sourness of the day had to be an omen that meeting with the woman he had always despised would be even more unpleasant than usual. He had often wondered why his mother hated her children. A shame she hadn't chosen to ignore them and leave them to the innumerable nannies, governesses, and tutors employed to care for them during their tender years. Instead, she had despised Vivvy and him so much that she made it her duty to torment them at every opportunity. Father had turned a blind eye to it all, saying it was not his place to intervene.

Alec knew better. Even his father had feared his mother.

He squinted through the deluge, trying to make out the outline of Douglas Manor through the dismal gray blanket of foggy wetness cloaking the land. Up ahead, perched on top of the rise and silhouetted against the murky sky, stood the black shape of the structure that had always reminded him of a demonic toad squatting on the hill. The mansion of stone was now crumbling in spots but still quite habitable—the perfect place for his dearest mother to live out her final days.

He rode up to the front entrance and stared at the place. The candlelit windows glowed like great, evil eyes staring back at him, daring him to reenter the hell of his childhood. With a nudge of his knee, he urged his mount around the house to the stables.

An old man with his hat pulled low and clutching a wrap around his bent shoulders emerged with a lantern held high. "Who be ye coming onto the Duke of Lionwraith's property?"

Even with the steady drizzle increasing to a hard rain, Alec swept off his hat and smiled down at the man. "Do you not recognize your own master, Estes?"

"Your Grace!" Estes doffed his hat and bowed several times in a row. "Welcome home, Your Grace. Thought ye might come here soon enough."

"And why is that?" Alec dismounted and followed the man who had been the head groom at the manor house for as far back as he could remember.

Estes hung his lantern on a hook, then led Alec's horse into the stall beside it. He swiped an arthritic hand across his face, shoving his thinning hair out of his eyes. "Heard the dowager is doing poorly." He puckered his toothless mouth, making his gaunt cheeks look even more sunken. "Dinna ken for sure, mind ye. Try not to go up to the main house less'n I have to."

"You are as wise as you are old." Alec pointed at the pouch hanging from his saddle. "There is a fresh flask of whisky in there for you. This dreadful weather warranted it. Warm your bones once you get old Raider settled in and fed."

The old groom smiled and bobbed his head. "I thank ye, Your Grace. Ye always was the one most apt to be kind 'round here."

"I am off to meet the demoness now," Alec told him. "I shall inform you whether or not celebrations are in order."

The man chuckled and made the sign of the cross in midair as though blessing him. "Saints protect ye, Your Grace."

"Thank you, Estes. I am sure I shall need it." Alec charged back out into the rain and loped up the stone path to the back entrance of the house. He had always found the back entrance less intimidating. Perhaps that was because it was considered the servants' entrance, and even though they could not do very much to shield Vivvy and himself from his parents' wrath, those working at the manor had always tried to do whatever they could to make the unbearable more bearable.

He pushed his way into the back hall that led to the downstairs kitchens and smiled at the mouth-watering aroma of freshly baked bread, the unmistakable smell of his favorite mutton stew, and the sweet fragrance of some sort of pie. He hoped dear old Mistress Lucy lived forever. The woman could boil a stone and turn it into a delectable meal.

"Lore A'mighty!" screeched a maid he didn't recognize. "There is a man done come in the back way! Mr. Beckers!"

Alec smiled as he took off his hat and coat, shook the water from them, and waited.

Mr. Beckers, Douglas Manor's ancient butler, rounded the corner with a meat cleaver raised. "Good heavens!" He hid the kitchen weapon behind his back and bowed. "Your Grace! What a wonderful surprise." He turned and shoved the blade at someone Alec couldn't see. "Take this! It is His Grace!"

The downstairs kitchen came to life, more abuzz than an overactive beehive.

"How have you been, Beckers?" Alec held out his hat and coat.

"Quite well, Your Grace," the butler said as he expertly gathered the wet things into his arms without getting a drop of moisture on either his clothing or the floor. He offered another polite bow. "Forgive us for our lacking a proper welcome. I fear your arrival completely slipped our minds."

"Rest easy, Beckers." Alec meandered down the hallway, reveling in the mouth-watering aromas. "The dowager was not aware of my visit, so you had no way of knowing. Might there be an extra bowl of stew and a slice of Mistress Lucy's wondrous yeast bread available?"

"Of course, Your Grace. I shall see to it at once. Do you wish to dine in the parlor or the dining room?"

"In the kitchen, old man. Like I used to when I was a defenseless young cub hiding from the monsters."

Mr. Beckers bowed his head in a poor attempt at hiding a sad smile. "Mistress Lucy will be delighted. Follow me."

As Alec stepped into the kitchen, silence fell. Until the silvery-haired woman chucking wood into the stove straightened and spotted him.

"Bless my soul, the young lion has returned to the manor." The portly woman clapped a hand to her ample chest and barreled toward him. "It is so good to see ye, Your Grace. So verra good."

"It is good to see you too, Mistress Lucy, but it would be even better with a bowl of your delicious mutton stew and a warm slice of your freshly baked bread." He seated himself at the worktable where he had spent many a dinner before escaping to boarding school and university, then become the Duke of Lionwraith and built his own lair. The kitchen had always been his sanctuary whenever he came home for the holidays too. He and Vivvy loved Mistress Lucy as though she were their grandmother rather than a servant.

"I shall have ye fed in no time." The cook hurried back to the stove, dished up a hearty portion of stew, and grabbed a board of bread. "Butter and jam for His Grace, Ellen!" she called back over her shoulder. She set his dinner in front of him, then stood there smiling and shaking her head. "Lore A'mighty, ye are a sight for sore eyes, indeed."

"I am glad to see you doing so well," he said, then shoveled a huge spoonful of the rich stew with its thick brown gravy into his mouth. He followed it with a big bite of bread, then closed his eyes and breathed in, enjoying the wondrous flavors dancing across his palate. "I need you at Lionwraith, Mistress Lucy." He paused for a sip of ale. "My lovely wife and I are expecting a little one who would thrive even more if you were there to add to the spoiling."

The cook clapped her hands, delight dancing in her eyes. "Congratulations, Your Grace. A bairn on the way. Such a wonderful blessing, and I ken ye will be the best father that ever was."

"I shall do my best." He thoughtfully stirred his spoon through the thick stew. "I damn sure know what *not* to do."

"Aye, well…" Mistress Lucy crossed herself, then settled on a stool beside him. "Old Martha says herself is not long for this world."

"Good." At the older woman's gasp, he fixed her with a look he knew she would understand. "Who once told me it is just as much a sin if you think it, so you might as well say it?"

Mistress Lucy chuckled, then her mirth died away. "Begging your pardon for being bold, but what will happen to the manor once herself is gone? Will ye be keeping it up? I ken well enough that ye have always hated the place, and I also understand why."

"I will leave Douglas Manor to rot. I meant what I said about needing you at Lionwraith." He used the thick, golden crust of bread to sop up the last of the stew from the bowl. "And anyone else employed here is welcome to come along as well. I will provide a generous pension to those who think themselves too old to relocate. They earned it for serving so long in this hell."

"Ye are a good man, Your Grace." She huffed a snorting laugh as she pushed up from the stool. "All those prayers I said over ye whilst ye were a bairn must have done some good."

"Apparently so." With a heavy sigh, he rose and offered the kindly woman a bow. "Thank you for the delicious meal. I am off now to face the demoness."

Mistress Lucy made the sign of the cross over him just as old Estes had done. "God be with ye, Your Grace."

Alec decided not to upset the dear old woman by informing

her he doubted very much that the Almighty would have anything to do with the battle between him and his mother. Instead, he accepted her blessing with a smile and a nod, then turned and headed up the back staircase to the first floor. He tensed more with every step—just as he had when charging into battle.

A bitter snort escaped him. He *was* charging into battle.

As he reached the door of his mother's private sitting room, he pulled the bundle of letters out from his waistcoat and held them ready as he announced his arrival with a sharp knock.

Hurried footsteps thumped across the creaking floorboards. The door opened, and his mother's maid peered out. "Your Grace!" She threw the door open wide and gave a proper curtsy. "Welcome, Your Grace. It is good you are here. Her Grace is not well at all."

"I doubt my presence will improve her condition. Tell her I am here and that she *will* see me immediately." He tipped his head at the bedroom door. "I apologize if this causes you any mistreatment, Martha, but I tire of the demoness's games."

The elderly maid's eyes flared wide open. "Yes, Your Grace. A moment, please."

He glared at the bedroom door while he waited, willing his mother to feel the depth of his animosity and disgust for her.

After a surprisingly brief amount of time, Martha opened it and curtsied again. "Do come in, Your Grace."

He entered and almost recoiled at the pungent aroma permeating the space. The room reeked of something rancid and foul. "What the deuce is that smell?"

"Greetings to you as well," his mother rasped from her bed, where she sat propped among an abundance of pillows. "It is lavender mixed with the snake oil Estes uses for horse liniment." She glared at him with the old, familiar hatred, her eyes dark and beady. "I did not expect you to respond so quickly." A phlegmy cough choked her, making her clutch her chest and grimace in pain. Gasping for breath, she flailed a weak hand toward the bedside table. "Give it to him, Martha."

The maid picked up an unsealed letter and held it out. Instead of taking it, he threw the bundle of letters proving his mother's guilt onto the bed. "You first, Mother. I always understood you were many things—all of them bad, of course. But I had yet to think of you as a murderess and an attempted destroyer of other people's businesses."

She scowled down at the correspondences, her gaunt face tinged a sickly gray. With a flick of her hand, she knocked them off the bed and gurgled out a malicious cackle. "What? You are amazed that a mere woman is capable of such power? Who the devil do you think built Lionwraith Shipping into the empire it was when you took over? It was not your father. He was too busy with ladybirds, parties, and gambling. You should thank me, you ungrateful whelp."

"West Belgium International never threatened Lionwraith Shipping's business. What you did makes no sense. And how can you show no remorse whatsoever for ordering a member of your own family murdered?"

"Sandilands was no family of mine. That waste of flesh came from your father's side." Another coughing spell took hold of her, making her rattle and wheeze until Martha rushed forward and gave her a few sips of a thick, noxious-looking liquid. Whatever it was, it appeared to be potent, because the dowager cleared her throat and continued, "And West Belgium International never threatened my business, you fool. That scheme was for the pure pleasure of ruining the old Dowager Marchioness of Ardsmere for stealing the life I almost had. Damn Emmeline straight to hell for stealing my George from me." She thumped her chest. "He loved *me* until he caught the scent of her dowry." She curled her lip as though ready to spit at him. "Of course, I would have exacted my revenge sooner if not for having to deal with this prison of your father's making. That and the fact that Emmeline took refuge in Belgium and made it quite difficult for me to take aim at her. But once your father died and got out of my way, finally, I could exact my revenge."

His mother sagged deeper into the pillows, gloating with a smirk of pure evil. "And when I finally came upon the perfect scheme, little did I realize how it would cut you both to the quick." With a twitch of her bony finger, she pointed at the letter Martha held. "I am quite proud of my handiwork, if I do say so myself. Not only did I give Emmeline her long-overdue comeuppance, I proved you to be the incompetent fool I always knew you were. First, you married that senseless whore Charlotte, and now you make yourself vulnerable to a deceptive little chit capable of anything in the name of riches and status in Polite Society." A rasping laugh escaped her. "You are so weak-minded. Just like your father. I should have drowned you and your sister both when he brought you into this house, you pair of unwanted bastards."

"Either your laudanum addiction or the snake oil is making you babble nonsense." Alec resettled his stance, wishing the old demoness was in much better health. A more stringent cut of her funds and imprisoning her in her chambers would not result in the desired level of misery for her in her current condition. After all, she was too weak to go anywhere.

"Show him the box," the dowager ordered Martha. She cackled out another wheezy laugh that left her gasping for breath. "He can keep it with the letter from his dearest mother-in-law."

Martha ran a finger behind her collar and pulled a ribbon out from where it was hidden under her clothing. Attached to the ribbon was a key. She went to a small cabinet in the corner, unlocked the top drawer, and drew out a plain wooden box that was barely large enough to hold a pair of gloves. With the mysterious letter that was supposedly from Lady Emmeline resting on top of the box, she brought both to him and waited for him to accept them.

Alec slowly shook his head. He regretted Martha being caught in the middle of this ridiculous altercation, but there was no helping it. He settled his glare on his mother. "Enough with your games. Admit your guilt. Maybe then, when you die, your next residence will not be as fiery hot."

His mother sat there looking entirely too proud of herself. Her smile taunted him, seemed somehow even crueler than usual. "Look inside the box. Or are you afraid?"

Bracing himself, he snatched the correspondence off the top and flipped open the lid while Martha held the tiny chest. A sealed document and a ring with the Lionwraith crest were inside. He picked up the ring and compared it to the one Father had given him years ago. The two were identical.

"Match it to the wax seal, fool," his mother rasped.

"I recognize the Lionwraith seal when I see it." It was the same one he used to add credence to his own documents. He pulled the yellowed parchment from the box and held it up. "What is this?"

"Read it." She struggled to clear her throat, coughing so hard that he wondered if the end was at hand. Unfortunately, it was not. She shifted among the pillows but kept her beady-eyed gaze fixed on him while fighting to catch her breath.

He broke the wax, then ran his finger under the seam to open the letter. The identity of the writer was unmistakable. His father wrote with an odd, elongated way of forming his letters. Even without the seal and his father's signature at the bottom of the page, Alec knew who'd authored the missive.

He clenched his teeth as the broken sentences jumped out at him. *Children of the only woman he had ever truly loved. Devoted mistress. Married a cruel, cold-hearted wife. Agreement to secure an heir. No one knows but Henrietta and her maid.* He looked up at his mother, noting how her dark eyes glittered even brighter as if waiting to feed off his pain and confusion. He held up the letter. "Did you come up with this lie to escape your boredom?"

"That is your father's writing. You know that as well as I." She laced her bony fingers together and rested her folded hands in her lap. "The man who sired you and your sister with that whore from Dumfries loved only two things in this life. That harlot and my dowry of land where your illustrious Lionwraith Estate now sits. He consummated our marriage, then returned to my bed only one other time, and I hated him both times. The brutal, heartless bastard enjoyed my pain and humiliation. Thank God Almighty, he never came to me again after he found his whore. He took his pleasure with her, the mistress he kept close enough to visit every night if he wished to."

Another coughing fit interrupted her. The handkerchief she held to her mouth reddened with flecks of blood. "When she told him she carried his child, he threatened to divorce me and ruin me with scandal if I did not make everyone believe it was I who was pregnant and then accept you as my own when he brought you into the household, and her as well. The harlot posed as a chambermaid and then your wet nurse after she gave birth to you." Eyes shut but still sneering, she rolled her head back and forth across the pillows. "And then he forced me to do it again when the whore found herself poisoned with your sister in her belly." She wheezed out a bitter, railing laugh. "At least your sister killed the doxy with her birth, and that ended the danger of any more bastards."

She opened her eyes and looked at him with more hatred and loathing than she had ever thrown upon him before. "Your father was a cunning devil, threatening me and keeping me trapped in this uncivilized place to ensure no one ever doubted your legitimacy. None of this would ever have happened to me if Emmeline had kept her promise to stay away from my Georgie, and I had married him instead, become the Marchioness of Ardsmere, the woman he would have truly loved as much as I loved him." Her cruel mouth twisted to one side. "You are nothing but a bastard and a duped fool. How does it feel?"

Alec treated her to a gloating smile of his own. "Quite a relief, actually, to know that none of your blood runs in my veins." It didn't matter that his real mother had never married his father. He was born of love—not bred in hatred. And whatever Mother—no, not Mother, but the dowager—was babbling about his being duped was more than likely brought on by her latest dose of laudanum.

"Read Emmeline's letter," she screeched. "She hates you as much as I do. Hates you enough to reveal the truth!" A more violent attack of coughing took hold of her, making her curl to one side to fight to wheeze in some air.

Martha rushed to her with the dark brown vial.

Before opening Lady Emmeline's letter, he tossed his father's confession and the wooden box into the hearth and watched them catch fire and burn. With no evidence, it would be his word against that of an elderly maid and her addled mistress. After all, he was his father's son and the rightful heir, whether England's legalities recognized that or not.

"Your Grace?"

He turned at Martha's quiet call and discovered the woman he had always known as his mother had become very still and somehow diminished.

"Gone?" he said, finding it impossible to feel anything but a satisfied sense of finality.

Martha nodded and backed away from the bed. She hurried over to him and bowed her head. "I beg you, Your Grace. Please do not kill me."

"Kill you?" He helped the distraught woman to a chair. "I fear that serving the demoness has caused you to take leave of your senses. Why would I kill you?"

With her hands tightly clasped and her head still bowed, she shuddered. "Because I know," she whispered.

"Is there additional proof other than what I tossed into the fire?" He went over to the cabinet and rifled through its contents. Nothing but paltry baubles, frayed ribbons, and bits of broken jewelry filled the drawers.

"No, Your Grace."

He studied the maid for a long moment and believed her. How such a gentle person could tolerate so many years with the cruel woman who had posed as his mother was beyond him.

"Consider yourself free. You have fully served your sentence.

She pushed up from the chair and curtsied. "Thank you, Your Grace."

"You will be provided a generous pension, Martha. You earned it." And he wasn't paying her to keep her quiet. The woman had wasted years of her life serving a bitterly cruel mistress. She deserved to live out what time she had left in peace and comfort.

The maid curtsied again and hurried out of the room with tears streaming down her face.

Alec realized he still held the letter that the dowager had so badly wanted him to read in front of her. A rueful smile came to him. At least he had denied her that pleasure. He unfolded the paper and squinted at the messy script that proved difficult to read. Lady Emmeline's penmanship was sorely lacking. The blots of ink and broken lines betrayed a trembling hand.

He moved into the sitting room not only for better light but to escape the medicinal stench of the departed demoness's room. "Much better." Or possibly not. The more he read, the more confused he became. "Never in all my days have I ever heard of such a far-fetched scheme."

He read the letter again, then carefully refolded it and tucked it inside his waistcoat. It couldn't be true. None of it. Frannie would have told him. And what about Sophie and Celia? They were Frannie's closest friends, her *sisters of choice*, by her own definition. Did they know that the Marquess of Ardsmere supposedly had never existed? That Frannie was presumably Lady Emmeline's daughter and not her ward?

"Balderdash! The lot of it." He strode over to the liquor cabinet and poured himself a generous splash of port. The letter could not be true. It was a product of a hysterical woman's pettiness fueled by one too many glasses of brandy. And why on earth would Lady Emmeline share such dangerous information with a woman known for her deviousness and cruelty? Had she hoped the demoness would use it to torment him?

He took another deep drink of the port and slowly shook his head. He had neither hoped nor cared if Lady Emmeline ever liked him or held him in high regard. The woman was irrelevant.

A bitter laugh huffed free of him. Not only was she irrelevant, but she knew it and hated it with a passion. He could tell it by the way she flitted about, vying for everyone's attention whenever she was sober enough to do so. But to make up such a story… A story that, if true, could be so extraordinarily dangerous was foolhardy. All of it had to be a lie.

"Frannie will sort it." He downed the last of his port, set the glass aside, and headed out. There was much to be done before he could leave Douglas Manor for the very last time.

CHAPTER SEVENTEEN

"I KNOW, WELLINGTON. I miss him too." Frannie scratched the loudly purring cat behind his only ear.

Alec had yet to return from Douglas Manor, what with having to see to his mother's burial and boarding up the place he had always hated. According to his sister, they both despised it because of their miserable childhoods.

Time spent with Vivvy and Dunkeld and their blossoming love only made Frannie miss him more, so she had made it a habit of taking refuge in the conservatory as often as possible.

"And where are your children today?" she asked the cat while rubbing under his chin until his whiskers twitched with delight.

The feline closed his eyes and flipped his tail, refusing to give even so much as a glance in the direction of his young.

"Kitties?" Frannie called, and was immediately rewarded with three small yet plump likenesses of Wellington. They tumbled out of the nearest herb bed, playfully wrestling with each other in the process. She couldn't tell them apart, so she merely addressed them as *kitties*. "Sir Henry will not appreciate your trampling of the parsley." She picked one of them up and held it close until it squirmed and spat with an audacious little hiss in a bid to rejoin its siblings. "Fine, angry little sir. Back to your brothers."

"Your Grace?" Daisy called from the doorway of the conservatory.

"Here, Daisy. Through the dark purple lilacs. Beside the

basil."

The young maid pushed through the last of the foliage and shook her head. "His Grace said that I was to ensure you ate properly and took care of yourself. Sitting out here with Wellington and his family when you have had nothing but a half-cup of chocolate all day is neither eating properly nor caring for yourself."

"I am not hungry." Frannie pinched off a stem of basil and dangled it over the kittens, smiling as they pounced and batted at the leaves. "If you wish to sit and have a pleasant visit, you may stay and enjoy not only my company but also that of the Wellingtons. If you are determined to scold, go away."

A long, loud huff yanked her attention from the felines and focused it on the determined maid. "You may go, Daisy. And do not send Mrs. MacGinnis out here in your stead."

The girl huffed again, but softer this time, as she sat on the bench beside her. "Sorry, Your Grace. May I stay?"

"Under the conditions I stated."

"Yes, Your Grace."

They sat in silence for a long while, playing with the kittens until the fluffy little beasts tired of them and disappeared deeper into the conservatory.

"Did His Grace say when he might return?" Daisy asked.

"No." Frannie leaned forward in a very unladylike way, braced her elbows on her knees, and propped her chin on her fists. "It has been well over a week now, but I am not certain how long it might take. He had to see to the burial, the welfare of the servants, and the closing up of the place."

"Will he sell it?" Daisy mimicked Frannie's pose.

"I don't know that either." Frannie chewed on the corner of her lip. "According to his letter, when he leaves the manor this time, he means to never return."

"Your Grace?" Mrs. MacGinnis's voice rang out, echoing through the conservatory. "I've brought tea and cakes for ye."

Frannie shifted and settled an accusing glare on Daisy.

The smiling maid hopped to her feet and urged her to follow. "The cakes are lemon with a drizzle of honey. Your favorite, and just baked today."

"Do not start conspiring against me," Frannie warned as she rose from the bench and followed Daisy to the table where Mrs. MacGinnis was busy serving the tea.

"Here ye are, Your Grace." The housekeeper smiled as she added an extra dollop of milk to the delicate porcelain cup of tea beside a plate holding a large slice of lemon cake. "And what better place to enjoy a wee bit of cake?"

"A *wee* bit?" Frannie gave Mrs. MacGinnis a dubious glare.

"Listen!" Mrs. MacGinnis stepped to the door and barely opened it. "Horses, and sounds like a carriage, too."

"Perhaps it is word from His Grace." Frannie hopped up, but the housekeeper blocked the door and waggled a finger back and forth.

"If it is word from His Grace, Mr. MacGinnis will bring it to ye straightaway," she said. "Ye dinna wish for your tea to grow cold, or the cake, either."

"You two are impossible." Frannie plopped back into the chair and glared at the staff who had turned on her. "I shall be speaking to His Grace about this ridiculous and completely unacceptable development of my being treated like a child."

Both the housekeeper and the maid smiled and nodded like indulgent nannies.

Frannie rolled her eyes, then sipped her tea. She was outnumbered by those two and might as well keep to her word and speak with Alec about this silliness later. As soon as the lemony, rich cake touched her tongue, her stomach grumbled and clenched, making her set down her fork and press a napkin to her mouth. She closed her eyes, pulled in a deep breath through her nose, and let it ease out her mouth. When she had confided her fears of expecting a baby to Celia, her dear sister had warned her there might be times such as this, but Frannie had scoffed at the notion. She had a hearty constitution. Where on earth had this weakness come from?

"Sip the tea, Your Grace," Mrs. MacGinnis instructed her with a knowing look. "It will help settle ye. Ye can always eat the cake when the bairn decides to let ye."

Frannie slid the cake as far away as the table allowed. Even the smell of it did not sit well with her. She bowed her head, closed her eyes, and concentrated on not embarrassing herself by casting up her accounts in the conservatory. If it came to that, she would strive to make it to the door in time to heave outside. She ignored the creaking bang of the conservatory door, feeling certain that Mrs. MacGinnis had sent Daisy for a cool, wet cloth to stave off the sickness.

Then another scent, the familiar, comforting fragrance of leather, sandalwood, and fresh, clean citrus wafted across her just as Alec said, "My love, are you all right?"

She lifted her head and discovered him crouching beside her. She dove into his arms, nearly knocking him onto his backside. "Alec! You are home!"

"Indeed, I am." He laughed, catching her in a tight hug. "Why are you having your tea out here?"

"Because Daisy and Mrs. MacGinnis are treating me like a child. I was out here visiting with Wellington and telling him how terribly I missed you, and they insisted on following me with tea and cake."

"Good on them." He smiled down at her, but something in his eyes, worried shadows that she had never seen before, gave her pause.

Her stomach clenched again, but she did her best to ignore it. Gently resting her hand on his cheek, she stroked the bristles of his day's growth of beard. "I am so very glad you are home."

"I too, my darling." But his slight frown and heavy sigh said otherwise as he eased away from her and seated himself in the chair next to hers. "Did your sisters of choice and Lady Emmeline have a safe journey back to London?"

His question struck her as odd, but perhaps he was struggling with weariness. This past week couldn't have been easy for him. She forced a smile she didn't feel. "I received word from Sophie yesterday. She sent it off right before leaving for France. The trip went well, and they actually arrived in London a day early."

"That is good." He studied her with a piercing look that made her feel like squirming. "And your mother?"

"My mother?" With an uneasy laugh, she lightly patted his arm. "My former *mother-in-law*, you mean. Lady Emmeline?"

When he didn't answer, she swallowed hard, then took a sip of tea, praying Mrs. MacGinnis was right about it preventing her from becoming ill.

"Why didn't you tell me, Frannie?" he asked softly.

"Tell you what?" She flinched as her voice cracked. She cleared her throat, then took another bit of tea. "Excuse me. Must be all the wet weather of late."

He looked so sad and disappointed as he pulled a folded bit of parchment from inside his waistcoat and set it on the table between them. After he tapped it once, he slid it over to her. "From your mother. To the old demoness before she died."

She stared down at the broken seal, knowing what the letter held without reading a word of it. No wonder Mother Ardsmere had seemed so eager to leave for London. The cross old hen had wanted to make sure she was well on her way before Frannie discovered she had laid bare all their secrets.

"Why didn't you tell me?" he repeated, his tone still ominously quiet.

With her gaze locked on the letter, she whispered, "I meant to, but the right time never seemed to turn up, and then I was afraid because I knew you would hate me for the lie." She barely shook her head. "I am so sorry. I could not bear the thought of losing you."

"I see."

She couldn't look up, couldn't face what she knew she would see in his eyes—hatred. The same furious hatred she saw when he had spoken of his first wife and how she had lied to him.

His chair scraped across the floor, then the conservatory door creaked and banged.

With a desperate gulp of air, that she held in to keep from keening out a heartbreaking wail, Frannie pressed her clasped hands to her mouth.

"Just like that," she said in a tearful whisper. "All over, just like that."

"*Meowrrr.*"

"Yes, Wellington. I am a fool." She set the dish of cake on the floor and soaked it in cream from the petite pitcher that matched the teapot. At least the cat might get some enjoyment from tea and cakes in the conservatory. "Forgive me for not staying, Wellington, but I must walk now, and think about what to do."

The old cat didn't lift his head, just kept lapping the milk between snatching bites of the cake.

She wandered outside and headed away from the house across the eastern meadow. It didn't matter that only a few hours of daylight remained or that blustery winds had shoved fine, fat storm clouds all across the sky. A little rain never killed anyone, and she could not be so lucky as to be swept away from this world and all its misery.

Her throat ached with the need to cry, but she held the tears at bay. No. She would not cry, because she had brought this upon herself by not being honest with Alec. If she had but told him early on, then Mother Ardsmere's vengeful cut would have held no sting. Either that or she would have already been well on her way to learning to live without him.

She halted her tromping across the rough hillocks of thick grass long enough to squeeze her eyes shut and order her tears to go away. She had not earned the healing balm of a good cry.

Thunder rumbled in the distance as though shouting a hearty "Amen!" A snort escaped her. Even the world agreed that she was the worst sort of fool who should have known better.

She continued stumbling across the way. The lake was up ahead. Perhaps watching the rain hit the dancing waves would help her think of something to say, so he might forgive her. Or, at the very worst, she would decide where to go and how to go about freeing him of the burden of her presence.

A rickety wooden dock missing several planks caught her eye. Surely she didn't weigh enough to break through it. As she neared it, the clouds split open and dropped sheets of water reminiscent of Noah and the Great Flood. Her hair and clothes were soon plastered to her, but she forged onward, gathering up her drenched skirts as she gingerly made her way out onto the dilapidated pier.

The waters of the lake appeared as dark and threatening as an angry sea. It didn't matter. She would sit here for a bit and think. Even if the boards beneath her gave way, it couldn't be that deep here as close as it was to shore. And she doubted very much if the lake possessed anything as dangerous as the current of a river or the ocean's tide.

Lightning splintered the sky and made her cry out. She clapped her hands over her ears as thunder followed with a deafening boom. She worked her jaws to pop her ears, squinting as the deluge flooded her vision. It didn't matter. She stubbornly wiggled in place, determined not to relinquish this spot until she had a plan or a solution, or until the lightning granted her mercy by striking her dead.

She heard a faint shout over the storm, or, at least, she thought she did. But a hurried glance all around assured her it was merely wishful thinking on her part. Alec would not come looking for her, and storms terrified poor Daisy.

The winds blew the waves higher, slamming them across her and dousing her as much as if she had jumped into the lake itself. The board beneath her shuddered as if trying to rid itself of her weight. Perhaps she had best move back a board or two. Maybe this one had had enough of her.

As she tried to stand, it gave way. The back of her head slammed hard into something. The force of the painful blow dazed her so much that she forgot to close her mouth and hold her breath. Water rushed in to steal her air. She tried to cough it out, but that only brought in more. She fought to the surface but then soused back under. Where was the bottom? How could it be this deep? She flailed harder, trying to fight her way back to the blessed air. She so badly needed at least one breath.

Panic filled her as the murky darkness laughed at her burning lungs. Her foot hit something, and she tried to push upward. At least, she *prayed* it was upward to the surface. But her gown went taut and yanked her back. It was no use. She allowed herself to go limp as the cold blackness closed in. It was over.

"NO!" ALEC ROARED as Frannie disappeared into the angry waters. He tore off his coat while charging toward the lake at the hardest run of his life. Without hesitating, he dove in, knowing the water at the old dock was deep and well over her head. Damn her for being so foolhardy. She never thought about herself. She only cared for others.

He couldn't see through the murkiness stirred by the storm and, more than likely, her fight to keep from drowning. Arms outstretched, he felt for her in the depths, searching through the muddy blackness. At long last, his fingertips brushed against something soft and pliable like fabric. He pushed toward it, praying it was her.

It was, but God help him, she was limp as a rag. He wrapped his arms around her and pushed off the slimy bottom toward the surface. But something tugged her back, kept her from rising with him. Her skirts had to be snagged. He yanked with all his strength and tore her free, broke through the surface, and lifted her face to the sky.

Limp as a rag and gray as slate, she made no attempt to breathe. He clambered up on shore and laid her on her side, blinking the water from his eyes as he willed her chest to move with intakes of air.

"Francis Isabella Marie, you will not die! I forbid it!" He stared down at her, willing her to breathe, demanding her to live. "Water in her lungs," he muttered as panic churned through him. "What the devil did I read about saving those who had drowned?"

And then the words came back to him. Words he had read in an addition to his library from a few years ago. *Observations on Apparent Death from Drowning and Suffocation*, published by Dr. Curry in 1793. To resuscitate the victim, the lungs should be inflated with air by any means available. He had to get air into Frannie. He would worry about getting her warmed and to the house later.

The only way he could think to force her to take air was by sharing his own. He lifted her head, covered her mouth with his, and blew in as hard as possible. He rose, drew in another great lungful, and gusted it into her again. Over and over, as the rain washed down upon them, he sucked in huge gulps of air and forced them into her.

"Breathe, damn you! You will not die!" He hugged her to his chest. She was so very cold. With her head supported, he turned her to lie over his knees and rubbed her back and arms. "Breathe, Frannie! I beg you to breathe and live." He choked on tears and anguish. Never had he cried for anyone in his life. He kept rubbing and thumping her back, as he had seen done for a child when they choked on a bit of meat. The action had made the little one cough it up and breathe. God willing, it would work for Frannie.

"Please, my dear one," he sobbed while rocking her in his arms. "Please, do not leave me. I beg you."

Desperate for her to live, he went back to blowing into her mouth, thumping her on the back, and then forcing air into her again and again.

As he lifted his head to take in another breath, a muffled gurgling from deep within her caught his ear. At least, he prayed it was so. His prayers were answered as a violent torrent of water gushed out of her mouth, shaking her with hard spasms of uncontrollable coughing.

"Thank God Almighty." He held her as she expelled what seemed like gallons of water. "Frannie—thank God you are alive."

But she didn't speak, just hung there limp in his arms. He shifted her so she was face up and pressed an ear to her chest. He closed his eyes with relief. Her heartbeat thumped with a steady rhythm, and he heard the unmistakable wheezing of air in and out of her lungs. Time to get her to the house and get her warm. Maybe then she would open her beautiful eyes and treat him to one of her lovely smiles.

With her cradled to his chest, he carried her back across the field to the covered walkway between the conservatory and the dining room. It was then he noticed blood from the back of her head soaking into his sleeve. He quickened his pace, kicked in the door, and charged across the dining room roaring, "Boil water, stoke the fires, bring bandages, and get a doctor here now!"

Mrs. MacGinnis, Mr. MacGinnis, and several maids and footmen came running. Their expressions turned horrified as they recognized the precious bundle Alec carried.

Dunkeld and Vivvy rushed out of the parlor. Vivvy gasped, and Dun caught hold of her and hugged her to his chest, shielding her from taking in the frightful sight. "What can I do?" he shouted after Alec.

"Pray!" Alec bellowed without slowing in his climbing of the stairs. He charged down the hallway, kicked open the door to their suite, and barreled into their bedroom, startling the maids tidying the room. "Get out!"

After easing Frannie down onto the bed, he hurried to rid her of her shoes and every other soaked article of clothing. He had to get her dry, get her warm, get her awake, and see to the wound on the back of her head. With as much care as possible, he turned her and gently parted her matted hair. A long split in her flesh and a vicious purple swelling made him cringe. Whatever she had hit, she had hit it hard.

Daisy rushed in, carrying an armload of blankets and looking ready to cry. "More blankets, Your Grace, and I have a dry shift for her."

"Good," he said. "Help me get the shift on her. The bed needs drying as well. I will not have her uncomfortable in a bed wet with cold filth."

"Yes, Your Grace. If you would lift her, I shall change them straightaway."

He scooped Frannie up and took her closer to the hearth to keep her warm while Daisy sorted the bed.

A maid rushed in with an armload of wood and stoked the dwindling coals until the fireplace roared like a crackling inferno.

"Hot water, bandages, and a poultice, Your Grace." Mrs. MacGinnis trundled into the room, one arm clutching rolls of linen and the other balancing a basket overflowing with vials, jars, and dried herbs. "I shall do what I can till Lord Dunkeld gets back. He's gone to fetch Dr. Tramadorn, but it could be a while, depending on where the good doctor might be." With a sympathetic look, she nodded at the bed. "Let's see to her, Your Grace."

"Cover her pillow with linens that can easily be changed," he ordered her. "She has a wound on the back of her head. She must have hit it when the dock collapsed."

Daisy spread several layers across the pillow, then jumped back out of the way, standing with her hands clenched as he eased Frannie back down onto the bed.

"Go and get yourself dried and changed, Your Grace," Mrs. MacGinnis said. "We shall see to her."

"No. I will not leave her for a moment."

"If ye catch your death, what good will ye be to her, then?" the housekeeper countered.

"She has to live," he growled. "She has to be well just like she was before!"

"We will do our best, Your Grace," the old woman gently promised. "Off with ye now to your dressing room. I had the lads bring ye some hot water and put on extra to boil for Her Grace for later." She arched a wispy brow. "On wi' ye now."

"I shall return shortly." As much as he hated the thought of leaving Frannie's side, he grudgingly admitted that Mrs. MacGinnis was right. He strode into his dressing room, kicked off his waterlogged boots, and stripped out of his wet clothes. A bitter snort escaped him. Somewhere out in the east meadow, his jacket remained. It didn't matter. All that mattered was Frannie.

While propped against the long marble counter he'd had built into the elaborate dressing room complete with an oversized tub, he bowed his head and closed his eyes. The image of her crashing through that dock and disappearing beneath the angry waters played through his mind, over and over, as a torturous reminder that if he had but stayed in the conservatory and talked with her in a rational, reasonable manner, none of this would have happened. If she died—

He pushed away from the counter. "No! She will not die." He quickly washed, scrubbed himself dry, then donned an old pair of breeches and a linen shirt made soft as down from innumerable washings. These were his lounging-in-the-library clothes, or for mucking about in the stables or fields. It didn't matter that he did not look his station. All that mattered was getting back to Frannie.

Barefoot and not caring what anyone thought, he hurried back into the bedroom, praying he would find his lady love awake. Instead, she lay deathly still, covered up to her chin in piles of blankets, a thick bandage wrapped around her head.

"I didna stitch her wound," Mrs. MacGinnis said in a hushed tone. "My feelings were that Dr. Tramadorn might wish a wee look at it first. But I did put a poultice on her chest that should help warm her blood and stave off the ague from her getting so chilled."

"What about..." Alec went quiet. He couldn't bring himself to ask for the news that he couldn't bear to hear.

Mrs. MacGinnis studied him, then moved closer and lowered

her voice even more. "The bairn seems safe for now. No bleeding is a good sign."

He closed his eyes and deflated with relief. "Let us pray it stays that way, and that both of them will be as if this terrible day never happened."

Mrs. MacGinnis nodded, then crossed herself. With her worried frown fixed on her mistress, she clutched her hands to her chest. "All we can do now is wait for the good doctor and pray."

Alec dragged a chair close to the bedside and brushed a hesitant touch to Frannie's cheek. "At least she is warmer without being feverish."

"Aye, Your Grace, and her color looks to be a mite better than it was when ye first brought her inside."

"She was so gray," he whispered. "I feared her soul was already gone."

"Ye need a hearty dram, Your Grace." Mrs. MacGinnis toddled to the door, then paused with her hand on the latch. "Would ye be eating anything?"

"No, thank you, Mrs. MacGinnis. No food."

She shook her head. "I didna think so, but I shall have that whisky up here shortly." The door clicked quietly shut behind her, leaving the room silent.

"Open your eyes, sweetling," Alec pleaded as he leaned on the bed, drawing in as close to Frannie as he could. "We have much to talk about, you and I. Where we shall build the nursery. Names for a boy or a girl. What nannies, governesses, and tutors we shall have, because we will love our children so very much that we shall never send them off to boarding schools."

Frannie's pale lashes didn't twitch, but at least he detected the barest rise and fall of her chest with her steady breathing.

"I was a damned fool to confront you the way I did, Frannie. I am so sorry. By the time I listened to my heart instead of my past and returned to apologize, you were gone." A sad laugh almost choked him, making him swallow hard. He smoothed the wrinkles from the blankets and tucked them closer around her.

"You should find this most amusing—I discovered I am a bastard in every sense of the word. It pleases me to say that the old demoness is not my true mother. As it turns out, my father loved another. A lady from Dumfries. She was Vivvy's mother too. I am sure she had to be quite wonderful."

He kept his gaze locked on the curve of Frannie's sweet mouth, hoping for the merest twitch of a smile. But none came. "I know you are tired," he whispered. "I shall cease beating your ear and simply sit here with you until you have rested enough to open your eyes for me." He stretched closer and kissed her cheek. "I love you, dearest. Please find it in your heart to forgive me."

CHAPTER EIGHTEEN

"I F TRAMADORN CANNA help her, I shall fetch that doctor who married Celia's mother. I believe MacMaddenly is his name. Celia and Sophie both spoke quite highly of the man." Dunkeld paced alongside Alec. "He is a Scot trained in Edinburgh. Shall I leave now to fetch him?"

Alec was tempted. He would spare nothing to save his dear one. "Riding hard, it would take you at least a week to get him here. Probably more, since the good doctor would need to travel by carriage."

"Then let him leave now," Vivvy said. She anxiously circled the sitting room of Alec and Frannie's private suite along with them. "Dr. Tramadorn has been in there entirely too long. What on earth could he be doing?"

"A valid question, dear sister." Alec eyed the bedroom door, barely restraining himself from bursting into the room and demanding news. The only thing that held him back was fear. At the moment, the unknown was safest. Frannie could be much improved and on the verge of waking. But if he entered that room and interrupted the doctor, he risked discovering there was no hope for either her or their unborn child. That fear held him back. He was ashamed to be such a coward, but it came from the depth of love he felt for them both.

His heart almost stopped as the door swung open, and the doctor joined them. "Well?"

Dr. Tramadorn squinted at him and curled his upper lip as if trying to think of a way to escape without speaking to him. "All we can do is wait, Your Grace."

Alec turned to Dunkeld. "Get MacMaddenly here. Now."

Dun charged out of the room with Vivvy on his heels.

"MacMaddenly?" Dr. Tramadorn repeated as he buckled the straps on his black satchel.

"Dr. MacMaddenly from London." Alec couldn't care less if that insulted the man. His dear one needed better advice than *waiting*. "A friend of the family, and quite astute from what I understand. He studied at Edinburgh."

The doctor gave him a tight-lipped nod. "I understand, Your Grace." He rolled his shoulders and locked eyes with him. "But I assure you, the prognosis will be the same."

"We shall see, Dr. Tramadorn. Thank you for your time." Alec dismissed the man with a curt glare at the door, then rushed into the bedroom and returned to Frannie's bedside. His dear one was as he had left her. Her color was good, but her eyes remained closed. The bandage was no longer around her head, and he noticed fresh linens had been placed across the pillow.

Mrs. MacGinnis stepped out of the dressing room, drying her hands on her apron. "Doctor decided against stitches. Said it looked good enough to heal the way it was."

"Thank you for assisting him so you could watch over her." Alec sagged down into the chair next to the bed, keeping his hopes locked on Frannie's closed eyes, willing her to open them. "Lord Dunkeld is fetching Dr. MacMaddenly from London, since Tramadorn refuses to do anything but wait."

"Sometimes these things take God's time and not man's," the housekeeper quietly said as she picked up the bowl of discarded bandages and balanced them on her hip. "I know it seems like forever, but it's truly naught been but hours with her in this state. Give her time to find her way back to ye, Your Grace. She will come. Perhaps when the sun rises shortly, it will tempt her to open her eyes." The kindly old woman blessed him with an encouraging nod. "She loves ye more than those wee kittens out in the conservatory or her favorite lemon cake. She will come back to ye, Your Grace. Love will bring her through this."

With his stare still fixed on Frannie, he almost choked on the regret tearing his heart to shreds. "Do you promise?" he whispered. "Promise with all your heart?"

Mrs. MacGinnis shifted in place as though suddenly uncomfortable. "I will pray for her with all my heart. I can give ye that promise without a doubt, Your Grace."

He picked up Frannie's limp hand, hugged it to his cheek, and closed his eyes. "You may go, Mrs. MacGinnis."

"Yes, Your Grace." The door thumped shut and its latch clicked with ominous finality.

He leaned over and rested his head against Frannie's side, while still clinging to her hand. With his eyes closed, he listened to the softness of her heartbeat through the blankets. Still steady and strong—that brought him what little joy there was to be had.

Please, God. He left it at that, not knowing what else to say and not wishing to risk insult. In his opinion, the Almighty probably heard innumerable promises and oaths whenever someone needed a miracle from Him. Then they promptly forgot their words once the miracle was received. But he would never do that. An oath made was an oath kept. Hopefully, God would take that into account. *Please let her and the child stay with me. I shall cherish them as long as I draw breath. I swear it.*

He tucked her hand under his chin as he nestled closer and draped his arm across her. Her warmth comforted him, helped him push away the horrid memory of how cold she had been when he carried her back to the house.

"I love you," he whispered without opening his eyes. "I love you more than you will ever know."

"Are you sure?" she asked in a weak, raspy voice.

Still holding tight to her, he lifted his head and hovered over her, praying with all his heart that he hadn't imagined her speaking. "Frannie?"

Her eyelids fluttered, then she squinted with a pained grimace. "The light hurts," she groaned.

He promptly blew out the lamp beside the bed, dimming the room to only the night candle burning on the mantel. He returned to his hovering position. "Praise God Almighty." He kissed her hand and kept it held to his lips.

Still squinting, she gave him the saddest smile. "I am so sorry," she mouthed more than whispered. "Please forgive me."

"Shush." He kissed her forehead, then eased back to stare down into her face, unable to get enough of her wakefulness. "All that matters is that you came back to me."

"Came back?"

He bowed his head and swallowed hard, choking on the love and thankfulness coursing through him. "You almost left me, sweetling."

She frowned as though trying to remember. Her eyes went wide and filled with tears. "Our baby?"

"Shh… All is well. Our little one is strong and stubborn." He didn't even attempt to hold back a thankful smile. "Much like his Mother—praise God."

Squeezing her eyes shut, she drew in a hitching breath. "I love you," she whispered without opening her eyes. "Love you so much. Please understand that."

"As long as you understand that I love you more than life itself."

Her mouth relaxed, then lifted in a faint smile. "Thank you."

"For what?"

"A second chance." Her eyes fluttered open. Sadness filled them. "I am so sorry."

He kissed her eyelids to close them. "Sleep, my love," he whispered, "and know that I love you. If you can forgive me for being a fool, I can forgive a slight bit of creativity about your past."

She drew in another deep breath, flinched, then eased it out. "We will talk more when the pain goes away."

"Yes, my love. For now, sleep." He rested his head against her side and placed her hand upon his cheek. "I am right here and will not leave your side."

"Promise?"

"Promise with all my heart and soul."

⟫⟫⟩✕⟨⟪⟪

WITH EVERY RACKING cough, Frannie clutched her head and kept her eyes squeezed tightly shut. Coughing made the terrible ache worse and threatened to split her skull in two.

"She is suffering!" Alec bellowed from the next room. "I demand you help her!"

She couldn't hear Dr. MacMaddenly's response but was certain the stoic Scot had said something Alec didn't like, because her dear husband roared again, sounding like a tormented beast. It made her smile through the pain. He loved her. Even though she had deceived him, he had found it in his heart to forgive her for her life of lies.

"The doctor said ye could take more laudanum, Your Grace." Daisy held the bottle and spoon at the ready.

"No." Frannie lifted her hand to stop the maid. Shaking her head would be a terrible mistake. "That stuff is ghastly and only makes things worse," she croaked through another congested cough. "My head had stopped hurting so terribly before this dreadful sickness set in."

The maid set down the medicine and offered a steaming cup in its stead. "From what His Grace said about that day, you breathed in half the lake. Is it any wonder you ended up so sick?" She handed over a fresh handkerchief along with the cup. "Cough that nastiness up, spit it out, then drink this herbal down. It will clean your lungs just as it did Lord Dunkeld's when he suffered with that miserable ague. Leastwise, Mrs. MacGinnis said so, and so did his lordship."

Another muffled rant came from the next room, making Frannie release a congested sigh. "Please ask His Grace to come sit with me before Dr. MacMaddenly washes his hands of us. He is the Duchess of Hasterton's stepfather now. We must treat him accordingly."

With a dubious look, Daisy grudgingly went into the sitting room, but she closed the door behind her, preventing Frannie from eavesdropping on a single word.

"I must talk with her about leaving that door open. I am sick to death of being cut off from the entire world." She'd lost track of how long she had been abed. According to Daisy, it had been almost a fortnight, but it seemed so much longer. She exploded with a hard sneeze, then groaned and held her head. As gingerly as possible, she blew her nose, flinching against the pounding ache that surged through her skull like the coming in of the tide.

Alec entered, his face like thunder, albeit somewhat subdued. "Forgive me for disturbing you, my love." He eased down onto the side of the bed. Eyes flashing and teeth clenched, he took her hand. "That infuriating man said everything possible has been done for you." He huffed in disgust. "The best from Edinburgh. In whose opinion, I ask you!"

"Sometimes, it simply takes time." She hazarded a sip from the steaming cup and was thankful to discover that Mrs. MacGinnis had added copious amounts of honey. The last herbal the housekeeper had sent up had been impossible to keep down and was so sour it had nearly locked her jaws. "There is nothing to do but outlast it. Get my mind off it, won't you? You did promise that today you would tell me how you found out the truth about my life. I vaguely remember something. Something about a letter. But for the life of me, I cannot remember who it was from. Did I merely dream that you found out through a letter?"

"No. You did not dream it, my love. There was a letter. You saw it before the accident, but memories are sometimes lost after what you endured."

She chewed on her lip, bracing herself for the worst. "Was it someone from Chanticlare? Did they send a missive to Douglas Manor hoping to catch you there?" It was the only way she could think of that he had discovered her real identity. And she could hardly blame whoever it was. After all, even though he had protected the villagers as much as possible, she was sure Lord Vulture still made their lives a misery.

She squeezed his hand. "It was, wasn't it? Probably old Mrs. Peebles. Even though we did our best to ensure her shop was a success, her sour disposition made it next to impossible. People refused to deal with her."

He stared down at their joined hands, his expression unreadable. "It was not Mrs. Peebles."

She stopped the threat of a sneeze by pinching the end of her nose with the handkerchief. "Then who?" she asked through the linen.

He gently brushed her curls back from her face and shook his head. "It does not matter."

"You promised."

He looked away and bowed his head.

It was then she realized without a doubt who had done it. "It was my mother."

His sad nod drove the realization through her heart like a stake.

"But how? Did she leave the letter here for you?" Frannie made the mistake of shaking her head and flinched. "No. She couldn't have, or you would have confronted me before leaving for Douglas Manor."

He kissed her hand and squeezed it. "She wrote to the demoness. As it turns out, they were old enemies who competed for the attention of your father. Your mother won because of her dowry. That is why the demoness paid Sandilands to bring down West Belgium International. To exact revenge against your mother by bankrupting the Ardsmeres. Her hate for your mother was so profound that it took her years to plan the perfect scheme that could be launched as soon as my father did her the courtesy of dying and getting out of her way." He blew out a sad laugh. "But your mother hated me and decided to confess all to the demoness in an attempt to stir trouble between you and me." After a deep sigh, he frowned. "It appears your mother did not realize the demoness still hated her or was the one behind the fake Lord Ardsmere scheme. I truly think she was merely reacting to the fact that without her fake son's existence, she had faded into the background."

"Mother Ardsmere must always be the center of attention, heaven forbid otherwise." Frannie squinted her eyes shut, determined not to shed a tear about her own mother's betrayal. After all, Mother had never truly hidden the fact that Frannie merely served the purpose of keeping the title theirs. And if she gave in to tears, the insufferable congestion would only get worse and make her cough even more until she ended up casting up her accounts.

"I am sorry, my love." Alec drew her into his arms and cradled her against his chest. "I did not wish to tell you."

She kept the handkerchief clutched to her nose and mouth to muffle another coughing fit. "You forgave me. That is all that matters." She pushed back and fixed a bleary-eyed scowl on him. "But I will not have her near our baby. Ever. If she wishes to be so selfishly cruel, then let her do so alone." She unleashed a shuddering, hiccupping cry that made her head hurt even more. "What if she tells others and ends up getting me sent to prison?"

"No one else will ever believe her," he said with chilling conviction.

"You seem so certain."

"I am certain. She now resides in Bedford Asylum."

Frannie stared at him, sensing he was watching and waiting for her reaction. She swallowed hard, struggling to keep down what little of the herbal tea she had managed to swallow.

"Bedford Asylum?" she whispered. "I know she is petty, selfish, and mean-spirited, but an asylum?"

"She knew how I would react, Frannie, and didn't care that it almost killed you. Almost killed our child. Dun confronted her in London, and she showed no remorse or worry for you whatsoever."

"But—"

"No." He shook his head. "I will never allow anyone to endanger my family." His eyes narrowed. "She should count herself fortunate that I did not send her to an even worse situation. Or end her permanently."

"But an asylum." The thought of the awful treatment Mother Ardsmere would be subjected to filled her with guilt. "Have you any idea how terrible those places are? Have you not heard the stories?"

His frown deepened. "I know the truth about the Sisterhood of Independent Ladies. Lord Raines explained it to Dun, and Dun explained it to me. Do you truly wish to risk the welfare of so many by setting your mother loose in London?" He lifted her hand for another kiss, and his tone softened. "It is for the best, my love. She can say anything she wishes at Bedford, and no one will ever believe her."

Frannie sniffed, then blew her nose with a loud, unladylike snort. "Sorry. I know I am disgusting." She closed her eyes and silently apologized to her mother for not trying harder to understand her or help her be a better person—like Celia's mother or Sophie's.

"You are not disgusting." He pressed a tender kiss to her forehead. "You are alive, and I love you." His gaze turned affectionately stern. "And your mother's behavior is not your fault. We are all accountable for the choices we make. She attacked my family. I do not take that lightly."

Frannie whirled away and sneezed hard. "My, wasn't that a vulgar way to spoil a moment?"

"I believe you need a fresh coating of Mrs. MacGinnis's oil of peppermint salve, my love." He stretched for the jar on the table beside the bed. With a wicked grin, he scooped out a dollop and held it aloft. "Pull down your shift, and I shall rub it on your chest."

Taking her time to untie the neckline of her shift and slide it down off her shoulders, she offered him a teasing smile. "You make quite the nursemaid, husband. With such ardent attention, I may never get well."

"Indeed." He slathered the pungent ointment across her chest with a slow, seductive caress. "I need you to get well, sweetling." He leaned down, treated her nipple to a nibbling kiss, then straightened with a heavy sigh. "I cannot, in good conscience, return to our bed until you are fully recovered." He arched a brow. "I need you to recover *soon*."

She turned aside and exploded with a series of rapid-fire sneezes. "Yes, indeed. And to stop erupting with sneezing fits." She tried to breathe in the powerful scent of the mint salve fortified with camphor, but her head had become completely plugged.

He chuckled and gently applied some of the salve to her temples. "Patience, my love. We have the rest of our lives to be together."

"I rather like the sound of that," she rasped, her heart soaring.

"As do I, my love. As do I."

EPILOGUE

Lionwraith Estate
The northernmost border of the Lake District, England
May 1817

"WHY THE DEVIL is it taking so long?" Alec spun on his heel and glared at Dunkeld, Vivvy, and his six-month-old niece, Lily, where they all sat on the sofa. He pointed at his sister and then at the baby, chortling and clapping her chubby hands while Dun held her. "Lily came in no time at all."

"I dinna call from dawn to midnight no time at all," Dun said with a laughing snort. "It seemed quick to ye because it was not *your* bairn ye waited for."

"Frannie is in the best of hands," Vivvy reassured him. She eased baby Lily out of Dun's arms and took her to the nanny standing in the doorway. "Off to your nap, my sweet girl."

"It has been hours and hours," Alec said. "Entirely too long. If no word comes out of that room in the next few moments, I am going up there." He increased the fervor of his pacing while raking his hands through his hair. Dun and Vivvy didn't understand. Frannie and the babe were his everything. He couldn't bear it if something went wrong.

"You do not belong up there." Vivvy swatted him on the shoulder as he paced past her. "Mrs. MacGinnis and Dr. Tramadorn have everything in hand."

"How do you know?" he growled.

She caught hold of him and attempted to shake him. "Because they took such good care of Lily and me, silly man."

"I am going up there."

"No!" Dun barked.

Alec jerked free of his sister and shot Dun a glare. "To the sitting room, damn you. At least there I will be closer to Frannie." He charged out of the parlor and vaulted up the stairs to the room just outside his and Frannie's bedroom. A long, loud, pained groan stopped him just as he barreled through the door.

"God in heaven, help my Frannie," he whispered.

"Are ye certain ye wish to sit in here?" Dun asked from behind him. "That is why Vivvy and I were trying to keep ye downstairs."

Alec strode across the room to the bedroom door and pressed his hand on it, splaying his fingers wide. He bowed his head and willed Frannie and the child to feel his love, take from his strength, and, above all, survive. "Please watch over them," he begged in another whispered prayer. "Please do not take them from me."

A strong, loud baby's wail made him lift his head and hold his breath while soaking in the beautiful sound. He turned and stared at Dun, who gifted him with a smile and a nod.

Dunkeld waved him back from the door and pointed at a nearby chair. "Sit. It will still be a little while before ye can go in and see your wee one."

"Sit? Are you mad?" Alec paced back and forth in front of the door, clenching and unclenching his fists. He strained to pick up on the slightest noise from the other side. Damn the thick wood he'd used for the doors! He couldn't hear a bloody thing. He shot a glance at his friend. "The babe sounded strong."

"Aye." Dun grinned again. "A healthy set of lungs on that one. With Frannie determined to keep the bairn in a cradle in your room for a while, ye best get used to that sound. Remember how my Lily howled in the nursery, and that's just down the hall?"

"As long as they are both well and full of life, I will forgo as much sleep as necessary without a single complaint."

"Your Grace."

Alec jerked and faced the bedroom door. His every muscle tensed, but at the sight of Mrs. MacGinnis's smile, he exhaled a ragged breath. "They are well?"

"Aye, Your Grace. Come and meet your daughter."

"A daughter?" He caught hold of the doorframe to keep from dropping to his knees.

Mischief danced in the old housekeeper's eyes as her smile grew even broader. "And your fine son."

"What?"

"Ye heard me, Your Grace." Quietly chortling with glee, she stepped back and waved him inside. "Are ye coming in to meet your braw wee ones or not?"

Alec eased inside. An overwhelming sense of awe, love, and gratitude made it impossible for him to speak as he crept closer to the bed.

Frannie looked up at him with a weary smile. She sat propped among pillows against the headboard with a swaddled baby cradled in the crook of each arm. Damp curls framed her flushed face. "You have a daughter and a son, Your Grace."

"So I understand," he said in a rasping voice while eyeing his new family, unable to believe he was a father to not one but two babies.

"Are you going to come any closer and say hello?" She tilted her head and smiled down at her precious bundles.

With the greatest of care, he sat down beside her and stared in wonder at his children. Both had the blackest hair, little red faces, and tiny fists clenched up under their chins. "They are beyond compare," he whispered, then looked at Frannie. "As is their glorious mother."

"Your daughter was born first. Your son decided to take his time."

"Polite and thoughtful lad he is, allowing his sister to go first."

He stared at them, glancing back and forth between the two. "They truly are identical. Thank heavens God was merciful in making one a boy and one a girl so they shan't be able to pull the wool over our eyes."

Frannie gave a soft laugh. "Oh, I am certain they will still find ways to trick us. After all, they already surprised us by being two instead of one."

"A daughter and a son." He brushed a fingertip across the nearest baby's velvety cheek. "And this one is?"

"Your daughter, Isabella, since you insisted on that name if we had a girl."

He kissed Isabella's head. "And rightly so that she be named after her beautiful mother. Hello, my sweet Isabella."

The baby squirmed and grunted.

He reached over and touched the other baby's tiny fist. "And hello to you, Alexander."

Little Alexander yawned and nestled deeper into his mother's arms.

"It appears our son finds me boring." He softly chuckled, then turned his head to find Frannie staring at him with tears in her eyes. "Happy tears, I pray?"

"Overjoyed tears," she said. "I love you, my lion."

"And I love you, my precious one, with a fury that will never fade."

The End

About the Author

If you enjoyed TO STEAL A MARQUESS, please consider leaving a review on the site where you purchased your copy, or a reader site such as Goodreads, or BookBub.

If you'd like to receive my newsletter, here's the link to sign up:
maevegreyson.com/contact.html#newsletter

I love to hear from readers! Drop me a line at
maevegreyson@gmail.com

Or visit me on Facebook:
facebook.com/AuthorMaeveGreyson

Join my Facebook Group – Maeve's Corner:
facebook.com/groups/MaevesCorner

I'm also on Instagram:
maevegreyson

My website:
https://maevegreyson.com

Feel free to ask questions or leave some Reader Buzz on
bingebooks.com/author/maeve-greyson

Goodreads:
goodreads.com/maevegreyson

Follow me on these sites to get notifications about new releases, sales, and special deals:

Amazon:
amazon.com/Maeve-Greyson/e/B004PE9T9U

BookBub:
bookbub.com/authors/maeve-greyson

Many thanks and may your life always be filled with good books!
Maeve